# OMEGA II - A CRY FOR HELP

## A JACK DAVIDSON AND SHAY LYNN ADVENTURE

DAVID J. STORY

OMEGA BOOK SERIES

To contact David J. Story:

Omegabookseries@Hotmail.com or visit www.Omegabookseries.com or @OmegaBookSeries



This book contains some adult material, including adult themes, adult activity, hard language, intense or persistent violence, sexual orientation, drug abuse, or other elements.

1st Edition 2023

ISBN: 979-8-9880085-4-5

Edited by Gregg Stephenson

Cover Designed by Getcovers

# CONTENTS

# PREFACE

The story you are about to read is Fiction. Many of the situations depicted in this book are true. However, the names, some details, and locations have been changed to protect the identity of the victims.

Book two of the Omega series "A Cry for Help" explores the Omega team members and dives more deeply into some of their past. In "A Cry for Help" they continue their pursuit to stop the sexual exportation of children across the world. Jack, Shay, and the others, see firsthand the sexual abuse of the child sex trafficking culture. A culture that will bring back bad memories for Jack and Shay that the others cannot even begin to understand. This makes them more determined in their quest to put an end to sex trafficking whenever and wherever they can.

It also gives insight into the secret world of dominatrix and submissive sexual behavior in the world of BDSM.

This book series is dedicated to the thousands of missing children and adults who are forced into the Human Trafficking system each and every year. Forced to live in slavery every day in the world of Human Trafficking. Most never to be seen again buy their loved ones.

**The International signal for help.**

The signal is performed by holding one hand up with the thumb tucked into the palm, then folding the four other fingers down, symbolically trapping the thumb between the rest of the fingers and repeating continuously.

If you see someone performing this hand gesture, please call 911 or your local law enforcement authorities. Make sure you note each person's clothing, approximate age, sex, and race, along with the location, direction of travel, and vehicle if one is used. Your actions could save someone's life.

You may read some disturbing things in the following chapters, but not anywhere near the disturbing reality of what a sexually abused child goes through. As you read, try and put yourself in the shoes of a child that has been raped, and multiply that a thousand times over.

The punishment of these offenders doesn't come close to the pain and suffering that they have inflicted on young, defenseless children.

If you have been or know of someone who has been a victim of sex trafficking or sexual abuse, please contact:

The National Human Trafficking Resource Center at 1-800-373-7888. The confidential hotline is open 24 hours a day, every day, and helps identify, protect, and serve victims of trafficking.

Prevention and intervention are key to keeping children safer. After making a missing child report to law enforcement; law enforcement, parents and legal guardians are encouraged to report ALL missing children, especially children who have run away, to the National Center for Missing and Exploited Children, NCMEC by calling 1-800-THE-LOST (1-800-843-5678).

Next, if you are concerned about potential child sex trafficking activity or see situations including the indicators listed below, please make a report to or call 1-800-THE-LOST.

**Stockholm syndrome**

/ˈstäkˌhō(l)m,ˈstäkōm ˈsinˌdrōm/

*noun*

feelings of trust or affection felt in many cases of kidnapping or hostage-taking by a victim toward a captor.

**What is Stockholm syndrome?**

The term Stockholm syndrome is the name for a psychological response to captivity and abuse that people often associate with infamous kidnappings and hostage situations. A person can develop Stockholm syndrome when they experience significant threats to their physical or psychological well-being, where they develop positive associations with their captors or abusers.

A kidnapped person may develop positive associations with their captors if they have face-to-face contact with them.

If the person has experienced physical abuse from their captor, they may feel gratitude when the abuser treats them humanely or does not physically harm them.

A person may also attempt to appease an abuser in order to secure their safety. This strategy can positively reinforce the idea that they might be better off working with an abuser or captor.

There could be other factors behind the development of Stockholm syndrome. However, the vast majority of captives and survivors of abuse do not develop Stockholm syndrome.

**Symptoms**

Stockholm syndrome can manifest in several ways, including when the victims:

- Perceive kindness or compassion from their captor or abuser
- Develop positive feelings towards the individual or group of individuals holding them captive or abusing them
- Adopt the same goals, world views, and ideologies as the captors or abusers
- Feel pity toward the captors or abusers
- Refuse to leave their captors, even when given the opportunity to escape
- Have negative perceptions towards police, family, friends, and anyone else who may try to help them escape their situation
- Refuse to assist police and government authorities in prosecuting perpetrators of abuse or kidnapping

After release, a person with Stockholm syndrome may continue to have positive feelings towards their captor. However, they may also experience flashbacks, depression, anxiety, and post-traumatic stress disorder (PTSD).

There is no clear definition of Stockholm syndrome, experts have linked it to other psychological phenomena associated with abuse, such as:

- Trauma bonding
- Battered person syndrome
- Learned helplessness

An attempt to establish an association between Stockholm syndrome and sex trafficking. A study describes several conditions that have associations with Stockholm syndrome.

These include:

- Perceived threats to physical and psychological survival
- Perceived kindness from the trafficker or client
- Isolation from the outside world
- Perceived inability to escape

Some research has found evidence suggesting that victims of domestic violence may also experience Stockholm syndrome.

# Chapter One

# Help Me Please

The trial was in its third week, and it had drawn national attention. The court room was packed with local townspeople, many from the surrounding communities and news crews from all over.

One person was taking a special interest in the trial. The man was sitting in the back near the double doors leading out of the courtroom. He was dressed in blue jeans and a dark blue Boston Red Sox shirt, along with a solid dark blue windbreaker, zipped halfway up over his shirt. He sported a plain black baseball cap that covered his long shoulder length black hair, wire rimmed glasses and two weeks of stubble on his face.

When the court went into recess for the day, he stood and slowly walked out of the courtroom. Leaving the courthouse; he removed his cellphone out of his jacket pocket.

He walked about a hundred feet beyond the courthouse; coming to a stop under an oak tree that looked like it had been there since before the revolutionary war. He entered a number into the phone, that he had called so many times. Looking up to see if anyone was around; he then pressed dial. On the third ring a familiar person answered on the other end.

"Vicky; it's Jack. It's a go on the target. I do not know how the jury's verdict is going to go, but based on his history and what I've seen; he's guilty as hell.

However, the defense is mounting a good case. It could go either way at this point." Jack commented into the phone as he was looking around the small town.

"Ok, come on back. There's nothing more you can do there right now." Vicky said.

Jack disconnected the call and placed the phone back into his pocket. He continued to walk a couple blocks down main street towards his hotel. Jack came to a stop outside of this small country restaurant and looked in the window. The smell of the fresh country biscuits and fried bacon filled the air.

"*Man, that smells good.*" Jack said to himself. He looked on the door to see what time they opened for breakfast. "*Maybe I'll stop in the morning before heading back home.*" He thought.

Jack turned and continued walking towards his hotel. Tomorrow he would check out of the hotel and head home; having gathered all the information he needed.

The next morning, Jack woke up and grabbed his cell phone to check to see if he had received any messages or important emails during the night. Checking the local weather; he saw that it was a brisk forty-five degrees with a thirty percent chance of rain that morning. Next, he threw the covers off and walked into the bathroom to prepare for the long drive home. He had packed everything the night before, so all he had to do was throw his toothbrush and comb into his bag and head out the door.

It was just past eight in the morning when Jack exited the hotel lobby and stepped out onto the sidewalk. Pausing for a second as he headed to his car, he noticed how quiet the town was and smiled. He turned and started walking into the parking lot. As he reached his car, he opened the back door and threw his bags in the back seat. He opened the driver's side door; stopping before getting in. The smell of fresh country biscuits and fried bacon filled the air as it did the day before. He looked down the street towards where the aroma was coming from. "*A good breakfast would be great, before heading out.*" He thought to himself. He shut the car door and slowly walked down the sidewalk towards the small country restaurant with the delicious aromas.

He greeted several couples as he passed with a slight nod and a smile; noting how friendly and polite the people were. He reached the restaurant and pulled open the door, causing a small bell to ring over his head; announcing his entry to the staff.

A lady that looked to be in her fifties approached him, "Is it just you, young man?" she asked, with a big smile.

"Yes ma'am, it's only me." Jack replied, returning her smile.

"Follow me, is this table, ok?" she asked, pointing to one of the tables in the middle of the room.

"Yes ma'am, it's fine." Jack replied, taking a seat.

"Do you know what you want, or do you need a second?" she asked, placing a menu in front of him.

"I'll have the country biscuits, fried bacon, two eggs scramble, toast and some strawberry jelly if you have it." Jack said, looking briefly at the menu.

"Would you like grits with that too?" she asked as she was writing down his order.

"Yes please." He replied.

"How about some good old country sausage gravy with that biscuit?" she asked, looking up from her pad.

"Sure. And a large glass of orange juice too please." He replied, as he leaned back in the chair.

"I'll get this out to you as soon as I can." She said as she turned and headed towards the kitchen.

"Oh, could you make that bacon crispy?" Jack asked, looking up at the lady.

"Sure thing, dear." She replied.

Jack looked over at a booth down towards the back of the restaurant. There were two couples sitting together that looked to be in their mid-seventies. They were smiling and telling stories of their grand kids and sharing pictures. They looked like they had been best friends since before high school.

Another table had a young married couple with a baby girl. The baby looked to be about six months old sitting in an old wooden highchair. She was trying to feed herself some scrambled eggs, but with little success. She had more eggs on her face and hair than she had gotten into her mouth.

Another man was sitting alone, nursing a large cup of coffee, and reading the local newspaper.

He looked like he was just getting off from nightshift and stopped by, before heading home

Across from Jack and up towards the front, sat a middle-aged man and young girl that looked to be about thirteen. He was busy digging into his breakfast like he hadn't eaten in days. She was just sitting there, with what looked to be a bowl of cereal.

She was dressed in a wrinkled pink dress, with a pink bow in her reddish-brown hair. She had a sad look on her face like she had just lost her little puppy. She sat there looking down at the cereal bowl with her hands folded in her lap.

She glanced over at Jack, and they briefly made eye contact before the little girl quickly looked away.

Jack smiled. He just thought the little girl was very bashful, until he noticed her looking at him again.

"*She had the saddest eyes.*" Jack thought to himself, as he took a sip of his orange juice.

Jack went about eating his breakfast. A few seconds later, he looked up and saw the little girl looking at him again, but this time she had a terrified look on her face and her eyes were starting to tear up.

Jack stopped in mid bite as he saw the little girl look down towards the floor. She slowly held her left arm out to her side. She had her hand open and fingers pointing down at the floor.

Then Jack noticed something strange and turned his head slightly to one side.

The little girl slowly folded her left thumb into her palm of her left hand without taking her eyes off Jack this time.

She then folded her four small little fingers over the top of her thumb repeating this gesture several times so Jack could see.

Jack could not believe what he was seeing. The little girl sitting just ten feet away was crying for help.

This thirteen-year-old little girl had just given Jack, the international signal for help.

Jack put his fork down on the table and just looked at the little girl, who had now looked away.

" *Was this for real? Was this a real cry for help? Or was she just messing with me? Or maybe, she had gotten in trouble, because she had not turned in her homework in school.*" These thoughts were racing through Jacks mind. " *What should I do?*" Jack thought to himself. "*Should I get up and run over and grab the girl and run? Take her to the police station down the street.*" His mind was going in all different directions. "*No just call the police and let them handle it.*" He thought.

"*But what would I tell them? That I saw a sad little girl and she made a fist.*" His mind was rapidly weighing his options. "*Maybe I should just pay my bill, leave and not get involved.*" He thought for a second. "*But that's not me. That's not what I have spent the last couple of years doing. That's not what Omega was about. NO! I have to do something.*" Jack finally made up his mind.

The little girl looked over at Jack without lifting her head.

Jack gave her a wink and a slight nod. He placed two twenty-dollar bills underneath the bill. That would be more than enough money, to cover the meal and a generous tip too.

He gave the little girl another quick glance and headed for the door. As soon as he cleared the front of the restaurant, Jack sprinted back to where he had parked his car. Starting his car: he drove down towards the restaurant. He pulled over to the side of the road, just across the street from the restaurant, where he could clearly see the front of the restaurant, from where he parked.

Jack retrieved his cell phone, from his jacket pocket and placed a call to Vicky.

When she answered, Jack explained to her what he had seen.

"Vicky I'm not sure what to do. I'm parked across the street from the restaurant. I plan to follow them and see where maybe they live. Beyond that, I'm not sure."

"Call me back whenever you get any information and I'll have Ray do some digging." Vicky said.

"I'm just hoping, that if this is for real, the little girl doesn't think I ran out on her." He said, in an obviously concerned and somber voice.

"Jack she's lucky it was you that was sitting there and not someone else. Most people don't want to get involved." She said, trying to reassure him.

"I know."

"That's why we do what we do, Jack." She said, with a sad tone to her voice also.

"Hold on." Jack paused. "Vicky, they just exited the restaurant, I'll call you back." He said in a rush and ended the call.

Vicky entered Ray's number into her cell phone and pressed send.

"Yes Vicky." Ray answered.

"Jack just called, and he's got something developing. I told him to give me a call once he gets some additional information." Vicky said.

"What is it?" Ray asked.

"A possible child abduction." Vicky replied, with concern in her voice.

"I'm on it." Ray said, as he grabbed his laptop.

About fifteen minutes later, Vicky's cell phone rang, and the caller ID displayed Jack's number.

"What do you have so far, Jack? I've got Ray ready." She said.

"They got into a red Ford Explorer, license number X-ray, Charlie, Victor, 3, 6, 4, 9. I followed them for about six miles outside of town to a house located at 5027 Villas Drive. See what you can get." Jack said.

"I'm texting Ray the information now. I'll get back to you as soon as I hear something from Ray." Vicky said and ended the call.

Jack continued to sit in his car, watching the house from down the street. He was able to see the front and one side of the one-story brick house.

After about ten minutes, Jack's phone began to ring, it was Vicky.

"Jack, you did good." Vicky started.

"What?" Jack replied.

"The car is registered to a man named, Peter McCree. The house is a rental house, owned by a company over in the next town." Vickey started.

"Go on." Jack said.

"He's been arrested several times for child molestation, exposure, possession and distribution of child pornography." Vicky said.

"We need to go in and get that girl." Jack replied angerly.

"Jack there's more." Vicky said, with some concern in her voice.

"What?" Jack asked, now getting angrier.

"Her mother reported her missing over three weeks ago." Vicky replied. "The girls name is Jordan McCree, her father's Peter McCree. They have been divorced for over eight years."

"I'm going in after her." Jack said.

"NO! Wait Jack. We need to let the FBI handle this. I have Tony notifying the local field office now. Stay where you are at and keep a watch on the place." Vicky said, trying to calm Jack down.

"He's just going to get out again and hurt some other child." Jack replied, in a loud tone.

"We've got this Jack. Just stay put. Please." Vicky said, trying to reassure Jack.

"Fine." Jack replied, angerly. "I'll call you back if anything changes." He added, before ending the call.

Over two hours had passed when Jack noticed some movement down the road. About two hundred feet beyond the house, he saw several vehicles were pulling up and blocking the end of the street.

He noticed also that a helicopter was circling high above; just out of earshot.

A line of six or seven people, all dressed in black, slowly approached the house. They stopped behind some bushes, just out of sight of the house. He could see the lead person holding up a shield. Printed on the front of the shield were the letters "FBI".

It was the FBI's, Critical Incident Response Group (CIRG). The CIRG consists of a unit of special agents and professional support personnel. They provide expertise in crisis management, hostage rescue, surveillance and aviation, hazardous devices mitigation, crisis negotiations, behavioral analysis, and tactical operations.

Jack could see another group of three, all dressed the same, slowly working their way down the side of the house. They were using small telescopes to look inside each of the windows.

They were trying to find Jordan and make sure that she was safe. They also wanted to make sure that Peter was not near Jordan when the tactical team entered the house.

Jack could see one of them taking up a position under one of the windows. The agent continued to watch through his telescope at what was going on inside that room.

Jack noticed another person, doing the same thing, outside of a window in the front of the house.

Jack assumed that the two people, at the windows, had given the others an all-clear signal, because, he saw the tactical team slowly approaching the front door.

Three black SUVs came racing past where Jack was parked. They stopped just in front of the house, less than fifty feet from Jack.

The group positioned themselves just outside of the front door. One of the tactical team members, struck the door with a battering ram. As the door flew open the tactical team rushed inside. At the same time, other agents jumped out of the SUVs and ran towards the house.

Within two or three minutes, they had Peter McCree handcuffed and were escorting him out. They walked him to one of the nearby SUV's and placed him inside.

Jack exited his car and walk towards one of the other FBI vehicles. He stopped next to one and stepped up on the curb. He watched as one of the FBI agents escorted Jordan out of the house. They walked towards the SUV in front of where Jack was standing. Just before Jordan got in, she looked up and saw Jack standing on the sidewalk.

Jack smiled at her and gave her a slight nod. The little girl looked at Jack and mouthed the words. "Thank You." She smiled back at Jack and got into the SUV. Jack turned and slowly walked back to his car. Once he got in, he sat there for about five minutes before he headed home. Jack cried most of the trip back home. He kept thinking of the little girl back at the restaurant and of him seeing her signal.

He wondered to himself how many others like her have tried to signal for help, but their cries went unnoticed. Or about how many people just moved on, not wanting to get involved. He knew he came close to being one of them. He kept thinking what if, I had just decided to keep eating my breakfast and not do anything? What would that little girl's future be like?

Jack smiled, knowing he did the right thing. He was thinking about the happy reunion between Jordan and her mother. He wiped the tears that were running down his face and took a deep breath.

"One down and GOD only knows, how many to go." Jack said, aloud to himself.

Several hours later, Jack pulled into Omega headquarters and entered the building.

Shay was sitting in the conference room. She was watching Ray, as he gathered information. He was working on the original reason why Jack had made his trip.

"Hi." Shay said, as Jack entered the room.

"Heard you had some excitement before you left." Shay added.

"I just wish I could have gotten a shot at that scumbag myself." Jack said, as he flopped down in one of the chairs.

"Tony made some calls. I think that Peter is not going to have a particularly pleasant stay at his new home." Shay said, looking at Jack and giving him a big smile.

"Why, what did Tony do?" Jack asked, now very curious.

"Tony and Ray made some changes to Peter's transfer orders. They arranged for Peter McCree, to spend his first few days in general population, at the county jail." Shay said, rocking back and forth in her chair.

Ray raised his right hand above his head and gave Jack a thumbs-up.

"In general population, he's going to receive the justice that he so deserves." Ray said, turning towards Jack.

"Tony said, people like Peter, normally don't make it far once put in general population. The residents there, although not angels themselves, don't treat pedophiles with much love." Ray added, turning back to his laptop.

"Good!" Jack exclaimed and gave Ray two thumbs-up.

"Ray, what do we have on this Robert Jamerson fella? You know the reason that I originally made the trip." Jack asked, looking at Ray.

"You know he's on trial for distribution for child pornography, that's why you made the trip. That is not his first time either. He's been charged, but never have been convicted, for actually taking the pictures that he sells." Ray said, looking at his monitor.

"Right now, it looks fifty fifty, that he's going to be found guilty of this latest charge." Ray added, looking back at Jack.

"You were there during much of the trial, what do you think?" Shay asked, looking over at Jack.

"The prosecution did a decent job, but he had some high dollar defense attorney." Jack replied, shrugging his shoulders.

"It could go either way, like Ray said." Jack replied, scooting up to the table.

"If he walks, it looks like we'll have another job ahead of us." Shay said as she was looking down at her cell phone.

Jack looked at Ray, "And if he gets some jail time, maybe you and Tony can do that trick like you did with Peter McCree."

"We can do that." Ray replied.

"Hey guys." Vicky said, as she walked into the conference room.

"What's up." Jack replied, spinning his chair around to face her.

Ray, focusing on his laptop, just stuck his hand up in the air and waved.

Shay looked at Vicky and gave her a big smile, "Hey Aunt Vicky."

"Ray, I know you're busy working on the Robert Jamerson stuff. But did you ever get access to any of Clinton's bank accounts?" Vicky asked, as she walked up behind Ray.

"Not yet. The encryption code he is using is state of the art. I'm still working on it." Ray replied, as he stopped working and turned towards Vicky.

"I'm running everything I've got, trying to crack the login and password." Ray added, with a defeated look on his face.

"Try this login and password." Vicky said, as she passed a piece of paper to him.

Ray looked at Vicky with a look of confusion. He looked at the piece of paper, she was handing him and then looked back up at her. Ray reached for the small piece of paper and placed it in front of him.

"I'll try it, but if my program can't determine the correct login and password." Ray replied, before being cut short by Vicky.

Vicky placed both hands on his shoulders and leaned forward, "I know you don't think it will work, but just humor me."

Ray did not say anything else and pressed a few keys on his keyboard. The login screen to Michael Clinton's bank displayed on the screen.

Ray entered the two sets of random numbers, symbols, and letters, that were written on the paper.

He pressed enter and looked at the screen.

Welcome Michael Clinton, along with a list of several bank accounts and totals, filled the screen.

Ray just sat there staring at the screen, not saying a word.

As she leaned over, she whispered into his ear. "Thank you." And squeezed his shoulders.

Ray still in shock, looked up at her, as she turned and walked away.

As Vicky reached the door she stopped and turned back towards Ray, "Now do your Robin Hood stuff on those accounts." She said. "And don't forget to give some of the money to those girls from the Clinton's ranch." She added and then turned and walked out.

Shay started laughing as she reached over and popped Ray on the arm.

Jack; after he stopped laughing said, "Ray, I guess she made you her B I T C H." while slowly sounding out each letter of the word.

Vicky walked down the hallway towards the door leading outside. "*Score one for the Sandman.*" She said to herself and smiled.

After Vicky had left, Jack was curious about how much money Clinton had in his account.

"Ray." Jack asked, tossing a tennis ball up in the air and catching it, as he reclined back in his chair

"What?" Ray asked, looking back at Jack.

"How much?" Jack asked.

"How much what?" Ray asked; stopping what he was doing.

"Dude, how much money is in Clinton's bank accounts?" Jack asked, tossing the tennis ball over at Ray, hitting the back of his chair.

"Two-hundred and fifty dollars, right now." Ray answered, turning back to his computer.

"Come on man, how much did you move?" Jack insisted.

"In the ballpark of six-hundred and fifty million." Ray calmly said.

"Holy Crap!" Shay said, looking over at Jack and then back at Ray.

"Don't think he's going to be able to pay his lawyers and legal bills with only two-hundred and fifty dollars." Jack said, laughing loudly.

"I should say not." Ray replied, turning his focus back to his computer.

"Karma's a bitch." Shay said. "I'm hungry. Anyone up for pizza?" she asked.

"You buying?" Jack asked; looking over at her and folding his hands behind his head.

"I think Clinton can pick this one up." Shay said as she picked her phone up.

"Same as last time?" she asked, looking at both Ray and Jack.

"Extra cheese on my meat lovers. Oh, and some garlic bread too." Jack said.

"I'll have my usual." Ray replied.

Ray stopped what he was doing and spun around in his chair.

"How did Vicky know his login and password?" Ray said, looking at Jack.

"Guess you're not the only one with connections." Jack replied.

Two weeks had passed, and the jury in the Robert Jamerson case was still in deliberations. They had asked several times, for certain parts of the trial to be clarified and had requested to review some of the evidence again.

There were reports that there was one juror, that was holding out. The other eleven jurors were all in agreement, all but the one.

The one juror; Thomas Payne would not change his vote to guilty.

After over two weeks of deliberations by the jury, the judge declared a mis-trial.

"Vicky." Ray called out, from behind his computer.

"Yes Ray, what's up?" Vicky asked as she walked into the room.

"The judge declared a mistrial, in the Jamerson case." Ray said, looking over at her as she entered the room.

"What happened?" she asked, walking up behind him.

"One of the jurors, refused to vote guilty." Ray replied.

"Interesting. Do we know who this juror is?" she asked, as she leaned over Rays shoulder to read the news article on his monitor.

"His name is Thomas Payne. He's single and runs a cleaning business in the area." Ray replied, as he pressed some keys on his keyboard.

"Any ties between Payne and Jamerson?" Vicky asked, as she stood back up.

"Nothing on the surface, or the prosecution would have picked up on it." Ray replied.

"What's going on?" Tony asked, as he, Jack and Shay entered the room.

"The judge declared a mistrial, in the Jamerson case." Ray said, looking over at the three new arrivals.

"What the hell happened?" Jack asked.

"Hung jury. One of the jurors refused to vote guilty." Vicky said, looking over at Jack.

"Ray, can you do a deep dive into that juror, to see if he has any ties to Jamerson?" Tony asked, walking over to Ray.

"Sure, give me some time." Ray replied, turning back to his computer, and starting his search.

"What ever happened to Peter McCree? Did he have a nice first couple of days in jail?" Jack asked.

"Oh yes, I forgot to tell you. He slipped on a bar of soap in the shower." Tony said.

"I hope he wasn't hurt." Shay said sarcastically.

"The report I saw. He suffered a fractured skull, multiple bruises, three broken ribs and severe injury to his genital area." Tony said, without cracking a smile.

“Damn. All that by just slipping on a little bar of soap.” Shay said, with a fake surprised look on her face.

“Should we send him a card?” Jack asked, looking around the room, at each of them.

Chapter Two

# FLASH FROM THE PAST

"What are we going to do about Robert Jamerson?" Hunter asked, looking at his file.

"Don't know yet." Vicky replied, looking over the top of her computer screen.

"And what about this juror, Thomas Payne? How does he fit in?" he asked, looking across the desk at Vicky.

Vicky reached over to the right side of her desk and picked up another folder. She checked the contents and handed it to Hunter.

"Here's the file we have on him." She said, turning her attention back to her computer.

Hunter opened the folder and started reading the information they had on Thomas Payne.

"Why didn't the prosecution find this out, before selecting him as one of the jurors?" Hunter asked.

"Because they don't have Ray." she replied, with a grin. "Ray did a deep dive into both him and Jamerson's background. He found out that they have known each other for several years."

"Really." Hunter replied, lifting an eyebrow.

Hunter flipped the page and started reading the second page of Payne's file. He looked up at Vicky and then back down at the file.

"Jamerson knows Payne, through Payne's cleaning business." He said as he scanned the page.

"And he also knows Peter McCree too." Vicky added, leaning back in her chair.

"So, this Peter McCree, the guy we helped put away. Knows Robert Jamerson and Thomas Payne?" Hunter said, leaning back and crossing his legs, with his right foot across his left knee.

"Looks that way." Vicky replied.

"I think we need to pay these two a visit." He said, matter-of-factly.

Vicky turned her chair around to face the window. She rose up from her chair and slowly walked over to the window; standing there without saying a word. She continued to stand there looking out the window for about a minute before she spoke.

"What is it, Vicky?" Hunter asked, seeing that something was bothering her.

"I want Jack to head this operation up." She said, calmly and without emotion.

"Sure thing, I don't have a problem with it." He replied.

"Thank you, Hunter. It is nothing that you've done. I just want Jack to take more of a lead in our operations." She said as she turned and faced him.

"No problem." Hunter replied.

"I still want you to advise him. Also make sure he is not doing anything stupid." She said, turning back towards the window.

He stood up and walked over and stood next to Vicky. "You know I will."

They both stood there looking out the window.

"What are you not telling me?" he asked, turning his head slightly, so he could see her reaction.

She stood there without moving or saying a word. Finally, she turned and looked at him and gave him a slight smile.

"Vicky, I've known you for most of your life. I know you are holding something back. What's wrong?" he said softly as he placed his arm around her shoulders.

"I had a visit from someone a couple of weeks ago." She replied, not looking at him.

"Who?" he asked.

"One late afternoon, I couldn't sleep so I came into my office here to do some work." She began, as she turned and walked over and sat down on the couch.

He turned towards her. "And?"

"And." She paused without looking over at him. "There was this man sitting here on the couch."

"There was someone here and you're not telling me until now!" Hunter said, in a concerned and somewhat angry tone.

She sat there for a few seconds, before she continued. "Do you know anyone by the name or is called. Sandman?" she asked, finally looking over at him.

"Sandman? No never heard the name. What did he want?"

She went over the conversation that she had with him. She told Hunter about how he removed her gun from the desk drawer and the cell phone and envelope that he left.

"He didn't harm you or threaten you in any way?" Hunter asked, now moving over towards the couch.

"No. And you know the login and password to the Clinton's bank accounts." She said.

"Yes." He replied.

She looked at him with a puzzled look. "They were in the envelope he left."

"And he's not contacted you since?"

"No, not a word."

"And you've waited this long before you told me." He said, now with more anger in his tone.

She lowered her head and looked away. "Sorry. I didn't know what to do."

"Tell me what this person looked like."

"I couldn't tell, it was dark. The only light that was on was the one on the desk."

"So, you didn't get a good look at him."

"No."

"Could you tell how tall he was?"

"When he walked out the door, I could tell he was tall, maybe six feet."

"Light or Dark?" he asked, leaning over towards her.

"Light or dark what?"

"Skin, hair. Both."

"He had light skin. His hair was light." She replied, trying to recall.

"Light colored hair. Blond or grey?"

"All I could really see was the back of his head when he left. He had a hat on, it could be grey."

"Ok, Ok. I'm going to have one of the team members stay here at all times." He paused. "When was the last time you've had your office searched for bugs?"

"Not since before the Clinton issue." She replied.

He reached for his phone. "You said he knows all about Omega?" Hunter entered some numbers on his phone and pressed send.

"What's up Hunter?" Kevin replied.

"I need you to bring your bug scanning equipment over to Vicky's ASAP."

"Something wrong?" Kevin asked.

"Not sure. I need you to scan the entire house, barn, and vehicles, everything. Then I need you to do the same thing at Omega." Hunter said.

"On my way." Kevin replied. Hunter ended the call and turned towards Vicky.

Hunter said in a stern tone. “If this ever happens again, you better call me then. Not weeks later. Do you understand me missy?”

“Yes sir.” She replied, with a sheepish smile.

“I’m going to check into this Sandman character and see what I can find. I’ll let Jack know he’s running this operation.” Hunter said, leaning forward and placing his elbows on his knees.

“I’ve already told Jack and he’s already working on a plan.” Vicky said, looking at Hunter.

Hunter stood up, “Ok then. I’m going to investigate this mystery man. Kevin is going to be here soon to scan the place.”

“Oh Hunter. Let’s keep this Sandman thing between you and me. I don’t want the team to know, until we find out more.”

Shay’s phone rang and she put down her sandwich and answered the call.

“Hello.” She said, not recognizing the number.

“Is this Marine Staff Sergeant Lynn?” the caller asked.

“Yes. Who is this?” Shay asked, puzzled that someone calling would refer to her with her rank during her time in the Marines.

“This is Master Gunnery Sergeant Steven Post.” The reply came.

“How can I help you Master Gunny?” she replied, now confused as to why she was receiving a call.

“You were friends with Staff Sergeant Silvers?” the Master Gunny asked.

“Yes, we were good friends. I’ve not heard from him in almost a year. Is everything ok?” Shay asked.

“I’m sorry to inform you that Staff Sergeant Silvers was killed in action three weeks ago.” He replied.

“Oh my GOD! How?” Shay said, shocked and surprised.

“An IED. He was killed instantly.” He replied.

"What can I help you with?" she asked.

"Staff Sergeant Silvers left you something and I've been tasked to deliver it to you." The Master Gunny replied.

"Sure. Do you have my address?"

"Yes, I do. Would 0900 tomorrow be fine, Staff Sergeant Lynn?"

At nine the next morning the doorbell rang, and Shay went to the door. When she opened it, there stood Master Gunnery Sergeant Steven Post.

"Staff Sergeant Lynn?" he asked. "I'm Master Gunnery Sergeant Steven Post and this is Sergeant Sam." The Mater Gunny replied, looking to his right.

Shay looked down and saw this beautiful Belgian Malinois with its right shoulder bandaged.

"SAM!" Shay yelled and dropped down to her knees and hugged her four-legged friend. Sam was also happy to see her, as he began licking her face and knocking her over.

"I take it you two have met." The Master Gunny said.

"Yes. He was only a puppy when Bobby, I meant Staff Sergeant Silvers got him." Shay said, as she sat on the floor petting Sam.

"Staff Sergeant Silvers had indicated in his papers. That if anything ever happened to him, then Sergeant Sam was to go to you." The Master Gunny replied.

"Was Sam wounded too?" she asked, looking at the bandage on Sam's shoulder.

"He was also wounded." He replied.

"Yes of course I'll take Sam. Is there anything I need to do or sign?" Shay asked.

He handed the clipboard to her. "Please sign here and here. These are his discharge papers, and the box here holds Sergeant Sam's Purple Heart, a couple other accommodations and a chew toy."

"Sergeant Sam, your service to the United States Marine Corps is officially complete. Thank you for your service." The Master Gunny leaned over and gave

Sam a good rub on his neck and patted him on his head. "Thank you, ma'am. Sam is now all yours." The Master Gunny turned and left.

Shay and Sam spent a few moments sitting on the front door landing getting reacquainted again.

"Come on boy, let's go meet your Aunt Vicky." She said, as she stood, and the two of them entered the house.

"Aunt Vicky, we have a new member of Omega." She yelled, as she and Sam ran up the stairs towards Vicky's office.

The next morning Vicky and Jack were standing in her kitchen, discussing Robert Jamerson.

"Vicky, I would like to have Jim and Robert, head over and do some investigation on Robert Jamerson, before Nicholas and I go." Jack said, standing in the kitchen with Vicky.

"Sure thing. I'll have them leave tomorrow. Anything special you need them to do?" Vicky asked.

"No, just the usual stuff, habits, where he likes to hang out. Gets some pictures of the neighborhood. Things like that." Jack replied.

"That shouldn't be a problem." Vicky said, taking a sip of her coffee.

About that time Sam came trotting into the kitchen and right up to Vicky. She reached down and gave Sam a short rub behind his ear.

"Where's Shay at Sam?" Vicky asked, kneeling to one knee.

"Here I am." Shay said, as she entered the kitchen. "What are you two cooking up?" she asked, walking over, and pouring herself a glass of orange juice.

"This Jamerson thing." Jack replied, giving Sam a little slap on his butt as the new member of the team walked by, heading to where Shay sitting.

"What's the plan?" Shay asked.

"I'm sending Jim and Robert there to get some intel first. I'm already familiar with the town somewhat." Jack replied.

She rubbed Sam on both sides of his neck and gave him a kiss on the top of his head. "Then what?"

"Then we'll see, once I get everything." Jack replied, looking over at Shay and Sam.

Shay looked at Vicky. "Where is Hunter?"

"He's off looking into something else. He's going to be tied up for a few weeks." Vicky replied, taking another sip of her coffee.

"That mistrial that Jamerson ended up with sure has several people in that town upset. Someone might get to him before we do." Vicky said, placing her coffee cup in the sink.

"A little street justice is a good thing." Jack replied, pouring himself another glass of orange juice.

"True. But things go much deeper than just Jamerson." Shay replied, reaching for a chocolate donut on the table.

Jack pulled out one of the chairs next to Shay and sat down. "That's what we're hoping to find out." Jack looked down at Sam. "Did you eat the last chocolate donut?"

It was a cloudy night, the temperature was in the low 70's, a perfect night for a walk. It was a little over half a mile walk, from the bar to his house, and Robert Jamerson had walked this path many a Friday and Saturday night. It was a four-block walk west, down Queens Mill Drive., then north on Cleveland past the Roseville cemetery to Lee Road. Then a left on Lee Road for three blocks and he's home.

At that time of the night there was very little traffic, on that side of town. As he turned and walked up Cleveland; a dog started barking two houses down, announcing his passing.

A shadowy figure, dressed in black pants and black hoodie, lurked about fifty feet behind, as Jamerson walked past the house with the dog.

"Target approaching." Came the call over the radio. Jamerson was being watched by someone in a black panel van, just over seventy feet away.

"Copy, I have him." Came the reply. He was dressed in all black from head to toe, with a ski mask covering his face.

As Jamerson was slowly approaching; the figure crouched down behind one of the tombstones about ten feet off the road.

"Hold your position, Hold!" came the voice from within the van. "I've spotted someone closing fast on the target from behind."

Jamerson was now passing right in front of the person behind the tombstone.

The attacker was now within thirty feet of Jamerson and started pulling a gun out of their right coat pocket.

"They have a gun. GUN! GUN! GUN! ABORT! ABORT!" shouted the voice from the van into the radio.

"*What the hell is going on*?" was racing through the mind of the person behind the tombstone.

"To your left. Your left." The voice from the van shouted over the radio.

The attacker was rapidly closing on Jamerson and was now right in front of the tombstone.

He pounced from the shadows of the graveyard and grabbed the gun with his right hand. He wrapped his left arm over the left shoulder and across the chest of the gun wielding attacker. He pulled back hard towards his body and drug the attacker back into the darkness.

Jamerson could barely hear the commotion behind him, over the barking dog. He turned his head slightly to his left but did not see anything. So, he continued his uneventful walk home.

The two dark cladded figures fell to the ground in a struggle for their lives. The attackers gun fell to the ground out of reach of the two. The attacker started biting and scratching, the other person, trying to break the bear like grip he had.

A headbutt to the face, caused the ski masked assailant to loosen his grip a little. They both continued to fight and struggle. One was trying to break free, while the other was trying to keep his opponent from fighting and getting away.

"A little help." Cried out the man, in the ski mask.

As the man from the van ran up to the two wrestling on the ground, he stopped. He stood about six feet away and looked down at the two fighting.

"Whatcha got there Jack?" Nicholas said, with a laugh.

"Will you please grab her." Jack replied, still trying to hold onto the struggling woman.

Jack was on his back with the girl laying across the top of him. He had his legs hooked around hers and his left arm over her left shoulder and holding on to her right wrist. His right arm was trying to get control of the thrashing jabbing and pinching left hand of his assailant.

"Looks like you've got everything under control." Nicholas said, leaning against a nearby tombstone.

"WILL YOU DO SOMETHING?" Jack said, in a plea. "Ouch! SHIT! She just bit me again!" Jack yelled out.

"Whenever you get finished playing, I'll be in the van." Nicolas replied, as he turned and walked off toward the van.

"Wait!" Jack yelled out. He was having trouble seeing. The girl's hoodie had come off her head, during the struggle and her hair was now covering Jacks eyes and in his mouth.

"Listen, listen!" Jack repeated to the struggling girl. "If I let you go, will you promise to stop fighting?" Jack pleaded.

"*Do bisa!*" (Fuck you!) she replied, still trying to break free.

"I don't know what you just said, but I don't think it was I love you." Jack replied. "*Shay makes this crap look so easy.*" Jack said to himself.

"Look. I'm going to let you go, so stop fighting." Jack pleaded with her.

"*Do bisa!*" (Fuck you!) she repeated, still struggling.

Jack reached up with his right hand and grabbed a hand full of her long brown hair and pulled. Her head bent to the right side and Jack whispered into her left ear. "Please stop. I'm going to release you and you're coming with me." He said, as she looked at Jack out of the corner of her left eye.

She gave Jack a nod and he slowly removed his legs that were wrapped around hers. Then he released his grip on her right arm, still holding onto her hair.

They both struggled to get up, as Jack kept a hand full of her hair in his hand. Once they both got steady on their feet Jack said, "Now walk." As he pushed her towards the van.

She turned quickly to her left and with an opened hand swung back, catching Jack on the jaw with the back of her hand.

"Damn-it, that hurt!" Jack said, and he slapped the left side of her head with his open left hand.

"Walk!" Jack repeated and grabbed her by the collar with his left hand and shoved her forward.

Once they reached the van, Jack opened the sliding side door, pushed her in and climbed in behind her.

Jack pointed towards the back of the van. "Sit down!"

Jack looked at Nicholas, who was sitting in the driver's seat. "Thanks for all the help."

"French fry?" Nicholas asked, holding up one in his right hand.

"No! Thank you. Where's the M99?" Jack asked, turning his attention back to the girl.

"In the tacklebox behind you." Nicholas replied and took a bite of one of the French fries.

Jack reached for the tacklebox and retrieved the M99 tranquilizer that had been meant for Jamerson and injected it into the arm of the girl.

"You sure you don't want a French fry?" Nicholas asked, turning towards Jack.

A tired but agitated voice replied, "No.... just drive."

"Where to, boss man?" Nicholas asked, as he started the van.

"Home. Just drive. We'll come back for our things and Jamerson later." Jack said, as he reached for the first aid kit. "Oh, and thanks for all the help back there." He said, sarcastically.

"No problem, glad I could help." Nicholas replied. "It looked to me like you had everything under control."

"Did you at least pick up her gun?" Jack asked.

"In the glove box." Nicholas replied.

Jack cut him a glance, as he cleaned his bite wound, on his left arm.

Jack zip tied the girl's arms and feet, and slid into the front passenger's seat. They drove the entire way back; only stopping for gas and snacks.

Jack called ahead and told Vicky what had happened and that they were bringing the would-be attacker back with them.

Once back at Omega, Nicholas pulled the van into the hanger area. They got out of the van and escorted the awake, but very groggy girl to the conference room. They sat the girl in one of the chairs and Jack and Nicholas took another seat.

Vicky and Hunter entered the conference room and looked over at the girl. "Who do we have" Vicky stopped in mid-sentence when she saw Jack, "here?" she continued.

"What the hell happened to you?" she asked, looking at Jack's swollen lip, black eye, and bandage on his left arm.

Jack just cut his eyes over and looked at her without saying a word.

"She did it." Nicholas said, as he pointed at the young girl sitting in the chair.

Hunter looked over at the girl and back at Jack. "I don't see a scratch on her. Did she have two or three guys helping her?" Hunter asked, as he looked at the battle wounds on Jack.

"Nope it was just her." Nicholas said, laughing aloud.

Jack had both hands resting on the arms of the chair. He rolled both of his hands at the wrist and flipped Nicholas the bird with both hands.

Hunter turned his attention back to the girl and walked over to the table where she was sitting. "Do we know anything about her?" He asked, looking over at Nicholas and then at Jack.

"Nope, she's not said a word." Nicholas replied.

"The only thing I've heard her say was, Polish no hurry. Or some crap like that." Jack said, from his chair back in the corner.

"Poshel na huy." The girl replied, looking at Hunter.

"Does anyone understand what she just said?" Hunter asked, looking around.

Everyone shook their heads.

"Poshel na huy, means Fuck you in your language." The girl replied. "My baby sister could whip his ass." She said, motioning over at Jack with her head.

Jack just closed his eyes and shook his head, "I was trying not to hurt her." He shouted, motioning towards her with his right hand.

Everyone looked over at Jack, except for Hunter, who didn't take his eyes off the girl.

"So, you do speak English." Hunter said, looking at her. "What is your name?"

The girl looked at him and said, "Jane Doe."

"Why were you trying to kill that man, Ms. Jane Doe?" Hunter asked.

"Lawyer." The girl replied, looking at Hunter.

"We are not law enforcement. A lawyer is not going to do you any good. So, you may as well tell us. Who you are, and why you were trying to kill him?" Hunter asked, in a sterner tone.

She just sat there not saying a word, every time Hunter would ask her a question, she just looked straight ahead.

"I'll be glad to interrogate her, like I did the dude in the cabin." Jack suggested.

Hunter looked back at Jack, "I don't think that's going to be necessary. Have Ray get in here and see if he can run her prints or do that facial recognition thing." Hunter said, looking over at Nicholas.

Nicholas got up and walked out the door. About three minutes later, he returned followed by Ray.

"I'll get her picture and run it against the State Departments database. It's got a record of all driver's license and passport photos." Ray said, as he positioned the camera of his laptop on the girl. "It shouldn't take much time. We should have an answer in a couple of minutes."

Just then Shay entered the room. "I hear that Jack and Nicholas brought someone back with them." Shay said, as she walked over to the table. Shay looked at the girl and cocked her head to one side.

"Wait a second, I know you." Shay said, as the girl looked away.

"Got it, Bohdana Kovalenko." Ray said, looking up from his laptop.

Shay looked at the girl and over to Hunter and back at the girl, "I knew it. I know I've seen you before." She said as she looked at the others.

"You're." Shay stopped and did a double take at Jack, who was still sitting in the back of the room. "What the hell happened to you?" she asked, looking at him.

Jack rolled his eyes, turned his head slightly and threw up his arms.

"Let's get back to the girl. Who is she?" Hunter asked, looking at Shay.

Shay turned back towards the girl and said, "Dana. She's one of the girls we freed at Sutton's house."

"You, I remember from hotel." Dana replied, smiling slightly, "Are you those people too?" she asked with a Ukrainian accent and looking over at the others.

"Yes, we are." Vicky replied, stepping over to the table.

"Sissy boy too?" Dana asked, pointing over to Jack.

"Well, he's a work in progress." Vicky replied, looking at Jack; who dropped his head and shook it side to side.

"Back to the questions, Ms. Kovalenko." Hunter said, taking a seat next to her.

"Please call me Dana, it's much easier." She replied with a smile.

"Ok, Dana, why were you trying to kill Robert Jamerson?" Hunter asked, leaning back in his chair.

"He took my baby sister and posted her nude pictures on the internet, for Pedarasti to see." Dana replied, looking down at the table.

"Pedarasti? What is that?" Vicky asked.

"I don't know your word. It's someone that has sex with children and likes to see them naked." Dana said, looking back and forth from Shay to Vicky.

"Pedophiles; we call them pedophiles." Shay said.

"How do you know he took your sister?" Hunter asked while glancing over at Vicky.

"I do not know for sure that he took her. But I know for sure that he posted the pictures." Dana said.

"So, you came back over here to kill him?" Vicky asked, leaning forward.

"Yes." Dana replied.

"It's a good thing Jack was there to stop you." Hunter said.

Dana looked at Hunter, "Why is that?"

"We were going to snatch him along with some others. We want to find out just where him and his friends operate and shut them all down." He said.

"You do this like you did for me?" Dana asked.

"Yes." Vicky said, taking Dana's hand.

"You help find my little sister?" Dana asked, as tears started rolling down her face.

"Yes, we will try." Vicky replied.

Dana reached up and wiped the tears off her face with her shirt sleeve. In a faint voice, she said, "Thank you." She looked over at Jack and gave him a smile, "I'm sorry I hurt you."

"Don't worry, Dana, he's accustomed to girls beating him up." Shay said, looking back at Jack and laughed.

"I don't understand?" Dana replied, looking at Shay and then at Jack.

Shay walked over and took Dana's hand, "Come with me, I'm going to show you around. I'll tell you all about it." Shay said as the two of them walked out of the room together.

"SSHHHAAAAYYYY!" Jack called out.

# Chapter Three

# PAY BACK'S A PLEASURE

"Looks like we have a new team member." Vicky said, looking over at Hunter.

"Oh my God. Someone shoot me please. Are we going to let that crazy woman join our team?" Jack said as he stood and limped out of the conference room. "I'm going to go and do inventory or bang my head against the wall."

"What's his problem?" Hunter asked, looking back at Jack as the door closed.

"Guess his male ego got hurt by Dana back at the graveyard." Vicky replied; cracking a smile and continuing to work.

Turning back towards Vicky; Hunter asked "So, you think Dana would be a good addition to the group?".

Vicky stopped what she was doing and looked at Hunter. "I think she will be. She had spent a little time as a captive at Sutton's. I know that she wasn't captive long, but she does have that insight on how they lure people into their system." She said, placing both hands on her lap.

"You don't think she'll take things too personal? You know, because of her little sister." Hunter asked as he leaned back in his chair.

Staring intensely at him; Vicky exclaimed "And you don't think that Jack and Shay don't take this personal? We wouldn't be here if they didn't take things personal." She said, folding her arms across her chest.

Hunter held up his right hand in submission, "You're right; there is really no way a person can't take it personal."

"Damn right it's personal." She said in a raised voice. "Nobody can come close to imagining what they, or anyone else has been through. Being molested by your stepfather or family member; someone that is supposed to protect you." Vicky started getting very emotional. "That's the hard part of it all. Majority of the time it's by someone you know or love. Or even someone in authority, like law enforcement, someone in the church or even a teacher at school."

Hunter looked at Vicky, "I can't even fathom what it would be like." He replied; reaching over to the table and pulling a magazine and newspaper over towards him.

"Jack had to endure years of abuse along with his sister. Then having to deal with his sister committing suicide; along with how it destroyed his mother as well." Vicky stopped and looked away.

"Shay won't even talk about what she went through. I can tell when it resurfaces again. She'll spend hours in her workout room, or at the gym with Stan; pounding the bag and taking it out on some poor sparring partner." She added, her eyes starting to tear up.

Hunter stood up, walked over, and took a bottle of water out of a cooler, "Jack seems to handle his past ok."

Vicky looked over at Hunter, "Can you grab me one too? Jack had his uncle Tony to help him through it. Besides, Jack compartmentalizes everything. He likes to let on as if nothing bothers him. But I can see it in his eyes sometimes." She said; watching Hunter return to the table.

"Never noticed. I guess I should pay closer attention." Hunter replied, as he sat back down.

Vicky took the bottle of water from Hunter and screwed off the top, "He hides it well." She said, then took a drink of water.

"You don't think Dana will be a loose cannon?" Hunter asked, picking the newspaper up.

"I don't know. Time will tell, I guess." Vicky replied, returning to her work.

They sat there for about an hour. Vicky was checking things on her cell phone and Hunter was reading his newspaper.

"Have you had a chance yet to look into that Sandman guy?" Vicky asked, looking over at him.

Without looking up from his newspaper; Hunter replied "Not yet, I'm going to talk to Stan in a couple of hours. I want to see if he knows anything about him."

"You know Hunter, most people don't read a physical newspaper anymore. They read it on their phone." Vicky said, looking over at him with a smile.

Hunter lowered one side of his newspaper so he could see Vicky, "What can I say, I'm old fashion." He said and returned to his reading.

Jack had gone into the armory and was taking inventory of the guns, ammo, and other various equipment, when he heard Shay's voice, just outside the door.

"And this is our armory." Shay was saying as the door opened and the two of them entered.

"Oh, hey Jack, I was going to show Dana our armory." She said, as they stood just inside of the armory's doorway.

"Fine come on in, show away." He replied, not turning around to look, and kept working.

They both smiled at each other and walked on in. They walked over to Jack and stood on each side of him. Shay on his left and Dana on his right.

Jack, trying not to acknowledge their presence, kept checking over the ammo.

"Jack." Dana said, as she watched what he was doing.

Jack leaned over and retrieved another box of ammo, from underneath the counter, "Yes." He replied; not looking at her.

"I want to apologize again for the other day." Dana said, turning and facing him. "I grew up with two older brothers and three cousins. We lived in a rough neighborhood. When you grabbed me, I just reacted, will you forgive me? Please."

Jack, without looking at her, said "Sure, no problem." And continued working.

"We are going over to Stan's gym and spar a little, you want to come?" Shay asked, smiling and gave Dana a wink.

Shay and Dana both put their head on Jack's shoulder and looked up at him, "Please." They both said simultaneously while batting their eyes.

Shay leaned forward a little and looked at Jack's face, "It will be fun." She added.

"I'm sure the two of you, would enjoy the hell out of it." Jack replied, still not looking at them and continued working. Jack put the box of ammo back under the counter. "Look, I've got work to do. Why don't you two go and beat each other up or something." He said; trying his best to ignore their presence.

"Come on Dana, let's leave grumpy pants alone with his ammo." The two of them then proceeded to walk out of the armory together.

Jack paused for a second after they left, "God help me." He said, and then continued his inventory.

Dana quickly became like one of the family; she was a natural fit. She brought things to the group that they were missing. She spoke the language that most of their past adversaries spoke. She saw firsthand how they recruited people into their system. She was also fearless and could handle herself.

Vicky insisted that she was welcome to stay there on the ranch if she wanted to. She could train with Shay and learn more about the team. And hopefully soon, Jack would accept her also.

Shay had something that had been eating away at her for some time now. She woke up that morning and decided to approach Vicky on the matter. After she finished breakfast, she walked upstairs to Vicky's office. Vicky was working behind her desk, as she was almost always doing.

Shay walked over to the front of Vicky's desk, "Aunt Vicky. Can I ask you something?"

"Sure dear, what is it?" Vicky replied, putting her work down on her desk.

"We've given money to the girls who were held by Sutton and the New Orleans girls." Shay said, standing there with her arms folded.

"Yes, go on." She said, not knowing where Shay was going.

"The little girl in Macon. Did she get anything?" Shay asked, shifting back and forth on her feet.

"You're talking about Crystal Lockman, right?" Vicky replied.

Shay looked at Vicky and nodded, "Yes."

"No, I don't believe we gave her anything. When we first started, we didn't give the victims anything." Vicky said, in a remorseful tone.

"Why not?" Shay asked, cocking her head to one side.

"We started giving the victims part of the assets that their captors had. I forget his name. Anyway, he didn't have any assets." Vicky replied, now seeing where Shay was going.

"Charles Darwood was his name." Shay said. "He was my first. I will never forget."

"I'm sure." Vicky leaned back in her chair, "So, you're proposing that we go back and give her something?"

"Yes." Shay replied, placing both hands on top of Vicky's desk and leaning forward. "Now that we have the assets available now."

Vicky held up the index finger of her right hand and picked up her phone. She entered Ray's number and after a few rings Ray answered.

"Yes Vicky, what's up?" Ray asked.

"Do you remember the little girl in Macon? Her name was Crystal Lockman." Vicky said, as she looked up at Shay.

"I think so." Ray replied.

"Shay has a great idea." Vicky said, shifting forward in her chair.

"What's that?" Ray asked.

"Track her down and her family. Find out what happened to them after the trial." Vicky said and smiled at Shay.

"I'm on it. Give me a couple of hours and I'll get back to you." Ray said.

"Send me the information as soon as you get it." Vicky replied and she ended the call.

"Thank you, Aunt Vicky." Shay said, with a big smile on her face.

"I'll have Ray also go back and do some research on the ones in Florida too. We'll see if he can track them down." Vicky replied, smiling at Shay. She had not seen Shay smile so big in a long time.

"Can I wait here, until Ray calls back?" Shay asked, now with her spirits lifted.

"Sure dear, I'd love the company." Vicky replied, returning to her work.

Shay walked over to one of the couches in Vicky's office and flopped down. She pulled out her cell phone and began reading a book she had started.

After about an hour, Vicky's phone rang, it was Ray with his results.

"I just sent you the information on the Lockman's." Ray said. "Is there anything else?"

"Not right now. But I'll need you to do some of your Robin Hood stuff later." Vicky replied.

"Just let me know and how much." He replied, and they ended the call.

Vicky pulled up the file on her computer, "Come over here and let's see what Ray dug up."

Shay put her phone in her pocket and walked over to Vicky's desk. She took a seat in one of the chairs in front of the desk and leaned forward.

Vicky sat there quietly reading the report that Ray had sent her. Shay could tell by the look on Vicky's face that it was not good.

"Well?" Shay asked, anxiously.

"It says here, that shortly after the trial ended, the Lockman's filed Chapter 7 bankruptcy. They lost their house and everything." Vicky said, stopping and wiping a tear off her face.

"Oh no!" Shay replied, leaning back hard in her chair, causing it to slide back an inch.

"That's not all. It looks like Sue; the mother, had to drop out of nursing school. Crystal's father lost his job soon after the trial." Vicky said, wiping another tear off her face. "Sue is working as a waitress at a small restaurant outside of Macon. And Bill is doing odd jobs and whatever he can find, to bring in money."

"What about Crystal?" Shay asked, trying to fight back the tears.

Vicky looked over at Shay, "It doesn't say. She's a minor, so there's not much information on her."

"We need to do something Aunt Vicky." Shay said in a loud tone.

"And we will. Give me a second to think." Vicky said, as she turned in her chair and looked out the window.

Shay stood up and walked over to the window. She stood there just staring for a few minutes, not really seeing anything, just thinking. "There is so much evil out there, Aunt Vicky. I wish we could do more." She finally said.

Vicky stood, walked over next to Shay, and put her arm around Shay's shoulder. "I know Shay, but we can only do so much. Just look at the ones that we have been able to save."

"I've got an idea." Vicky said as she returned to her desk. She sat down and took a note pad out of her desk drawer. She started writing down notes on the pad. She stopped and leaned back in her chair in thought. After a few seconds she leaned forward to make a few additional notes.

Shay walked over and sat back down in the chair in front of Vicky's desk. She watched as Vicky would write something on the pad and then look something up on her computer. This went on for close to half an hour, until Vicky stopped and looked at Shay and smiled.

Vicky picked up her phone and called Ray.

"Robin Hood; what does my queen require of thy servant?" Ray said, when he answered.

"Here's what I want Robin Hood to do." Vicky started. "Find them a nice house in a good neighborhood and buy it for them. I do not want any mortgage for them. Then set up a trust fund to pay them a monthly income for five years. Next, any debt they have, take care of it. Next, I want you to find out where Sue was going to nursing school. Set up a fund that will pay for her school and supplies. Then find out what Bill was doing before he lost his job. Find him something in the same field and take care of any training he will need. Lastly; set Crystal up with a trust fund so that she'll be taken care of."

"Anything else?" Ray asked.

"Oh, and make sure they have good transportation." She added, glancing over at Shay.

"Consider it done." Ray replied.

"Make sure they never find out where the money came from. Also, see what you can dig up on the children down in Florida too. Just do your magic Ray." Vicky said and ended the call. She looked over at Shay and said, "Well?"

Shay looked at Vicky, and while fighting back the tears said, "Thank you Aunt Vicky. I'm going to take Phantom for a ride. I need to get some fresh air."

Phantom was a solid jet-black Mustang stallion, that Shay had fallen in love with, shortly after the Sutton house raid. They were a perfect match. Both were free spirited, stubborn, hard to control and powerful. Shay, Phantom, and Sam would run and ride through the countryside for hours. When the three were together; nothing got in their way. She felt free and left the troubles of the world behind.

Hunter entered the front door of the gym and walked directly to Stan's office.

"Hunter my old friend, what brings you to see me. It's been a long time?" Stan said, as he stood up behind his desk. Stan stuck his hand out to shake Hunters.

"How are you, Stan?" Hunter asked, grasping Stan's hand, and shaking it.

"Getting old, getting old. Here sit, please." Stan said, pointing with his hand over to a chair.

"How's your sister back in Israel?" Hunter asked, as he sat and pulled the chair closer to the desk.

"Same old thing. Complains about this and that. It's either too hot or too cold; always has something to complain about." Stan replied, waving his right hand from left to right.

"How have you been?" Stan asked, "Forgive me, would you like something to drink?"

"No, I'm fine thank you." Hunter replied, looking around the room.

"What brings you here? It's not a social visit, I can tell." Stan replied, as the smile melted away from his face.

"No, business." Hunter said, his smile now replaced with a serious look.

"Always business with you." Stan replied, leaning to his right and resting his right elbow on the arm of his chair. "Tell me what brings you here today."

"What do you know about a man who calls himself Sandman?" He asked, watching Stan's face for any reaction.

Stan sat there for a few seconds, before responding, "What makes you think I know someone by this name?"

"Surely you've run across this person somewhere in your past." Hunter replied, still watching for some reaction from Stan.

"The only Sandman I know of is a mythical character in European folklore. He would put people to sleep and encourages and inspires beautiful dreams by sprinkling magical sand onto their eyes. Is this whom you're speaking of?" Stan asked, returning Hunter's gaze.

"No." Hunter replied, locking gazes with Stan.

"Then I do not know of this Sandman." Stan said, "Why the interest in him anyway?"

"He paid Vicky a visit, late one night and made her some offers." He replied, still not taking his eyes off Stan's face.

Stan finally broke Hunter's gaze and turned his head slightly to the right. He placed his chin on his right hand, between the thumb and forefinger. He sat like that for over a minute, cutting his eyes back to Hunter and then away a couple of time.

The two sat there not moving or saying a word to each other for several minutes. Stan finally stood-up and slowly walked over to his office door. He closed it and walked over to the radio on top of a file cabinet in the corner. He turned on the radio and took a seat next to Hunter in front of his desk.

He sat there for a few seconds before speaking. He leaned over closer to Hunter, "I do recall someone that went by the name of Sandman." Stan said, in a low and humble voice.

"I thought you might." Hunter replied, nodding his head slightly. "Is he like, an enforcer?"

"No, no, he's more like a go between. A supplier of sorts." Stan replied, looking at Hunter and waving his right hand back and forth.

"A go between for who?" Hunter asked, leaning back in the chair.

"That my friend, I do not know. But they are very powerful." He replied, looking Hunter square in the eyes.

"Government? Corporation? Terrorist Group? You've got to have some idea." Hunter asked, still watching the expression on Stan's face.

"Are they not, all one in the same, my friend?" He replied, now leaning back in his chair, and smiling at Hunter.

"Where can I find this Sandman character?" Hunter asked, leaning forward, and placing a hand on Stan's knee.

"Where do you find the wind? It is here and it is there. It appears from nowhere and suddenly it is gone." Stan said, "The Sandman will find you."

Tony had returned to his FBI job in Houston but was on stand-by if Vicky needed anything. Vicky added Red, Nicholas and Dana to Vickers Private Investigation payroll to justify their income. Hunter devoted most of his time trying to find out who the Sandman was.

Since Hunter was spending his time looking for the Sandman; Vicky had put Jack in charge of the Robert Jamerson issue.

It had been just over a month since Jack and Dana had met on that crisp fall night. Jack had sent Jim, Dana, and Robert back to gather more information on Robert Jamerson.

After the trio had spent over two weeks, investigating Jamerson; Jim sent Vicky an update.

"Jack, I just got this report on Jamerson from the team." Vicky said as she entered the conference room.

Jack had been looking over some of the reports from their earlier investigation. "What now?" Jack asked as he looked up from the reports.

Vicky walked over to the table and took a seat, "Robert Jamerson and Thomas Payne along with three or four others, are all in a hunting club together." She replied.

"Interesting. Where at?" Jack asked, looking at her.

"It's about seventy-five miles south of town. Jim and the others are heading down there now to check it out." She slid the file over to Jack. "According to court records, Payne bought the property about ten years ago. It's got a five-bedroom three bath ranch style house, sitting on hundred-seventy-five acres of woods."

"Nice little get-away." He replied.

"And get this." Vicky paused, "The co-owner of the land is Bill Mason."

"Where have I heard that name before?" He asked, looking up thinking to himself. "Wasn't that."

Vicky interrupted him, "Yes. He was the attorney for the prosecution, in the Jamerson's trial."

"Wait, wait, wait, time-out." Jack said, scratching the side of his neck under his right ear. "Jamerson was on trial for sex crimes and Bill Mason was the prosecuting attorney. And one of the Juror's, this Thomas Payne, is a co-owner on some property with the lawyer?"

"And all three are members of the same hunting club." Vicky added. "That explains how Payne made his way on to the jury."

"Wonder how they kept this all a secret?" Jack asked, now showing great interest in the added information.

"Who knows, we still don't know just how deep this goes." She said, as she stood up. "I'll let you know something as soon as Jim calls, with an update on the hunting property." She turned and walked out.

After she left, Jack sent Ray a text, asking for everything he had on Jamerson, Payne and District Attorney Mason. Ray replied, telling Jack to give him about 30 minutes and he will send it to him.

Soon Jack's laptop beeped, letting him know that he had received an email from Ray. The email had three attachments with each of the men's names.

He clicked on the one entitled Robert Jamerson, and the file opened on his laptop. Jack began reading aloud to himself. "Jamerson, date of birth, check. Address, check. Education, check. Nothing new. Ok, family. This is new. Let's see what we have here." Jack continued reading to himself. "*Married for seventeen years to Susan Jamerson. Two boys, Robert Jr., age fourteen and Thomas Jamerson age twelve. Both kids are home schooled. Nothing else new.*"

Jack closed the file and opened the one titled, Thomas Payne. "Ok, let's see what Mr. Payne has." Jack read down the file, birthdate, address, education. "*Ok now family.*" Jack said to himself. "*Wife April, died three years ago of cancer. One son by the name of Jackson age nine. Nothing about his school. No arrests other than a couple of speeding tickets.*"

"*Let's see what Mr. DA Mason has for us.*" Jack said to himself, opening that file. "*Birthdate, address, same old crap, he's got a nice house.*" He thought as he read the file. "*Here we go, family...... Wife Judy, married ten years, stepdaughter Amy Mason age thirteen and stepson Jacob Mason age eleven. Says here he adopted Amy and Jacob soon after Judy and he got married. Both kids are home schooled.*" Jack leaned back in his chair and read aloud, "Seems like a nice family. But why are you, hanging out with a known child sex photographer? What am I not seeing?" He sat there pondering to himself for a few minutes.

Jack's phone rang, "Go for Jack."

"Jack, it's Vicky." She started.

"You know Vicky, your name pops up on my phone when you call. You don't have to tell me who you are."

In a hurried tone, "Shut-up Jack, I've got Jim on the other line. He called me with an update, he's got another piece of the puzzle. I'm on my way over to you. I am going to transfer Jim over to you. See you in a few minutes." She said and ended the call.

"Jack, it's Jim." He said.

"What's up Jim, why is Vicky all keyed up?" Jack asked.

"Here's what we found at the hunting property, Jack, you're not going to like it." Jim said and continued filling him in on their discovery.

Jack had just gotten off the phone, just before Vicky came into the conference room. "Well?" she said, taking a seat across from Jack. "Are you ok?" she asked, tilting her head slightly to one side.

"Yes why?" he replied, looking down at his papers.

"Looks like you've been crying." She said, looking closely at him.

"No. I'm fine, allergies." He replied, turning slightly away.

"What do you think about what Jim and the others found out?" Vicky asked, still showing some concern over Jack.

"Disturbing. We need to get some eyes on that place."

"I'm sending Red and Nicholas there. They are going to pick up some cameras from Ray." She replied. "Jim and the others were able to place four cameras, that they had with them."

"You know, deer season opens in two weeks." Jack said, finally looking at Vicky.

"What about the other four small cabins, that are remotely scattered throughout the property, Jim told you about?" Vicky asked, with a concern look on her face.

"I'm afraid to imagine Vicky, what might be going on inside." Jack replied, softly, batting his eyes quickly.

"Jack, are you sure you're ok?" she asked again.

## Chapter Four

# CAMP PEDOPHILE

Everyone had returned from the hunting property and were preparing to head back in a week or so. They had placed several cameras throughout the property. They setup cameras outside at the main house and around the four cabins. They were able to place cameras and microphones inside some of the cabins, to catch what happened inside.

With deer season starting in just a few days, they will hopefully find out more about what happens at the hunting club. Now it was wait and see.

Nicholas, Jack, Shay, and Dana were relaxing in the conference room. They were there to start preparing for the Jamerson case, based on the added information. They had been waiting to see if someone would show up at the hunting property before the start of deer season.

"Dana, now that you're in the group, we're going to have to assign you an operational code name." Shay said, looking at her.

"What is operational code name, I do not understand?" Dana replied, with a puzzled look on her face.

"It's what we'll call you whenever we are out on a mission. We don't want to use your real name. My code name is Viper." Shay said, smiling.

"Viper. I like name." Dana replied with a smile.

"What can we call you?" Shay asked, leaning back in her chair, and rubbing her chin in thought.

"How about Hemorrhoid." Jack said in a faint voice, from the back of the room.

Nicholas who was sitting next to Jack, popped Jack on his right leg with his left backhand.

"What?" Jack said, throwing up both hands.

Shay glancing over at Jack and said, "I know a good code name for you, Dana." Giving Jack an evil look.

"What is it?" Dana asked, smiling, and sitting upright in her chair.

"Well since you almost buried Jack in that graveyard. How about Grave Digger?" Shay said, smiling and gave Jack a glance.

Jack rolled his eyes and said, "I like Hemorrhoid better."

"I like Grave Digger." Dana replied, with a big smile.

"What is Jacks?" Dana asked, looking over at him, smiling.

"Stryker." Jack responded, with pride in his voice.

"Striker? Does he protest a lot?" Dana asked, looking back at Shay, with a confused look.

"NO, Stryker, like the military's armored fighting vehicle! Not Striker." Jack replied in a defensive tone.

Both Shay and Nicholas were laughing, "I kind of like Dana's definition better." Nicholas said.

"Whatever." Jack said, as he picked his cell phone up.

"We could just call you Batman." Shay blurted out in laughter.

"And what is yours Nicholas?" Dana asked, trying to hold back a laugh.

“Shadow or Zeus.” Nicholas replied.

“Why is Shadow and also Zeus?” she asked.

“I got the nickname of Shadow because I was the tallest member of my Olympic team. And when I stood next to some of the others, I casted a shadow over them. And Zeus, because when I’m on overwatch, I am God of who lives and who dies.” He replied.

“What is overwatch?” Dana asked, looking back at Shay.

“Overwatch is when someone, like Nicholas, hides with his sniper rifle and waits for a target or enemy to wonder into his kill zone.” Shay replied. “He’s there to watch over the others in the team and protect them for the bad guys.”

“Yes, I protect the team, from a bad guy from sneaking up on them.” Nicholas added.

Just then Jack’s phone rang, “Hey, Ray what’s up?” Jack said, as he gave Shay the stink-eye look.

“You need to see this. We’ve got activity at the hunting property.” Ray replied.

“Ok, I’m on my way.” Jack said and disconnected the call.

“You know what. We’ve got work to do.” Jack said as he stood up and turned towards the door.

“Is he always so delicate?” Dana asked, looking back at Shay.

“He’s got a lot on him right now. Vicky put him in charge, while Hunter is gone. He’s a little wound tight right now.” Shay replied, looking at her.

“A little?” Nicholas replied.

Jack walked into Ray’s office, “What’s up Ray?”

Ray turned towards Jack, “Looks like they are arriving at the hunting camp.”

“Who is?” Jack asked, as he walked up behind Ray.

“So far it looks like Jamerson and his two boys. They arrived about half an hour ago. And Mason just has arrived with his stepdaughter and stepson.” Ray replied, turning back to his laptop.

“Where are they?” Jack asked, leaning over Ray’s shoulder.

"Looks like they are all gathering inside the main house, right now." Ray replied, looking up at the video feed on the wall monitor.

"Ok, keep me posted. I'm going to get the others ready to move out. Can you send a text blast out to everyone and have them meet here ASAP?" Jack said, as he turned and headed back to the conference room.

Jack stuck his head back into the conference room. "Hey guys, I hate to break up your party, but our guests are arriving at the hunting camp." He said, "I'm calling everyone in, we've got to be ready to move fast."

Within two hours the entire team, minus Tony, and Hunter, had assembled in the conference room. The team had gathered around the conference table, waiting for Vicky and Jack to enter.

"Ok, guys. Ray's going to give us an update on who's arrived at the camp." Jack said, as he and Vicky entered, Jack taking a seat at the table. "Tony is joining us via video call and Vicky will be filling Hunter in after we finish our meeting."

"Hey guys." Tony said. "Sorry I can't be with you personally. But I've got a case I'm working on and can't break away at this time."

"No problem." Jack replied. "We might need your FBI support later. You can help us from there."

Jack gave a nod to Ray to start.

Ray began, "So far, we have Jamerson and his two kids, Mason and his two. Payne arrived along with his son, about ten minutes ago. One other single male arrived shortly after Payne. I've not identified him yet."

"Ray, can you bring his picture up on the screen?" Vicky asked.

"Sure thing." He replied, and with a couple of keystrokes, the man's picture displayed on the wall monitor.

"So right now, we have a total of nine people at the main house. Four adults and five children, including one girl." Vicky said, as she stood in the back of the room.

"Any unusual activity yet?" Robert asked, looking at the monitor.

"Nothing yet. As you can see, there are a few of them gathering around the fire pit behind the house. Some of the kids are cooking hotdogs and other stuff over the fire." Ray replied, looking over at Robert.

"Looks like a normal family and friends get together." Kevin replied, looking at Ray.

"There's nothing normal about this group." Jack added, looking around at Kevin, and then looking back at the monitor.

"Until we see something unusual or alarming, we can't do anything." Vicky said, leaning against the wall with her arms crossed.

"Agree, but we need to be ready if it does." Jack replied. "Kevin, have you made any preflight arrangements?"

"We're, going to have to take Omega Two. I have fitted her with extra fuel tanks as we should be able to make it in one hop. There's a field next to their property we can use. There are no houses close by. If we fly in low, they will not be able to hear us." Kevin replied.

"What is Omega Two?" Dana asked, looking at Kevin.

"It's a Blackhawk helicopter that we acquired from a previous encounter we had." Kevin replied, looking over at Dana.

"Sounds exciting." Dana replied, with a smile.

"You'll have your chance to ride in it later. But for this outing, you'll be staying here and helping Ray and Vicky." Jack replied, looking at Dana.

"You've not worked together with anyone on the team yet. When they get back, we will put you through some team workouts. That way you'll know how the team works together." Vicky said, looking at Dana.

Dana nodded her head, looking extremely disappointed.

"Jim, Robert, Kevin, Red, Nicholas, Shay, and I, will be going on this trip. So, you guys need to be ready to go. We will only need minimum equipment, so pack light." Jack said, looking at each of the team members.

"What about Sam?" Shay asked. "He's coming too."

Jack looked over at Shay, "Is he ready?"

"Yes, I've been working with him for several weeks now."

"He's going to be your responsibility then." Jack replied.

Shay gave him a thumbs up and leaned back in her chair.

"Jack, I've got the single man identified." Ray said, looking over his shoulder towards Jack.

"Who is it?" Jack asked, without looking away from the wall monitor.

"Jeffery Moon." Ray said, bringing a recent DMV photo of him on the monitor.

"Where have I heard that name before?" Vicky asked, looking closely at the picture.

"He's the former State Speaker of the House." Tony said. "He retired two years ago."

"Lovely." Vicky said. "As if the Clinton fiasco, didn't uncover enough government degenerates."

"Ray, keep an eye on the cameras, if we see any of them touching one of the kids, we're going in." Jack declared. "We need to keep a twenty-four-hour watch on all the cameras."

"Don't underestimate these guys. It's not going to be a walk in the park." Jim said. "We are going into a hunting camp. These guys will be armed, with high powered rifles. Our body armor will not stop those bullets." Jim said, looking at each person.

"Hopefully, we'll have surprise on our side again." Jack said. "When we move, we'll go in at night."

"What about weapons?" Red asked, looking at Jack.

"Our primary weapon will be non-lethal. But, if we have to, take them down anyway you can." Jack said, looking at Red and then at the others.

"Keep in mind, there will be children there. Our number one concern is the safety of the children." Vicky replied, with concern in her voice.

"Ray, we'll need Mother Hawk and a couple of her babies to take with us." Jack said, looking over at Ray. "We'll do two-hour watches. Dana, how about you take first camera watch with Robert. Jim and Nicholas, you two take the next. Then Kevin and I will take the third. Red you and Shay do the next?" Jack said, as everyone nodded in agreement. "Let me know if you see anything out of the norm." Jack added.

"Before we get out of here," Vicky said, before everyone left. "Ray has produced each of you cover names. He has created a complete background history, driver's license, passports etc... Make sure you use these names when asked. We don't want to use out real names, because someone might be able to trace you back to Omega." Vicky started passing out the files to each of the team members.

They each took their folders and looked inside to see what their new cover names were. Vicky's is Linda Smith, Hunter's is Bill Davis, Tony's is Stanley Cleveland, Jim is now Doug Elliot, Robert will be known as Clay Webster, Kevin as Stewart Breedman, Nicholas as Larry Decker, Christopher (Red) as Edward Little, Ray's new cover name is Eric Hudgins, Jack's is David Martin, Shay will use Sharon Story, Dana is Jane Kolenski.

"Make sure you study your history and back stories. Make them part of you." Vicky added. "When we finish this mission, I want each one of you to sit down with Ray and fine tune your cover stories."

They started getting up and heading to check their equipment and to make sure everything was set and ready to go at a moment's notice.

"Vicky, can you contact Dr. Wilson and have him heading that way." Jack asked. "I want to use the main house to hold them, if need be, until we sort things out." He added.

"I'll give him a call now. Oh, and Jack." Vicky said, placing her hand on his shoulder. "You've done a fantastic job on this so far. I'm very proud of you and I'm sure Tony and Hunter are too." She ended with a smile and walked away.

Jack stood there watching as Vicky walked away. He slowly closed his eyes and took a deep breath. He tried his best to fight the tears from rolling down his face. He thought back to his childhood and how his sister, Judy and he suffered the sexual abuse of his stepfather. After his sister couldn't take the pain anymore, she took her own life.

Jack wiped the tears from his eyes with his shirt sleeve and looked around to make sure no one was watching. He took a couple of deep breaths and headed to the armory. "*I need some ammo therapy*." He said to himself.

Jack spent almost two hours in "therapy" on the Omega firing range. Until he was interrupted by a call from Nicholas.

"What's up?" Jack said, as he answered his phone.

"Something is not right. You need to see this." Nicholas said, in an anxious voice.

Jack put his gun down and ran to the conference room. He pushed the door open not slowing, causing it to crash against the wall.

"What is it?" Jack said, as he walked up behind Jim and Nicholas.

Jim with a puzzled voice, "They all finally came out and sat around the fire pit. After a while they paired up."

"What do you mean, paired up?" Jack asked, now getting agitated.

"Jamerson's son Thomas, went over and sat down next to Thomas Payne. Then Robert Jr., went to Bill Mason." Jim looking up at Jack.

"Then Amy and Jackson went over and sat down with Robert Sr... Then Jacob went to Jeffery Moon." Nicholas said, finishing the matching.

"DAMN IT!" Jack screamed out. "Get the team in here, we are out of here first thing in the morning." Jack just stood there looking at the monitor. He knew, from past experience, what was instore later for those children.

Forty-five minutes later the team was all back at Omega, Vicky being the last to arrive.

"What's happening Jack?" Vicky asked as she watched Jack pace the floor.

Jack took a deep breath and looked up at the ceiling, trying his best to control his emotions.

"Jack are you alright?" Vicky asked, showing concern for Jack.

"Earlier the children were divided up among the adults. They sat around the fire pit together in pairs for another fifteen minutes. They began leaving that area," Jack said, fighting back the tears and taking a long swig of his water. "They began leaving and took four-wheelers to the various cabins located on the property." Jack paused and took another drink of his water, not looking at anyone.

"Did any of the children fight or resist? Kevin asked, looking around at the others.

"No." Nicholas replied. "They all went willingly."

"Do we know for sure what they are doing?" Robert asked, trying to clarify what was going on.

"We were able to see inside one of the cabins with one of the cameras." Jim started.

"And?" Shay asked, not really wanting to know the answer.

"We saw Amy Mason taking off her clothes in front of Robert Jamerson." Jack replied, in an angry voice.

"The lights went out after that, so we can only imagine what happened next. We were able to pick up voices, crying and other sounds inside the cabin." Jim said. "But I don't want to repeat what I heard."

"You think Bill Mason knows?" Red asked, showing some discomfort in what he was watching.

"I'm sure he does and he's doing the same thing to Robert Jr." Jack replied, looking directly at Red. And the others are doing the same thing to whoever they have!" Jack added.

"We saw and heard similar actions from the other cabins." Jim replied. "They know. They all know."

"But why?" Vicky said, fighting the tears back.

"They feel it's ok to molest other children but not their own. They satisfy their sickness by swapping their kids with other kids." Jack replied, then downing the remainder of his water.

"But why don't the kids resist or run or do something?" Vicky asked, wiping the tears away.

"Stockholm syndrome." Dana replied. "I saw it when I was held by Sutton. We have another problem." She added, looking at Vicky.

"What is that?" Vicky asked, as she wiped away a tear.

"The children may fight you if you try to separate them or stop them. They are basically brain washed. In order to break someone, you must first destroy their hope." Dana added, looking at Vicky and then up at Jack. "We don't have four threats to worry about, we have nine."

Those words weighed heavy on everyone in the room. No one said a word for over a minute, as each person looked at the monitor but not really seeing it.

"Ok, we are going non-lethal. I don't care what, we are not harming the kids. We'll leave Vicky's ranch at noon tomorrow." Jack said, looking at each person's face.

"We'll go in, with teams of two. One team member will carry a Kel-Tec KSG shotgun, loaded with ten rounds of simunition. Each person will still carry your standard CZ P-10 pistol. You'll have two mags of simunition for your CZ. And as a backup, just in case, you'll also carry your standard number of mags with lethal rounds. Make sure you keep them separated. And only use them as a last resort." Jack explained.

"Dana." Jack said, "I've changed my mind. You're coming with us. We're one person short since we don't have Hunter or Tony. We've got four cabins to hit and only seven of us to do it. Besides, we might need your knowledge on this Stockholm Syndrome stuff." Jack said, looking at Dana.

"I would love to come along." Dana replied with a smile. Then she looked over at Shay, who was sitting across the table. Shay gave her a wink and a smile.

"We will have to fly in and land in a field about two miles away. When it starts getting dark, we will leave from there and fly low to the field next to the property." Kevin said. "We don't want to get to the area before dark."

"Let's all try and get some rest. Tomorrow is going to be a long and stressful day." Jack said, looking at each person.

"Dana, come with me, I'm going to get you fitted and equipped with what you're going to need." Jack said, as he started to walk out the door. "Ray, can you give her a once over with the helmet camera and other gadgets?"

"Sure thing boss." Ray replied, getting up and headed toward the door.

Jack looked over at Jim, "Jim, can you grab Dana tomorrow morning and work with her on the equipment? Run some drills with her and check her out on the range."

"Be more than happy to." Jim replied, looking over at Dana and giving her a nod.

The next morning, Jim and Dana arrived about three hours early at Omega. They shot on the Omega indoor firing range. Jim worked with Dana doing room clearing, using the rooms at Omega headquarters.

Jack was the first one to arrive at the Blackhawk, parked about a hundred yards behind Vicky's ranch house. "How's she doing?" Jack asked, as Jim and Dana walked-up.

"She did fine. She'll be ok." Jim replied, looking at Dana and then back at Jack.

"Good, you two will be paired-up, when we go in." Jack said, as he looked at Dana. "Grab your stuff and load up, Grave Digger."

The others started arriving shortly after that and proceeded to store their gear in the helicopter.

"Hey guys, I've got some food prepared for you, over in the house. You need to eat something before you go." Vicky said, always being the mother hen to the group.

They all sat around eating without saying a word, until Jack stood and finally broke the silence.

"Ok, I hope everyone got a least a few minutes sleep last night. I have each one of you a folder with the pictures of each of the men and children. Also, a layout of the property along with the cabins and main house location." Jack said as he passed out the folders to the team.

They sat there for a few minutes looking over the information contained inside the folder. Every now and then, looking up and making a comment to the person sitting next to them.

"Ray and I will be monitoring the cameras the entire time. We're assuming that during the day, they will be doing some hunting. And that evening they will return to the same cabins. We will keep you updated if we see anything change." Vicky said, sitting next to the fireplace.

"I'll have the Hawks up and flying the best I can. The woods are thick, and I'll have trouble getting them in some areas." Ray said, leading back in one of the couches.

"Here's the teams.' Jack said. "Kevin and Nicholas, you'll be Bravo One and Two. Your target is Bill Mason, he's Tango Two. Jim and Dana, you are Charlie One and Two. Your target is Robert Jamerson, he's Tango Three. Shay you and Robert are Delta One and Two. Your target is Thomas Payne, he's Tango Four. Red and I will be Alpha One and Two, our target is Jeffery Moon, Tango One." Jack looked around. "Any questions?"

Dana looked up from her file, "What are we doing with them once we have them?"

"Each one of you will have zip ties, gags, and blindfolds. You'll need to zip tie and blindfold your targets and possibly the children. Then take them to the main house." Jack replied.

"Why the children?" Robert asked, with a concerned look.

Jack looked over at Robert. "As Dana explained yesterday. If they are suffering from this Stockholm Syndrome, we don't know how they are going to respond.

To be safe, we need to consider them as a threat also. Once we get them back to the house, we can reassess the situation."

"Gotcha." Robert replied.

"Dana, Ray tells me that you attended, Kharkiv Karazin National University and majored in Psychology?" Vicky said, looking over at her.

"Yes, when I returned to the Ukraine, I took some of the money that you gave me and used it for college." Dana replied, smiling at Vicky.

"That is great, I'm glad we could help. You will also be a terrific addition to the team too, a very valuable tool to help us in the future." Vicky added, smiling at Dana.

Dana's face turning red slightly, "Thank you." She replied, looking down at the floor.

"When you get back, I want you to continue your education. Texas A&M here in College Station, has a great Psychology program. I want you to consider going. We're going to pay for everything." Vicky said, watching Dana's reaction.

"I don't know what to say!" Dana replied, smiling ear to ear.

"Think about it. And like Vicky said, you'll be a very valuable addition to the team." Jack said.

Dana smile at Jack, "Thank you, I will."

"You'll need to evaluate the children, once we get them back to the main house." Jack said, looking over at Dana.

"Will do Stryker." Dana replied, still smiling, and gave Jack a two-finger salute.

Jack looked around the room at each person, "If there's nothing else, lets finish up here and meet at the helicopter in thirty minutes."

"Listen up guys." Kevin said. "We're going to fly a little over three quarters of the way there and stop to refuel. Then we're going to proceed from there to the field about two miles from the property. We'll wait there until dark, then take off and head to the field next to the property. We're going to fly from there at tree top level."

"Wouldn't the radar pick us up dropping down and thinking we crashed?" Jim asked, as he walked by Kevin.

"No. I filed a flight plan to that area and showing us landing. I logged us as a chartered hunting group. From there we'll be flying in at tree top level, we will turn nighty degrees east. We'll be flying under the radar at that point." Kevin explained.

The flight from Vicky's ranch to the fueling stop was quiet. The only sound that was heard, was the thump thump sound of the helicopter's rotor blades slicing through the air.

It took about thirty minutes to refuel the chopper and get back underway. They landed at the designated landing location, that Kevin had filed. When it got dark, they took off for the last leg of their journey, flying at tree top level. It was very nerve-racking to most of the passengers, but it was nothing to Kevin. He had done this type of flying, many times during his years in the military.

Those last two miles only took a couple of minutes, but it felt like a roller-coaster ride at Six Flags. The helicopter pitched back and forth, up, and down, several times. They thought they would clip the top of several trees as they flew past. But soon the helicopter, carrying its passengers, slowed and made a wide circle before gently touching down back on solid ground.

Once they finally touched down in the field, Red jumped out of the helicopter. He immediately dropped down and kissed the ground. "Thank ye o God! If man werst met to fly amongst the trees, he would have made us birds. Dear God, I need a drink."

They spent the next couple of hours checking over each other's equipment and reviewing their file. The past missions, they knew what to expect. But they did not know how the children would react. This was a common concern among the entire team.

Would they welcome the team with open arms? Or would they see the team as a threat and attack?

His phone rang and he reached over and picked it up. He glanced at the caller ID and pressed the answer button. "What's up Vicky?" Hunter said.

"Just wanted to give you an update. By the way. How are things in Germany?" Vicky asked.

# CHAPTER FIVE

# FROM THE DARKNESS

It had been dark now for several hours. "Hey guys gather around." Jack said quietly. They gathered in their two person teams, and joined Jack and Red.

"Let's get these boxes out of the chopper." Jack said, turning towards the open door of the helicopter.

They helped Jack unload four docking stations for Ray's Hawks. They placed them on the ground about fifteen feet from the helicopter and opened the top of the boxes.

"Is everyone ready?" Jack asked, looking at each team. "Any questions? Remember we are using non-lethal force. Take it slow going through the woods, we don't want to alert them that we are coming."

No one said a word, they just nodded their heads.

"Remember we don't know how these kids are going to react to us. So be ready but try your best not to hurt the kids." Jack reminding them of the situation. Jack looked over at Kevin and Nicholas, "Kevin, Nicholas, you may have the most trouble out of them all. Robert Jr. is fourteen and he has been exposed the longest to this situation. He's also a big kid, so watch yourselves."

"Jim you and Dana have three people to contend with. Amy, Jackson, and Robert Sr." Jack said, now looking at them.

"I'm thinking that Amy will head to Jackson and try and protect him." Dana replied.

"What about OC spray?" Red asked, looking at the group.

"No." Shay replied, "If we set off OC spray inside, it will affect us too. Use your stun gun first against the kids, if you have to."

"Most people will stop once they hear that crackling sound of a stun gun. Let's hope we don't have to use them." Kevin said, looking around at everyone.

"If no one has any other questions or comments let's get ready. Mask-up and turn your night vision on and your IR strobes. Shay, don't forget to turn Sam's strobe on too so we can keep track of him." Jack said, as he pulled down his mask and place his communications helmet on.

The Infra-Red strobes were small lights attached to their helmet's. The "near infra-red" (NIR) spectrum of light is invisible to the human eye – but it can be easily seen using , but invisible to others. This makes it easy for your team mates to identify you and to know your position.

They gave each other a high five and set out on their way. Each team heading in a different direction.

As Jack and Red entered the woods, "Alpha One to all, radio check." Jack said into his mic.

"Alpha Two, copy" Red replied.

"Bravo One, clear" Kevin said.

"Bravo Two, clear" Replied Nicholas.

"Charlie One, Copy." Jim said.

There was a long pause and Jack stopped, "Charlie Two, do you copy?" Jack said into his mic.

"Sorry.... Charlie Two, I hear you." Dana replied, after Jim gave her a slight nudge.

"Delta One, clear." Shay said.

"Delta Two, copy." Came Roberts reply, completing the teams radio check.

"Eagles Nest, copy." Ray replied. "We received all teams loud and clear.

"Alpha One, copy." Jack said, and the other teams replied in their order, confirming that they received the transmission from Eagles Nest.

"Alpha One to Eagles Nest, Mother Hawk One, Two, Three and Four are free and cage doors are open."

"Copy Alpha One, Eagles Nest has control." Vicky replied, as she powered up Mother Hawks One and Two. "Hawk's One and Two are outbound to their target locations."

"Copy Eagles Nest, let us know when you have confirmed target's locations." Jack said.

About twenty minutes later, "Eagles Nest to all, we have confirmed all tangos are in their cabins and no change from previous intel." Ray radioed the team, after checking all the cameras that were setup at each cabin.

"Alpha One to Eagles Nest, copy no change. Bravo copy, Charlie copy, Delta copy."

Each team moved slowly through the darkness towards their targets. Stopping every few yards to check the surrounding area. All they could hear, was the deafening sound of thousands of crickets that surrounded them. An occasional hooting sound of a nearby owl, added to the nighttime music. Lighting bugs filled the air and gave an eerie twinkle to the forest around them.

They would catch a glimpse, of one of the many nocturnal animals, that inhabited the woods. As they kept a watchful eye, on the strange glowing green-eyed humans, slowly invading their territory.

"Eagles Nest to all, Targets Alpha, Charlie, Delta have gone lights out. Bravo still active." Ray informed the teams.

Nothing else was said between the teams, as they slowly advanced towards their prey. It took over an hour before the first team reached their target. Then the first words came over the radio.

"Charlie One to Eagles Nest.... Go Charlie One.... We are in position.... Copy, hold your position." Jim and Dana positioned themselves behind some thick brush about two-hundred feet from their cabin.

Twenty minutes later, Delta One called in. As Shay and Robert took cover behind some trees about hundred and fifty feet from their target.

Two teams were now set and ready. The time slowly ticked by when Alpha One called in fifteen minutes later. Jack and Red holding up behind a small hill just a hundred feet away from their target.

Thirty minutes went by, and still no status from Bravo. "Alpha One to Bravo One...." There was no reply. "Alpha One to Bravo Two, do you copy?"

"Eagles Nest to Alpha One, we have a location on Bravo, they have been holding their current position for eight minutes." Vicky said, tracking their GPS location on her monitor.

"Eagles Nest, do you have a visual?" Jack asked.

"Negative Alpha One, we currently have no eyes overhead at their location." Ray replied.

"Bravo One to Alpha One, copy." Kevin whispered into his mic.

"What is your status, Bravo One?" Jack asked, kneeling behind a tree.

"We had to stop and make an adjustment to our direction. We ran into a local, and he didn't want to give up his ground." Kevin replied.

"Bravo One are you compromised?" Jack asked, with a hint of stress in his voice.

"Negative Alpha One, it was a bear. I don't think he's going to rat on us. We'll be in position in about ten mikes." Kevin replied, continuing their slow progress towards their target.

Fifteen long minutes later, "Bravo One to Eagles Nest, we are in position. Copy Bravo One, glad you can join us." Vicky replied.

"Eagles Nest to all Teams, hold your position, until further instructions."

"Eagles Nest to all, Mother Hawk One and Two have returned to their nest." Ray informed the teams. Ray had extended the battery life of the drones before the last mission. He also landed the drones after they had done their first areal recon of the area. He wanted to save as much power just in case, they were needed again.

The two Mother Hawks, slowly lifted from their positions and above the trees. The two flew silently back to their cages to recharge.

"Eagles Nest to all, Mother Hawks Three and Four will be on station in ten mikes. Mother Hawks One and Two are in their nest and recharging. They will be operational in forty-five mikes." Ray informed the teams.

"Alpha One to Eagles Nest.... Go Alpha One .... Can you bring up the cabin's audio and videos on the inside of each of the cabins? And relay it to the assigned teams?"

Within seconds, each team member, had the inside camera view of their assigned cabin, displayed on their two-inch heads-up display screen.

"Eagles Nest to all, switch to silent communication, unless urgent response is needed."

The teams would no longer use verbal communication except in an emergency. Instead, they would communicate by using text messages on their units attached to their forearm. Eagles Nest would still be using voice communication with the teams.

All was quiet inside two of the cabins, the occupants had all turned in for the night. Disturbingly sharing the one bed in each of the cabins. Except for the one that Thomas Payne and 12-year-old Thomas Jamerson was in. Shay and Robert could hear the conversation between the two.

"Come on." Payne said, standing in the middle of the cabin, dressed only in his underwear.

"You know the drill, Thomas." He said to the young boy.

"But I don't want to." The terrified young boy pleaded.

"I didn't come here and pay money to just sleep." Payne replied.

Shay and Robert could hear the conversation and were increasingly getting furious.

"I don't like doing that anymore." Replied, the young boy.

"I don't really care! Take your clothes off now and get over here right this second." Ordered Payne.

The sound of the young boy crying was heard over Shay and Robert's earpieces. Ray and Vicky could also hear and see what was happing inside the cabin too.

The faint image of the young boy slowly walking over to Payne played on the small display on their helmets and on the monitors back at Omega.

"We've got to do something." Shay whispered to Robert. "We can't just sit here while that sick bastard molests him." Looking back at Robert; she could see the anger on his face.

"Well, I'm not going to wait any longer." Shay said, as she started to stand.

They could see the boy just inches away from Payne now. Payne reached out and pulled the boy up against his body. They saw the young helpless boy try and push himself away as Payne started kissing the boy's neck. Payne took his hands and placed them on top of the boy's shoulders. He then pressed down and forced the young trembling boy down on his knees.

"You know what to do." Payne said, once the boy was on his knees.

"Delta One to Eagles Nest, we're going in!" Shay said, this time not so quiet, and she started moving towards the cabin.

Vicky was caught off guard by the sudden, unexpected transmission from Shay. Everyone could hear the stress in Shay's voice, and everyone got ready.

"Eagles Nest to Delta. Hold your position!" They could see on their monitor that Shay and Robert were not stopping. "Shit!" Vicky said to Ray, "Send them in!"

"Eagles Nest to all! EAGLES NEST TO ALL! INITIATE IN 3... 2... 1...EXECUTE! EXECUTE! EXECUTE!" Ray screamed over the radio.

Earlier that morning, Tony was in his office, located at 1 Justice Dr. in Houston Texas. He was trying to catch up on some of the cases that he had fallen behind on. He was also following the action, via an earpiece, of the progress of the Omega team. He soon found, that listening to what was going on and concentrating on his work in front of him posed a problem.

The team was about to leave Vicky's ranch, when Tony was interrupted. His office phone rang, and he picked up the receiver, "SSA James." He said.

"SSA James, you have a visitor." Came the voice of Jane, the floor receptionist.

Tony thought for a second and looked for his day planner. Finally finding it and turning to the days date. He wanted to make sure he didn't have an appointment, and just forgot. "Who is it? I'm not expecting anyone." Tony asked, looking up in thought.

"It's SSA Roger Basiliano, from the New Orleans field office." Jane replied.

Tony paused for a few seconds before he replied, "Send him in."

Tony removed his earpiece and looked around on his desk to make sure he didn't have anything Omega related. Then came the knock on the door.

"Come on in." Tony said as he stood up and walked around to the front of his desk.

Tony stuck out his hand, "I'm SSA Tony James, come in." Tony said, as the two shook hands.

"Glad to meet you, I'm SSA Roger Basiliano from the New Orleans field office." He replied, as he shook Tony's hand.

"Have a seat." Tony said, motioning over to one of the chairs. "What brings you to Houston and the great state of Texas?" Tony asked, as he took the other chair.

"I'm following up on some cases. I wanted to drop by to see if you can shed any light on any of them." Roger replied, leaning back in his chair.

"I'll be glad to help in any way I can." Tony replied, interested in knowing what Roger had and why he came to him.

"Can I get you anything to drink? Water, Coffee, Coke?" Tony asked.

"You wouldn't happen to have a Big Shot soda?" Roger asked, looking hopeful.

"I don't have any. I'll ask Jane if she can have someone track one down for you." Tony replied, as he started to get up from his chair.

"No No, please don't bother, a water will be fine." Roger said, waving his hand.

Tony got up and walked over, to the small refrigerator in his office, and pulled out two cold bottles of water. "Here you go, I'm going to have one myself." Tony said as he took his seat again.

"Thanks." Roger said, as he took the bottle of water and removed the top.

"So, what is it that you need?" Tony asked; taking a swig of his water.

"I understand you head up the sex trafficking team, here in Houston." Roger said and took a drink.

"Yes, I do, how may I help you?" Tony replied, placing his right ankle on top of his left knee, and leaning back in his chair.

"I'm looking into a series of killings that may or may not be linked." Roger said; as he opened his notebook.

"Are we talking about a serial killer?" Tony asked, showing some concern.

"I'm not really sure at this time." Roger replied, looking through his notes. He reached up with his right hand and patted his jacket's left breast pocket.

"Need a pen?" Tony asked, reaching for one of his.

"No thank you, I found it." Roger replied, pulling the pen out of his shirt pocket.

"Well, tell me what you have, and I'll see if I can help." Tony said, trying to look helpful and not seem nervous.

"There have been four shootings over the past two years. One in south central Florida, one outside of New Orleans, and one in a town north of Texarkana, Arkansas." Roger said, reading from his notes.

"Interesting, you think those three are linked somehow?" Tony asked, leaning back in his chair. Tony was thinking to himself, "*They sure are linked. I just hope like hell you've not linked them back to us*!"

"Local law enforcement has written the shooting in Florida as gang related." Roger said, as he looked around Tony's office.

"So do you think differently?"

Roger looked back at Tony, "Maybe."

"The one down in my area, we found two dead in the house and two more located in a warehouse a few miles away." Roger replied.

"You said two were found in a warehouse. I'm assuming they were dead too?" Tony asked, shifting in his chair.

"Very dead. Looks like they were tortured before they were killed." Roger replied.

"Tortured?" Tony asked, sounding shocked.

"Never seen anything like it before in my years with the Bureau. Or even during my tour in the military." Roger said; shifting uncomfortably in his chair.

"How?" Tony asked, still trying to show the shock.

"Get this. They were shocked by some kind of electrical device. But that is not what killed them. They were eaten alive by rats!" Roger said, shaking his head.

"My God! What kind of sadistic person would do that to someone?" Tony asked, knowing who that sick sadistic person was. "Any leads on who did that?"

"Nope, they were last seen at a local bar harassing two college kids. The funny thing is the girl cleaned the floor with both of them." Roger said, with a slight grin.

"Do you think they may have tracked down the two guys and tortured them?" Tony asked, now really getting interested in what Roger knew.

"They were both just some young college kids out for some drinks. They said the girl was about five foot nothing and looked to be about nineteen or twenty. The guy just sat at the bar, while his girlfriend took care of the two guys. After she was finished cleaning the floor with the two. The two college kids left."

"Sounds like it just wasn't a good night for those two guys." Tony replied.

"Nope, wasn't their night. There has been a common thread in the three." Roger replied, looking up at Tony.

Tony thought to himself, "*Here it comes. Stay calm Tony. If he suspected you, you'd be in handcuffs right now.*"

"What's that?" Tony asked, not knowing if he really wanted to know.

"A middleman by the name of Craig Sutton seems to be a common link to the three." Roger replied, looking back down to his notes.

Tony took a long swig of his water; trying to give his heart time to restart.

"Do you have this Sutton in custody?" Tony asked, knowing the answer, or at least hoping Sutton hadn't survived his South American trip.

"No, as a matter of fact, his place, the location near Texarkana, was blown-up." Roger said, looking back up at Tony.

"Wow, that is strange. Did you recover his body?" Tony asked, now trying to probe Roger for what he had.

"No, we don't think so." He replied, closing his notebook.

"What do you mean, you don't think so?" Tony asked, cocking his head to one side.

"We recovered three bodies from the blast. However, one was burned beyond recognition. We're not 100% sure, if it was Sutton." He said; placing his pen into his shirt pocket.

"What about DNA?" Tony asked.

"The bone fragments were highly degraded, making it too difficult and almost impossible to get a good DNA sample." Roger replied, in a disappointing tone.

"Sounds like it could be another rival gang trying to eliminate their competition." Tony suggested, trying to probe for information.

Roger, replied with a disheartened look, "We've not ruled that out, either."

"What other theories do you have?" Tony asked as he leaned forward in his chair, trying to show some concern. But not the concern that he is involved in any way with the killings.

"Another theory is, that we have a vigilante running around killing sex traffickers." Roger replied, leaning back in his chair, and grasping his right knee with both of his hands.

"Do you have any evidence pointing in that direction?" Tony asked, hoping that the answer was no.

"Nothing solid at this time." He replied.

"You said four? You've only mentioned three." Tony asked.

"I'm sure you heard about the Michael Clinton cluster fuck, several months ago." Roger said, shaking his head.

Tony chuckled, "How could you not. It was all over the news for weeks. There are still ongoing investigations into several prominent people all over the country." He said, glancing down at his watch.

"We've tied Sutton to that group too." Roger said, as he stood.

"Were there any witnesses at any of the crime scenes?" Tony asked, hoping to hear that there were none.

"We interviewed everyone. That is, everyone that lived. And they were of no help." Robert replied, shaking his head.

"I heard that there were several young girls that were found at the Clinton compound." Tony said, as he stood up also.

"Yes, but they only heard the shooting. They never saw anyone other than their captors." He replied, turning towards the door.

"On the surface; it looks like Sutton is behind it all." Tony said while walking with Roger to the door.

"I agree. Our forensic guys found that in each case, all bank accounts connected to them were drained. Michael Clinton claims he had over $650 million taken." Roger said, as he stopped at the door.

"What about Sutton's accounts?" Tony asked; stopping beside Roger.

"His accounts too. Along with the accounts of the ones in New Orleans. Everything's gone." Roger said as he stuck his hand out.

"I'm assuming that you've put out a BOLO on Sutton?" Tony asked, reaching out and shaking his hand.

"We have. But it looks like he's dropped off the face of the earth." He replied.

"Please keep me updated. If I run across anything, I'll let you know." Tony said, as he felt relieved.

As Roger walked down the hallway; he threw up his hand to wave goodbye to Tony. Tony turned and slowly closed his door. He walked over to his desk, sat down, and leaned back in his chair. He closed his eyes and sat there; slowly rocking back and forth in the chair.

After several hours of trying to get his focus back on his work; Tony reached over and picked up his cell phone. Standing, he placed his phone in his jacket pocket and walked out of his office. As he walked by Jane, he said, "I'll be out in the field for the next couple of days; if anyone needs me."

"Yes sir." She replied, smiling at him.

Tony walked out into the lobby and pressed the elevator button. After a few seconds, the elevator doors opened, and he stepped inside. He pressed the garage level three button and the doors slowly closed.

Once Tony got into his car; he sat there thinking for several minutes. "*I really like what I do as an FBI agent. But I love what I do and can do in Omega.*" He started his car and exited the parking garage. He soon hit highway 290 heading northwest and into the normal Houston rush hour traffic. Before he knew it, he was turning off highway 6 and onto state 190 in Bryan Texas. Three hours after leaving his office, he was sitting in front of Omega headquarters.

He sat in his car in thought for about five minutes before exiting his vehicle. He stood next to his car and looked around. Everything was quiet as he started walking towards the door. He knew as soon as he entered Omega the world around him would be different.

The evil would still be there, but he had a new and better way to fight it. The laws he had to follow, when working for the FBI; many times slowed the process down. He understood the innocent until proven guilty and supported that 100%. But too many times, the victims suffered while the guilty got off scott-free. Too often a person would be set free, simply because someone didn't dot an I or crossed a T. The laws were setup to help protect an innocent person from going to jail. But many defense lawyers would use minor errors to get their guilty clients freed.

Here at Omega, there was no paperwork to mess-up. The innocent till proven guilty was still followed. But, if someone forgot to cross a T or missed reading someone their rights; that didn't matter. The only thing that mattered was innocence or guilt.

If you harmed a child or sexually exploited someone, and you were guilty; it didn't matter that the arresting officer didn't put the exact time in his report or not. If the crime was committed at 8:05 p.m. and not at 7:45 p.m., as was indicated in the report. This minor error sometimes allowed the perpetrator to be set free. The facts are that the person was guilty.

Yes, Omega did their homework before taking action. They just didn't have to deal with all the defense attorney crap that was pulled, just to get a truly guilty person off.

Is it right that a person who is caught read handed, molesting a child gets off scott-free because someone misfiled a report?

Tony walked up to the entrance into Omega and entered his code into the keypad. The door unlocked and he entered and walked down the hallway towards the conference room.

"Hey guys." Tony said as he entered the room.

Vicky and Ray looked up from their monitors. "What are you doing here? I thought you had some FBI work to get caught up on." Vicky asked, turning towards Tony, with a noticeably puzzled expression on her face.

"I couldn't stay away." Tony replied. "Besides, I had to fill you in on something."

"What's so important that you couldn't do it over the phone?" she asked.

"You'll never guess who paid me a visit this evening." Tony replied; looking at Vicky and then over at Ray.

"The Sandman?" Vicky asked, looking worried.

"Who?" Tony asked, now with a puzzled look on his face.

"Never mind." She replied.

"I was going to say Elvis." Ray said. "And who is Sandman?"

She leaned back in her chair, "Forget it. Tell us who came to visit you that is so mysterious that you couldn't call and tell us?"

"Ok, you've got to sit down." He said, showing some nervousness in his voice.

"Tony, we are sitting. Who has gotten you so keyed up?" Ray replied, with a laugh.

"Roger Basiliano." He said, as he took a seat.

"The FBI dude from New Orleans?" Ray asked, with his eyes wide open.

Vicky sat there for a second before she said anything, "What did he want?" she asked as the color drained from her face.

# Chapter Six

# Fur Missile Inbound

"Eagles Nest to all! EAGLES NEST TO ALL! INITIATE IN 3... 2... 1...EXECUTE! EXECUTE! EXECUTE!" came the frantic voice of Ray over the radio.

They knew that Shay and Robert, were already heading towards their target cabin to stop Payne from sexually assaulting the young boy. They had no choice but to send everyone in now. They wanted each team to strike their assigned cabins all at the same time.

Payne heard Shay's voice outside and immediately pushed the boy to the floor. Reaching over to a nearby table and retrieving a gun; he turned and headed toward the door.

Payne stormed out of the cabin, with his gun raised, ready to shoot whoever was lurking outside.

Shay was running full speed towards the cabin door when suddenly, the door opened, and she saw Payne charging out. She stopped twenty feet short of the cabins front porch and froze.

Payne stood there with his gun pointing in her direction. As soon as Shay saw the large figure, she dropped to one knee. As she did, she threw her right arm over her head forming a half circle and pointed towards Payne.

"*SAM FASS!*" (SAM ATTACK!) She screamed.

From out of the darkness behind her; Sam came charging full speed past Shay on a collision course towards his target.

Sam locked down on Payne's arm and took him down to the ground. Sam pulled at the man's arm as if he were trying to rip the arm off his body. Shay ran up and dropped down on the back of Payne, slamming her knee between his shoulder blades.

"*Sam Aus.*" (Sam Let Go.) Sam let go of the man's arm and knelt next to Payne's head. Sam growled, showing his teeth, just inches from the man's face,

Shay lifted her hand above her head and made a circular motion over her head, "*Sam Suchen!*" (Sam Seek!)

Sam stood and made a fast 50-foot circle around Shay, searching for any other threats. Sam returned to her side after making sure there were no threats around.

"*Braver Hund.*" (Good Dog.) Shay said as she reached over and scratched Sam's head.

"Are you ok?" Robert asked as he ran up to Shay.

"I'm fine, thanks to Sam. Payne had me dead to rights. If it wasn't for Sam, I'd be dead right now." Shay replied, noticeably shaken.

She reached into her cargo pants pocket and pulled out Sam's chew toy; tossing it on the porch. "*Lauf.*" (Go.) Sam jumped up, ran over to it, and picked it up with his mouth. He laid down and started chewing it.

"I'll take care of Payne; you go check on the boy." Robert said, as he reached down and grabbed Payne's left arm.

Shay rushed into the cabin and found the boy still on the floor crying. She slowly walked towards the boy and knelt next to him.

"It's ok now, Thomas. You're safe. He's never going to hurt you again." She said, as she gently rubbed the boy's head.

"Who... who are you?" the little boy asked, still crying.

Shay removed her helmet and pulled down her balaclava mask; exposing her face. "My name is Sharon, you're safe now."

"Delta One to Eagles Nest." Shay said, into her mic.

"Go ahead Delta One."

"Thunder?" she replied, sounding shocked to hear his voice.

"That's an affirmative. Delta One." Tony replied.

"Eagles Nest; Tango Four is secure." Shay said. "We'll be transporting to holding area in five mikes."

"Copy Delta One, Main House is clear. Good job." Tony replied.

Robert had Payne gagged and blindfolded, with his hands zip tied behind his back; sitting on the porch of the cabin.

Shay came walking out slowly with Thomas Jamerson by her side. Thomas stopped when he saw Payne sitting on the steps of the porch.

"It's ok." Robert said, "He's harmless now. We're not going to let him hurt you anymore."

"Eagles Nest to Delta One, do you have any injuries?" Vicky asked.

"Affirmative, Eagles Nest, we have one. Delta Three took a bite out of Tango Four. He's going to require a few stitches." Shay replied, then looked over at Sam, still chewing on his chew toy.

*"Sam Hier."* (Sam Come.) Sam stood and walked over to Shay with his ball still in his mouth.

"*Braver Hund.*" (Good Dog.) She said as she rubbed Sam's head.

"Can I pet him?" Thomas asked, as he looked up at Shay.

"Not right now. Let us get you back to the main house and cleaned up." Shay replied and gave Thomas as slight squeeze on the shoulder.

Robert grabbed Payne by the arm and the five of them loaded into the six-seat four-wheeler parked next to the cabin. Robert zip tied Payne's hands to the bar that went across the top of the four wheeler's roof. Once they were all loaded; they took the twenty-minute slow ride through the woods, to the main house.

As they got closer to the main house, the reports from the other teams started coming in.

As soon as they all heard the words "EXECUTE!" they started moving. Jim and Dana moved quietly around the side of the cabin and up on the front porch. They took their positions; one on each side of the door. Jim raised his left arm and looked down at this cell phone strapped to his forearm. He sent a text back to Ray asking for the status inside of the cabin.

"They are all in the bed. We do detect some voices but are unable to understand." Ray replied over their earpiece.

Jim reached for the doorknob and tried to open the door, "*Locked.*" He said to himself. He motioned to Dana letting her know. Just above the doorknob was a deadbolt lock. "*This must be what has the door locked.*" He thought and pointed to the deadbolt so Dana would see. He turned and placed his left shoulder against the door and leaned back. Jim put every ounce of power into the door when he crashed into it with his left shoulder.

As the door flew open, they both rushed into the dark cabin. "LET ME SEE YOUR HANDS!" they both screamed out as soon as they entered the cabin.

Robert Jamerson sat up in the bed, "WHAT IN THE HELL IS GOING ON?" he yelled.

Jim and Dana both had their handguns trained on Robert Jamerson. Their green laser lights dancing across his chest.

"LET ME SEE YOUR HANDS." Jim yelled out again.

Amy Mason and Jackson Payne, both let out a scream as they threw the covers over their heads.

"DON'T MOVE!" Jim said, not taking his eyes off Robert. "Jane, get the kids." He said as he slowly moved towards the bed that the three were in.

"AMY! JACKSON! It's ok, we're here to save you." Dana said, as she moved over to the left side of the bed.

Amy slowly brought the covers down that were covering her face and looked at Dana. "Who are you?" she asked.

"I'm here to take you to safety." Dana said.

"I don't understand. Who are you?" Amy repeated; now crying and confused.

"Amy you and Jackson come to me." Dana said, as she holstered her gun. "We're not going to hurt you." Dana stuck out her hand towards Amy, "Please trust me. We are not going to hurt you. You can call me Jane."

Amy slowly slid the covers off her almost naked body and stepped onto the floor. She was wearing nothing but her panties as she turned away from Dana.

Dana reached over and grabbed a sheet off the bed and handed it to Amy, "Here Amy put this around you. Where are your clothes?"

Amy pointed to a pile of clothes over in the corner of the room behind Dana.

Dana stepped back, picked the clothes up and handed them to her.

"Thank you, Jane." Amy said; still confused.

"Jackson, my man, your turn." Jim said not taking his eyes off Robert Jamerson.

Jackson, still uncertain as to what was going on, slowly slid his legs off the side of the bed and onto the floor. He too was wearing only his underwear.

"Get dressed." Jim said to Jackson, as he momentarily raised his aim off Jamerson, so that Jackson could walk past.

After Amy and Jackson were dressed; they stood there huddled together next to Dana.

"Ok Jamerson, your turn." Jim said, taking a couple steps back to keep some distance from Jamerson, so he too could get out of bed.

"My clothes are over on the chair." Jamerson said, as he pointed to a chair behind Jim.

"Standup." Jim ordered.

Jamerson slowly stood on the floor next to the bed. He too, was only wearing underwear.

"Turn around and lay face down on the bed." Jim ordered.

As soon as Jamerson laid face down on the bed; Jim moved over to Jamerson and placed the barrel of his gun against the back of Jamerson's head.

"Jane, come over here and put the zip cuffs on this shitbag." Jim said, as he grabbed one of Jamerson's hands and pulled it behind his back.

After Dana zipped tied both of Jamerson's hands behind him, Jim grabbed his left arm and pulled him up off the bed.

"Ok, let's go." Jim said, as he pushed Jamerson towards the door.

"What about my clothes?" Jamerson asked; looking back at both Jim and Dana.

"You don't need them, now get going." Jim replied, as he pushed Jamerson out the door.

"But it's like forty degrees out there." Jamerson exclaimed.

"Sucks to be you." Dana replied, "Amy, Jackson, get your jackets, it's cold outside."

Once outside they walked over to the four-wheeler. Jamerson jumped into the front passenger's seat.

"Was that Tony on the radio?" Dana whispered.

"Sounded like it." Jim replied.

"We have a problem." Dana said, as she looked at the four-wheeler.

"What's that?" Jim asked, as he walked up next to Dana.

"It only holds four people." Dana replied, looking at Jim and back at the four-wheeler.

"Not a problem," Jim said. "Jamerson, get your ass out, you're walking." He said, as he reached over and pulled Jamerson out of the seat.

"Amy, get in. Jackson you'll ride in the back with me." Dana said, as she pointed to the four-wheeler.

Jamerson stood there shivering from the cold, "What about me?" He asked.

"You're going to have to walk." Jim said, retrieving a rope from under the front seat. He tied one end to Jamerson's waist and the other end to the back of the four-wheeler.

"I'm going to have to walk?" Jamerson exclaimed.

"Either that, or I'll drag you." Jim replied. "If given a choice, I'd rather drag you." He added and pressed the accelerator.

"Charlie One to Eagles Nest." Jim said, into his mic.

"Go ahead Charlie One." Came the reply from Tony.

"Eagles Nest, Tango Three is secure." Jim said. "Transporting to holding area."

"Copy Charlie One, Main House is clear. Good job." Tony replied.

"Charlie One, do you have any injuries?" Vicky asked.

"None to report yet, but we still have a long trip to the main house." Jim replied.

The four slowly headed towards the main house in the four-wheeler. They were followed closely behind by Robert Jamerson; dressed only in his underwear and slippers.

They were the second team to report in. This left the Alpha and Bravo teams remaining.

As soon as they got the word; Nicholas approached the cabin followed by Kevin about ten feet behind. Once they reached the back corner, they both took a knee. They checked the camera feed of the inside of the cabin and saw that Bill Mason and fourteen-year-old Robert Jamerson Jr. was sitting at a table playing cards.

"They are just sitting there like nothing is going on." Kevin whispered to Nicholas.

"Maybe he's suffering from that Stockholm stuff that Dana talked about." Nicholas replied.

"Whatever the case, we need to be careful." Kevin whispered, as he glanced over his left shoulder.

The two inside, continued playing cards together as if nothing was wrong. Little did they know that two people were stalking them just outside the cabin.

"Where are we going to hunt tomorrow?" Robert asked, looking up from the cards in his hand and taking a sip of beer.

"I'm thinking the two deer stands down past the creek." Bill replied, as he finished off his beer. "We better head to bed if we're going to get up early and hit the woods."

"Ok, I'm getting tired anyway." Robert replied, as he placed his cards down on the table.

"You feel up to some playing before we go to sleep?" Bill asked, giving Robert a wink and a smile.

"I guess so." Robert replied, as he stood and walked over towards the bed. Robert removed his sweatpants and tossed them over on the floor next to the bed.

"Let me help you." Bill said as he walked up behind Robert and helped Robert remove his shirt. Bill reached around with his left hand and started rubbing Robert's chest while kissing him on his neck. With his right hand, Bill slid his hand into the front of Roberts underwear.

Robert reached back with his left hand and started rubbing Bills crotch with his hand.

"Eagles Nest to Bravo, are you receiving the video feed from inside of the cabin?" Tony asked, as he watched what was playing out inside the cabin on his monitor.

"Copy Eagles Nest, we see." Kevin replied, not believing what he's seeing.

"Robert may be succumbing due to years of abuse and programming." Tony said, looking back at Vicky. "So, he may fight Kevin and Nicholas, when they go in."

"Eagles Nest to Bravo, based on what we are seeing, you need to treat both as possible hostiles." Vicky said over the radio. She looked over at Tony with a disgusted look on her face.

"Bravo One, breach now! They are both facing away from the door." Tony instructed over the radio.

Kevin and Nicholas had already positioned themselves outside of the cabin's door. Nicholas kicked the door with his right foot, just to the side of the deadbolt lock. As the door flew open; Kevin ran past Nicholas through the open door. Nicholas was right on his heals after recovering his balance.

The crash startled both Robert and Bill. They both turned around facing the door, with Robert now standing behind Bill.

"WHAT THE HELL!" Exclaimed Bill, as he saw two armed figures come charging through the door.

"LET ME SEE YOUR HANDS!" Kevin and Nicholas both yelled as they came crashing through the door. After clearing the doorway; Nicholas went to the right and Kevin to the left. They stopped just eight feet from Bill and Robert; frozen by shock and fear, and whose eyes were as big as saucers.

"LET ME SEE YOUR HANDS!" The masked Kevin repeated, holding his gun on young Robert.

Robert glanced over to a hunting knife that was sitting on the nightstand next to the bed.

"DON'T DO IT ROBERT!" Kevin yelled as he noticed the knife, just out of Roberts reach.

"DON'T MOVE!" Nicholas shouted; still holding his gun on Bill, who had his hands up in the air.

Robert reached for the knife, grabbing it with his right hand and turning towards Kevin.

"PUT THE KNIFE DOWN!' Kevin commanded, aiming his gun at Robert's chest.

Bill immediately moved to his left, out of the way of Kevin's aim. This caught Kevin's attention and he glanced over at Bill. Robert lunged forward, towards Kevin with the knife, barely missing Kevin's left side. Robert lost his balance when he lunged and fell to one knee. Kevin stepped around behind Robert as he went past. He grabbed the hair on the back of Roberts head and forced him down on the ground. Once down, Kevin placed his right knee on Roberts right arm, pinning his arm and knife to the ground.

"NOW STOP RESISTING. I DON'T WANT TO HURT YOU!" Kevin said, placing his left knee in the middle of Roberts back.

Nicholas still had his focus on Bill; making sure he did not try anything. "Get on your knees." Nicholas commanded, keeping his gun trained on Bill.

"You alright bro?" Nicholas asked Kevin.

"I'm good." Kevin replied, as he holstered his gun. He reached down and removed the knife from Robert's hand. After tossing the knife a safe distance away he reached for a zip tie. He pulled Robert's left hand behind his back and slipped one end of the zip tie on and fastened it. He then did the same, with Robert's right arm.

Once Kevin had secured Robert, he rolled him onto his side and went to help Nicholas.

After securing the zip ties on Bill, Kevin went back and helped Robert up to his feet.

"Ok you two, let's go." Nicholas ordered and pushed Bill towards the door.

"Where are we going?" Asked Bill Mason, as he stumbled towards the open door.

"To hell I hope." Kevin replied, as he grabbed Robert by the right arm and led him out the door behind Robert and Nicholas.

"Eagles Nest, Tango Two is secure." Kevin said. "We're transporting to the holding area."

"Copy Bravo One, Main House is clear. Good job." Tony replied.

"Bravo One, do you have any injuries?" Vicky asked.

"None to report." Kevin replied. "Had a little resistance, but everything is under control."

They secured Robert in the passenger's seat of the four-wheeler and Bill in the driver's side back seat, next to Nicholas. Kevin started the four-wheeler and the four slowly headed towards the main house.

Once Jack and Red received the word to go; they both slowly approached the back of their target cabin.

"Hold up." Jack whispered to Red.

They both stopped and knelt next to each other. "Red you slip around to the right side, I'm going left." Jack said, signaling also with his hand.

Jack turned and started around the back. Once he reached the corner he turned and slowly crept up the left side.

"Alpha One to Eagles Nest, we've lost video inside of the cabin. Do you copy?" Jack said into the radio.

"Eagles Nest to Alpha One, we have also lost signal too, stand-by." Tony replied, as Ray was working trying to fix the problem.

"Alpha One to Alpha Two, hold your position." Jack whispered to Red over the radio.

Red had reached the side window where he could look inside. He saw the face of a young boy staring back at him. Red jumped back; startled at seeing the young boy's face just inches away. Eleven-year-old Jacob Mason was laying in the bed, tears streaming down his face.

Red pressed his back against the side of the cabin, trying to control the rage that was building up inside.

He slowly turned back towards the window and saw a man's arm draped over the naked boy's body.

Red didn't say a word. He just barreled around to the front of the cabin.

"Red, do you copy?" Jack whispered into the radio again but received no reply.

"Alpha One to Eagles Nest, do you have a fix on Alpha Two?" Jack asked over the radio.

"Affirmative, he's approaching the cabin's door." Tony said, with a bit of hesitation in his voice.

"Eagles Nest to Alpha Two, hold your position, do not enter. I repeat do not enter." Vicky said over the radio.

"*What the hell is going on.*" Jack said to himself, still positioned on the left side of the cabin.

"Eagles Nest to Alpha One, Alpha Two has gone dark, Alpha Two has gone dark." Tony replied with tension in his voice.

"What do you mean he's gone dark?" Jack replied.

"Alpha Two has switched off his cameras and equipment. We have no way of tracking his location. Our last location of him was just outside of the cabin, next to the front door." Ray replied, this time over the radio.

"Damn it, Eagles Nest, I'm going in." Jack said into the radio.

Jack came around the front of the cabin and headed for the cabin's door. He paused just for a second as he noticed the door was wide open. Jack slowly crept closer to the open door and stopped just inches from the opening.

"Alpha Two, do you hear me are you ok?" Jack whispered, while standing just outside the door. Jack heard a crash from inside of the cabin and took a quick peek around the door.

To his dismay, Jack saw Red walking out the door with Jeffery Moon draped over his left shoulder.

"What happened?" Jack asked; looking at Red in disbelief.

"He fell." Red replied, as he let Moon's limp body drop to the ground.

Jack looked down at the bloody face of the man. "He got all those bruises and cuts from falling?"

Red nodded; looking at Jack, and then down at Moon laying on the ground.

"Looks like he fell more than once." Jack said; looking at the man on the ground.

"Ok, he fell down two times." Red replied, cocking his head to one side.

Jack just looked at the man's bloody face. "Two times?" Jack questioned, still looking at Moon.

"Ok three times, maybe more. I don't know it was dark." Red replied, looking down at Moon.

"Is he dead?" Jack asked, as he looked up at Red.

"Nope, just unconscious. He must have had a wee too much to drink last night and fell." Red replied with a smile.

"I see, he must have fallen several times." Jack said, not believing a word.

Red reached down and picked Moon up causing Moon let out a moan. "Aye. Must have."

"I'm going in to get Jacob. You get Moon in the four-wheeler." Jack instructed Red, as he entered the cabin.

Jacob was still in the bed, staring out the window. He never moved during the entire time after Red entered the cabin.

"Jacob, come on. Let's go." Jack said softly, as he stood next to the bed. But Jacob did not answer. He just lay there.

Jack looked the young boy over for any physical injuries. He knew there were going to be major emotional injuries and a long road ahead of the young boy. Jack noticed ropes were attached to the foot and the head of the bed. A small stand next to the bed contained several sex toys and lubricants.

Jack stood there looking down at the naked eleven-year-old Jacob Mason. Jack's mind flashed back to when he was Jacob's age and what his stepfather had done to him.

"*What is this boy's future going to be like?*" Jack thought to himself. It was like Jack was reliving a nightmare of his own past, as he looked down at the boy.

Jack took a blanket and gently placed it over Jacob's naked body and gently picked him up. Jack cradled the boy in his arms as a tear rolled down the boy's face.

"It's going to be ok Jacob; he's never going to hurt you again." Jack whispered, as he turned and walked towards the door. Jacob opened his eyes and looked up at Jack's hood covered face. He didn't show any fear of the faceless man that was holding him. Instead, Jacob placed his left arm around Jack's neck and gave Jack a weak but loving hug.

"Who are you?" Jacob quietly whispered as he looked up at Jack.

"You can call me David." Jack replied, looking down at Jacob. "I'm going to take you back to the main house and get you taken care of." Jack was doing everything he could to fight back the tears, but it was a losing battle.

"How's the boy?" Red asked as Jack approached.

"Physically he seems to be fine." Jack replied with a shaky voice. "Let's get him back to the house."

Jack looked over at the front of the four-wheeler, as he slid into the back seat. He saw that Red had tied Moon across the hood of the four-wheeler like a gutted deer.

Jack looked over at Red, "Let's go."

Red climbed into the driver's seat and slowly drove towards the main house.

"Alpha Two to Eagles Nest." Red said into his radio.

"Go ahead Alpha Two." Tony replied.

"Glad to have you back online." Vicky added.

"Tango One is secure." Red said. "We're transporting to Main House."

"Copy Alpha Two, Main House is clear. Good job." Tony replied.

"Alpha One, do you have any injuries?" Vicky asked.

"Tango One did suffer a few cuts and bruises." Red replied, as he slowly drove down the narrow trail.

"A few cuts and bruises?" Vicky replied, in a questioning tone.

"Aye, maybe a broken nose too. It was an accident, he fell getting out of bed." Red tried to explain.

"Copy that Alpha Two. Try and make it back to the Main House without letting Tango One fall anymore." Vicky replied.

"Aye, I'll do me best." Red replied.

"Eagles Nest to all teams. All Tango's secure." Came the report over the radio.

From the word "Execute", the entire operation took less than ten minutes from start to finish.

The teams slowly started arriving at the Main House. They took the children and put them all in a room together. The four men, plus Robert Jamerson Jr., were placed into separate rooms. They remained gagged and bound for the time being. They were going to treat Jamerson Jr. as a hostile, until they had time to evaluate him further.

Vickie's phone rang and she picked it up off the table. "Yes, Jack how's it going?" she asked.

"We're all back at the main house. We're holding the children in one of the bedrooms. The others are in individual rooms tied up." Jack replied, as he stood in the kitchen of the main house.

"Jack I've got to ask." Vicky said, with curiosity in her voice.

"Shoot." Jack replied.

"Why did you put Dana on the team that went in to take Robert Jamerson?" Vicky began. "You do remember she just tried to kill him."

"How could I forget." He replied, with a slight laugh.

"And you did it anyway." Vicky replied.

"I wanted to see how she would react. Beside she had non-lethal rounds in her gun."

"She could have switched them." She replied.

"And?" he said.

"She could have killed him." Vicky said.

"And that's a problem how?" Jack replied, with a tone of sarcasm.

"Never mind, what about Jamerson Jr.?" Vicky asked, leaning back in her chair.

"We're going to hold him separate from the other children. I'm going to get Dana to talk to him and see where his head is at. He may be suffering from that Stockholm Syndrome crap." Jack replied as he opened the refrigerator door.

"That's a good idea. He's the oldest and probably been subjected to this sexual abuse the longest." Vicky said, scratching her forehead. "You need anything?" she added.

"Yes, we could use some food and our go bags of clean clothes." Jack replied, pulling a water bottle out of the refrigerator.

"Send Kevin back here in the chopper, that'll be the fastest way. I'll see that Tony and Ray have everything ready when he gets here." She replied. "Oh, and Jack."

"Yes." Jack said.

"You did a fantastic job. You saved those kids, and no one got hurt." She said, with a little pride in her voice.

"Well except for Payne and Moon." He replied, taking a swig from the water bottle, and placing it down on the counter.

"They don't count." Vicky replied. "The children are the only ones that matter."

"I'm afraid the wounds and scars that the children suffered will take a lot longer to heal." Jack replied in a soft voice, as he looked out the window, the tears streaming down his face.

## Chapter Seven

# Let Me Introduce Myself

Kevin woke up about an hour before sunrise and headed to the chopper. He wanted to be in the air as soon as light allowed. The first part of the flight back would be the same tree top level flying as it was coming in the day before. One short refueling stop and he'd be back at Omega. After loading up supplies; he would turn around and be heading right back. This reminded him of his old military days not so long ago. But hopefully; this time he would not be shot at, like he did back then.

Shay and Dana had bunked in the room with the children, while the guys took turns keeping a watch over the five others.

They had placed cameras in each of the rooms containing their adult male prisoners, so someone could keep a watch on them all.

Robert and Nicholas took the first watch, although none of the others got much sleep. After an operation like they just went through; it took a while to come down off the adrenaline rush that they experienced.

Around noon time they could hear the approach of Kevin flying just above treetop. He landed in a small clearing closer to the main house. Jack, Shay, and Red took three of the larger four-wheelers out to meet Kevin and help bring supplies back to the main house.

Once everyone was back at the house, and supplies were checked and put away; it was time to get started on the next phase of their mission. This would be to get whatever information about any sex trafficking they could get out of the four. They also had to determine to what extent Robert Jamerson Jr., had been broken and, if he was complacent in the activities of the group.

Shortly after the supplies were taken care of; there was a familiar sounding knock at the door. “Good evening gentlemen... and ladies. Good to see you again. I am looking forward to assisting you again.” He said, looking at each one. “Oh, I don’t think we’ve met before.” He said as he stuck his hand out.

“No, we haven’t, my name is Bohdana Kovalenko, everyone just calls me Dana.” She said reaching out to shake his hand.

“I’m Doctor Wilson, it’s a pleasure to meet you, Dana.” Wilson replied, with a big smile.

“Are you here to tend to the injuries to Moon and Payne?” Dana asked; smiling back at the new acquaintance.

Doctor Wilson; pausing before replying as Jack, Shay and the others, laughed. “Yes, I will be more than happy to look at their injuries.”

“I don’t think we’ve formally met, but I’ve heard a lot about you.” Nicholas said; walking over to greet the doctor.

Dana stepped aside as Nicholas and Red approached the new arrival to greet him. She moved over next to Shay and asked, “Why you laugh when I asked him if he was here to tend to injuries?” Dana was looking at Shay, who still had a grin on her face.

Shay leaned over towards Dana and whispered, "I'll tell you later."

Doctor Wilson stepped over to Dana and asked, "Dana, I understand that you've studied Psychology at Kharkiv Karazin National University, and you are planning on going to Texas A&M soon?"

"Yes. I've been interested in the human psychology and how people think and respond to different situations." Dana replied with a smile.

He smiled back at her, "I too have studied the human mind and how it responds to different stimulations."

"That sounds great! We can get together, and you can show me some of your procedures and ideas." Dana replied, with some excitement.

This got a loud uproar of laughter from everyone in the room except for Dana, who looked around trying to understand what was so funny.

"But of course, my dear. I would love for you to sit in and observe my work. I think you will find it very interesting." He replied with a smile.

Shay started to reach for Dana's arm to pull her aside, but Jack intervened. "I think that is a great idea, Dana. Why don't you help Doctor Wilson." Jack said; giving Shay a, '*Don't you say a word*' look.

Shay looked at Jack and mouthed the word, "NO!"

Jack smiled and held up his index finger in front of his lips; implying for her to keep quiet. Shay just shook her head and rolled her eyes at Jack.

"Well, there's no reason to put this off any longer. Dana, would you like to assist me?" Wilson said, looking back at Dana.

"I would love to." She replied, as she walked towards Wilson.

"Great, could you grab my bag and follow me. Jack; let's start with Mr. Payne. He's the one with the dog bite, correct?" Wilson asked.

"Yes sir, he's in the first room on the right." Jack said, smiling at Dana as she walked by.

"Dana, don't forget your face cover." Jack said, and Dana pulled her face mask down to hide her identity.

Wilson and Dana entered the room that held Thomas Payne and walked over to a small table against one of the walls.

"Please put my bag down on the table Ms...." He started to say Dana before Dana cut him off.

"Jane!" Dana said.

"Jane? But of course." He replied. "Jane, would you please remove Mr. Payne's blindfold and that gag from around his mouth." Wilson requested.

Dana stepped around behind Payne, who was still tied to a chair, and removed his blindfold and the rag used to gag him. She placed them on the bed, that had been moved aside when Payne was placed in the room.

"Good evening Mr. Payne, let me introduce myself. I'm Doctor Thanatos." He said with a smile. "May I look at your dog bite?"

"Yes." Payne replied, still in some pain.

Wilson started removing the bandage that covered Sam's bite. "I see that someone at least cleaned and bandaged the bite." Wilson commented.

"You're a doctor, right?" Payne asked; looking up at Wilson.

"Yes and No." Wilson replied with a somber look on his face.

"What do you mean, Yes and No?" Payne asked; looking over at Wilson and then over at Dana.

"A story for another time, Mr. Payne. Let's get this bite taken care of first." Wilson said while looking closely at the bite on Payne's arm.

Wilson reached over and retrieved a bottle of rubbing alcohol out of his bag. "This is going to sting some." He said and poured the alcohol over the wound.

"SHIT! Damn that hurts!" Payne yelled and withdrew his arm from Wilson the best he could with it still tied to the chair.

"Sorry my friend, you don't want it to get infected. You don't want to have to amputate it do you?" Wilson asked, as he patted down the wound.

"No. Thank you for taking care of it." Payne replied with a smile. "What are they going to do with me?" he asked; with a nervous tone in his voice.

"Just needing some information. They'll be asking you some questions soon." Wilson replied, as he stood and walked towards the door.

"I would rather you do the questioning, Doctor Thanatos. You are much more compassionate and understanding than those others." Payne said; looking up at Wilson.

Wilson stopped before opening the door and looked back at Payne. "Very well Mr. Payne. I'll be glad to handle your interview. Until then, try and relax the best you can." Wilson replied with a smile.

Wilson opened the door and he and Dana walked out into the hallway; proceeding to the next room where Jeffery Moon was being held.

"Doctor Wilson, may I ask you something?" Dana asked, after entering the hallway.

Wilson stopped and turned towards Dana. "Sure, my dear, what would you like to know?" He replied, looking at her.

"We have to cover our faces, so that they can't identify us." Dana started.

"Yes?" Wilson replied.

"Why don't you do the same? Aren't you afraid that someone will identify you?" Dana asked.

"I've been doing this type of work, way before you were born Dana. I've never had a problem." Wilson explained. "Let's look in on Mr. Moon. I understand that he fell out of bed or something; suffering some bruises and maybe a broken bone or two." He said, as he turned and walked towards the room that held Jeffery Moon.

"That's the story." Dana replied as she fell in behind Wilson.

"Do you think otherwise?" Wilson asked; not slowing his step.

"No comment." She replied.

He glanced back over his shoulder at Dana, "You'll learn working in this business, that nothing is as it seems, and no one is who you think they are." He paused for a second and opened the door.

"Mr. Moon." Wilson said, as he entered the room, "I'm told you had a nasty fall."

Moon was laying across the bed in the room. He wasn't bound or gagged like the others, since the chances of him trying to run were slim. His face was swollen, and his bruises were already starting to turn dark. His left eye was nearly swollen shut, and he sported a cut across this forehead about two inches long. The thought of Moon rolling out of bed and received all these injuries, was very farfetched. Unless of course, he fell out of a top of a bunk bed five or six times.

"THAT'S BULL SHIT!" Moon tried to say, but his swollen lips, muffled most of his words.

"Mr. Moon, I'm Doctor Thanatos. Sorry we had to meet under these conditions, but I'm going to look at your injuries and see what I can do."

Wilson walked over next to the bed and leaned over to get a better look at Moon's face. Dana also stood just next to Wilson looking at the swollen face.

"Yes, yes it looks like that cut on your forehead is going to need a couple of stitches." Wilson commented. "Let me check your ribs to see if there are any of them broken." Wilson gently moved his hands down along Moon's ribs, trying to see if any of them were broken. However, Moon didn't show any signs of pain, as his ribs were being checked.

"I shall be back shortly Mr. Moon. I'd like to ask you some questions if you don't mind?" Wilson said, as he stepped back from the bed.

"I'm not answering any questions without my lawyer, and I haven't been told who you are." Moon demanded through swollen lips.

"Who we are is the least of your worries. And as for getting lawyer, that may come in due time." Wilson replied, as he turned towards the door.

"Do you know who I am?" Moon demanded, as he tried to sit up in the bed with little success.

"Yes Mr. Moon, I do know who you are. You are the former State Speaker of the House and you've been caught having sex with a minor." Wilson turned and looked at him as he opened the door. "We know exactly who and what you are."

Dana and Wilson walked out of the room and into the hallway; closing the door behind them.

Jack was standing just outside of the room as Wilson approached.

"Jack, I heard you were trying your hand in my area of expertise?" Wilson said, looking at Jack.

"I don't know what you're talking about." Jack replied; showing a sheepish grin on his face.

Wilson smiled, "You know, the Russian gentleman in the cabin behind Clinton's place."

"Oh.... That." Jack said. "It didn't end like I was hoping it would."

They turned and started to walk down the hallway, "Many times, it doesn't." Wilson replied. "I've had many people die on me that I hadn't planned on. It's part of the risk; you never can tell."

"What are you two talking about?" Dana asked, as she stood there next to Wilson; looking at Jack and then at Wilson.

"Shop talk my dear." Wilson replied, looking over at Dana and smiling.

"I would love to sit in on some of your......" Jack started to say.

Wilson smiled, "Some of my interview sessions?"

"Yes, I would love to learn some of your... interview techniques someday. Just in case you're not around and I need some answers fast." Jack replied; winking at Wilson as he glanced over at Dana.

"It takes many many years to perfect the right technique. A lot of trial and error." Wilson replied.

"Maybe you can show me some simple things that I can use in a pinch." Jack said smiling at Wilson.

"Yes, I think I can give you some basic techniques that you can use." Wilson replied. "Well Dana, shall we look in on the children?" Wilson turned and started walking towards the room where the children were being held.

When Wilson and Dana entered the room; Amy Mason was sitting on the bed reading one of the novels that she had brought with her. Her brother Jacob was curled up next to her, asleep on the bed. Thomas Jamerson and Jackson Payne was sitting on the floor at the floor of the bed, playing cards.

"Hello Amy, this is Doctor Thanatos. He just wants to check you guys out; to make sure you're ok." Dana said; smiling at the kids as they looked up at her and Wilson.

"We're fine." Amy replied, looking at both Dana and Wilson.

"No cuts or bruises?" Wilson asked, as he walked over to Thomas and Jackson and knelt beside them.

"Nope." Thomas replied, glancing up at Wilson briefly from the card game. Jackson just shook his head and kept looking at the cards in his hand.

"Amy, are you and Jacob, ok?" Dana asked, taking a seat on the edge of the bed.

Amy closed her book, and placed it on her lap, "I said we're fine. What are you going to do with us?"

"We're going to make sure you're safe." Dana replied; looking at Amy and gently rubbing Jacob's back.

Amy was looking over at Wilson, who had walked over next to Dana, "When can we leave?"

"Soon I hope." Dana replied. "Can I get you anything?" she asked, looking at each of the kids.

Thomas looked up at Dana, "Something to eat."

"How does pizza sound?" she asked.

"Sure." Came the reply from the children.

"Peperoni please." Jackson shouted.

"Me too." Thomas chimed in. "Extra peperoni."

"Jacob and I will have a cheese pizza please." Amy said, nudging her brother on the shoulder.

Dana and Wilson walked towards the door, "I'll get this for you as soon as I can."

As Dana was closing the door behind her; Amy said, "Thank you." and smiled at Dana.

Dana looked back at Amy with a smile and closed the door.

Shay and Kevin were watching the cameras and listening to everything that was going on in the rooms. "You notice that none of the children have asked about their fathers." Shay asked; looking up from the monitor showing the kid's room.

Kevin leaned back in the chair, "Interesting; wonder why?"

Nicholas and Jim drove into the nearby town and picked up the pizza and a few other supplies that they needed. They returned about two hours later and took the pizza's that the kids ordered into their room.

After about forty-five minutes; Shay and Dana got Amy out of the room and placed her into one of the other rooms alone.

"Amy we would like to ask you a few questions." Dana said, taking a seat across from Amy.

"Like what? What do you want to know?" Amy replied, looking at Dana and then at Shay.

"We just want to talk and find out a little about you, your brother and the others." Dana replied, smiling through her face cover.

"Those masks are creepy." Amy said, looking down at the ground.

Shay reached up and slowly removed her mask and Dana followed. "There is that better?" Shay asked, giving Amy a smile.

"Yes." Amy replied, looking up at Shay, then she looked at Dana, "Thank you. You were the one who came into the cabin last night and rescued us?"

"Yes, I'm Jane." Dana replied.

"My name is Sharon." Shay added, sticking out her hand to shake Amy's.

"Nice to meet you." Amy replied, softly.

"Sorry we had to meet under these circumstances, but we need to find out what is going on here." Shay replied, leaning forward in her chair towards Amy.

Amy shifted her gaze towards Shay, "Yes."

"You said, 'Rescued' us?" Dana asked, looking a little puzzled. "Did you feel you needed rescuing?"

Amy looked at Dana, "I don't know what you mean?"

"When someone is being rescued, they are normally being saved from a dangerous or stressful situation." Dana said, looking intently at Amy.

"Did you feel you were in danger?" Shay asked. "You can be honest with us; no one is going to harm you."

Amy looked away, "Not as long as I obeyed."

"What do you mean, 'obeyed'?" Dana asked, glancing over at Shay.

Amy looked down at the floor, "Do what I'm told."

"Amy please tell us what you were told to do." Dana replied.

Amy didn't say anything, she just continued looking down at the floor.

"Take your time Amy, there's no rush." Shay said softly.

Amy sat there for a couple of minutes just staring down at the floor without saying a word. Finally, she mumbled something that neither Dana nor Shay could understand.

"I'm sorry Amy; we didn't understand what you said. Could you say it again a little louder?" Dana said while taking Amy's left hand in both of hers.

Without looking up; Amy said, "Sex."

"They forced you to have sex with them?" Shay asked and looked towards the camera.

Jack and the others had been sitting in the living room watching the interview on the monitor. Jack picked up his cell phone and called Vicky.

"Vicky, are you watching this?" Jack asked.

"Yes, Ray and Tony are too." Vicky replied.

"I've got an idea." Jack said. "Put me on speaker phone."

"You're on speaker Jack. What's your idea?" she said.

"Hey guys." Jack said. Ray and Tony replied, "How's it going?"

"Ray you're recording this, correct?" Jack asked, knowing the answer.

"You know I am, why" Ray asked, sounding puzzled.

"You're going to blur everyone on the teams faces, correct?" Jack asked.

"Yep, and doing a voice change too." Ray replied.

"How about also blurring everyone's right arm or hand too." Jack asked.

"What for?" Ray and Vicky both replied at the same time.

"I think I know where you're going with this." Tony said, with a tone of interest in his voice.

"Pray tell." Vicky said.

"If we blur the same spot on each of the team members arm or hand, even though there is nothing there; when we turn over the videos and they see those blurred image's, they will assume that the area has some kind of gang tattoo." Tony replied, enthusiastically.

"Yes, and they will be looking for people with tattoos on their arm or hand." Jack added.

"Great idea." Vicky replied. "Ray, can you do it?"

Ray smiled and looked at her, "Is the Pope Catholic?"

"Yes, they forced me." Amy replied.

"Was it only the men here?" Dana asked.

"No, it was at some parties too, and some women also." Amy Whispered.

"How old were you when this started?" Dana asked.

"Nine." Amy replied.

"Have you ever thought about running away or going to the police?"

"Many times." Amy replied, looking at Dana.

"Why didn't you?" Dana asked.

Amy looked around for a few seconds and looked back at Dana. "Because they said that they would hurt my mother and Jacob if I told anyone." Amy said, as tears started rolling down her face.

"Who told you this?" Shay asked in a stern voice.

Amy glanced over at Shay, "Some people. I don't remember who they were."

"Ok, we'll come back to this later." Dana said, trying to calm Amy down some.

"Amy let's talk about your mom and dad. Does your mother know what is going on?" Shay asked.

"I don't think so. I don't know. Maybe. She's never said anything about it." Amy replied looking up at Shay and shaking her head.

"Your dad adopted you and Jacob soon after he and your mother married." Dana asked.

"Yes." Amy replied.

"Your father started taking you to.... sex parties when you were nine?" Dana inquired.

"Yes." Amy replied, with tears starting to roll down her face again.

"I'm sorry to have to ask you these questions. But we need to know everything we can, so we can stop this from happening to other children like you and your brother." Dana added, as she passed Amy another tissue to wipe her face.

"Did your mother know about these parties?" Shay asked.

"Yes." Amy replied, softly and looking down. "Well... I did say something one time that some of my dad's friends touched me and I felt scared."

"What did she say?" Shay asked.

"She." Amy paused for a second. "She told me that it was just a part of growing up. That boys and men have special needs and that I'll grow to like it. She said that I was getting to be a big girl now and she didn't need to know what happened."

"What else?" Shay asked.

"I told her that it hurt." Amy replied, looking up at Shay.

"What did she say when you told her that?" Shay asked.

With a slight tone of resentment, Amy replied, "She said I was overreacting."

"Your mother knew about the sexual abuse?" Dana asked, looking at Amy and then over at Shay.

Amy didn't say anything and remained looking down at the floor. The hearts of everyone broke as a tear fell onto the floor.

"Amy, I know this is extremely hard for you. But we need to find out everything we can, so that something like this will never happen again." Dana said, as she handed Amy a tissue.

"What is your father's involvement in this group?" Dana asked.

Not looking up, Amy said, "My dad does all the paperwork for the adoption company."

"What adoption company?" Shay asked, glancing over at Dana and back at Amy.

"The one that Robert, Thomas, Jackson and the others came from." Amy said, as she took a swallow of her drink.

"Others?" Dana asked, leaning forward. "What others?"

"Liu, Mei, April, James. I don't remember the other's names." Amy replied, looking over at the table.

Shay tilted her head to one side and just looked at Amy for a few seconds. "What happened to them?" she asked, not sure if she wanted to know.

"I do not know. They were a few years older. I did text with Mei. But one day she stopped, and I never heard from her again. They don't like for us to talk to each other. Except during camp or house gatherings." Amy reluctantly said.

"Camp?" Shay asked.

"Yes, this Camp, this place is one of them." Amy said, now starting to get upset.

"Wait. You said one of them. Are there more camps like this?" Dana asked with a surprised tone.

"Yes, but I've only been to three." Amy replied.

"You've been to three of these camps?" Dana asked, with a shocked look on her face.

"Yes." Amy replied.

"How many camps are there?" Shay asked.

"I don't know." Amy replied and shrugged her shoulders.

"Do you know where the other camps are that you were taken?" Shay asked.

"No." Amy replied.

"Amy, the other kids you mentioned; were they part of the camp and house gatherings?" Shay asked, now starting to show some concern on her face, but trying not to show it. Shay leaned back in her chair and looked over at the camera in the corner of the room.

"Yes, some of them were." Amy replied.

"Amy, were they also adopted through the same agency?" Dana asked.

"Yes, I think so." Amy replied softly.

"And your father handled the placement of them too?" Dana asked.

With tears rolling down her face, "I don't know, maybe." Amy replied.

"Amy, I need to ask you one more question." Shay said, taking Amy's right hand in her hand.

Looking down, Amy gave a quick nod.

"Were they forced to have sex too?" Shay asked; fighting back the tears.

"Yes, we all were." Amy whispered and started crying.

Shay leaned over, pulled Amy close to her and held her. The three of them all hugged and cried for several minutes.

Shay leaned back and said, "Why don't we take a break. Can I get you anything Amy?" Shay stood-up and walked to the door. She slowly opened the door and glanced back at Amy who was still crying in Dana's arms. Shay closed the door behind her and walked down the hallway.

"OH Crap! GRAB HER!" Jack yelled out as he leaned forward in his chair. Jack had been watching Shay and Dana question Amy on the monitor.

"Who?" Robert and Red both yelled out at the same time.

"SHAY!" Jack replied, "she's going to kill him."

"WHO?" Robert yelled out as he and Red stood and started towards the hallway.

"Mason, she's going to..." Jack stopped in mid-sentence and ran towards Mason's room.

Shay opened the door to the room that Bill Mason was in. She walked over to where he was still tied to a chair in the middle of the room.

She grabbed Mason by the shirt and drew her right fist back, "YOU" she said as she punched Mason on the left side of his face. "FUCKING" she punched him again, "SON" and another strike to the face "OF A..." But before she was able to hit him again, Robert and Red grabbed Shay from behind and pulled her away.

"BITCH!" Shay yelled, as Robert and Red pulled her out of the room and into the hallway. Even though Shay only stood five feet one inches tall and weighed about a hundred and ten pounds soaking wet. She could pack a powerful punch.

Jack looked in the room at Mason's bloody face and closed the door. "Take Shay outside, so she can cool off."

Shay jerked away from Robert and Red and stormed out of the house, as they followed her.

Once outside the three stopped and Shay turned back towards Robert and Red.

"Chill little lady." Robert said, holding his hands up.

"DON'T YOU TELL ME TO CHILL. I'M GOING TO KILL THAT SON OF A BITCH." Shay yelled; now standing facing the house. Robert and Red stood between her and the house, trying to keep her calm and to keep her from going back inside, to finish what she started.

Inside of the house, Jack came walking back into the kitchen where Wilson was sitting and eating a slice of Pizza.

"You need to go check on Mason, Shay just beat the shit out of him." Jack said as he walked past Wilson and into the living room.

"When I finish my pizza." Wilson replied.

"No rush, he's not going anywhere." Jack said and disappeared around the corner.

"What in the hell is all this yelling?' Dana asked as she walked down the hallway.

"Shay just beat the crap out of Mason." Wilson replied with a mouth full of pizza.

"Where is she?" Dana asked; looking over at Wilson.

"Robert and Red took her outside." Wilson replied and pointed towards the door leading outside.

Jack picked up his phone and called Omega. "Jack." Came the reply from Vicky.

"Are you guys watching this?" Jack asked, as he took a seat.

"Yes, is Shay, ok?" Vicky asked.

"She'll be fine. Give her time to cool down. Robert, Red and Dana are out there with her now." He said, trying to replay the last several minutes over in his mind.

"I've got Ray trying to track down this adoption company." Vicky said.

"Vicky, is this ever going to stop? Every time we plug a hole, another one opens up." he said, noticeably upset.

"Jack are you ok?" she asked, with real concern in her voice.

"This is just bringing up bad memories from my past. I'll be ok." Jack tried to reassure her, but he was trying more to reassure himself. "You'd think by now it wouldn't affect me like this."

"Jack I'd be more worried if it didn't bother you. You're dealing with pure evil, and any normal person would be affected." She tried reassuring Jack. "I had the same conversation with Shay not too long ago. We can only do what we can. Focus on the ones we have saved."

"It's hard to relive the nightmares and know what these kids are going through. And knowing what they will have to live with the rest of their lives." he said as he looked down at the floor.

"Jack, you, and Shay have gone through what most people can't ever imagine. You two have survived and can now, do whatever you can to save others from suffering the same nightmares." Vicky said, trying to reassure him.

"I know. But it's hard Vicky." Jack replied, softly.

"Jack, think of the ones you have saved, and the hundreds if not thousands you have saved from ever having to go through this nightmare in the future." Vicky said, with all the compassion that she could muster.

"I will never understand how a father could molest their own children; much less allow someone else to do it." Jack added, thinking back to his stepfather.

"Get Doctor Wilson busy finding out everything he can from those guys. Ray will track down everything on this so-called adoption agency." She said with confidence.

"And once we get it?" Jack asked. "What are we going to do with the sick bastards and the kids?" he said, leaning back hard in his chair.

"I've got Tony working on ideas and options now. Jack; you are doing an excellent job." She said, reassuring him.

"Thanks" he replied, with a slight smile.

"Talk to Shay. You are the team leader." Vicky said, in a serious tone. "You need to get her under control."

"I'll try, but you know Shay. She's going to do what she's going to do." Jack replied with a slight chuckle.

"I know, she's got a good heart, but very head strong." Vicky replied.

"And stubborn too, you forgot stubborn." Jack said laughing.

"She gets that from her fathers' side." She replied.

Jack laughed, "Sure thing, whatever you say. I'll head out there. Maybe the four of us can handle her."

"Jack you're the only one who can relate to what she's been through. You both have that common connection. You both need to be there for each other." Vicky said, with some sadness in her voice.

Jack looked out the window and saw Shay sitting on one of the chairs around the fire pit. The others were sitting around her talking.

"*Well, I don't see any blood or bodies lying on the ground. So, I guess it's safe to go out.*" Jack thought to himself.

Jack opened the door and walked out towards the group. "Hey guys can I have a second with Shay?" he said, looking at each one of them.

Robert, Red and Dana all got up and walked towards the house. Dana stopped next to Jack and squeezed his arm and gave him a concerned look.

"She'll be fine." Jack said softly to Dana. "She just needs some time." He added and walked over to Shay.

"Can I sit?" Jack asked, as he stood in front of her.

She motioned with her head to her right and said, "Sure."

Jack took a seat next to her and reaching over, took her hand. After a few seconds, Shay leaned over and put her head on Jack shoulder.

"I'm sorry I lost it." She said softly.

"Don't worry about it. He deserved every lick, and then some. You only did what everyone else wanted to do."

Shay gave Jack's hand a slight squeeze and looked up at him. "But I lost control in front of everyone."

"No one is going to give it a second thought. If it had been me in there, I would have done the same thing."

"Jack, you hit like a girl. He would have just laughed at you." Shay said as she sat back up and smiled at him.

"Hey now, I've been working out. I've gotten much better." He replied and nudged her with his shoulder.

Shay looked away and wiped the tears from her face. “I know you’ve been through the same thing that I’ve been through. The others can’t really understand.”

“My stepfather did the same thing with me.” Jack said; wiping the tears from his face now.

“What do you mean. I know he molested you and your sister. You told me that.” She replied looking up at him.

“He also would take me to some of his friends and he would allow them to molest me too.” He said

as he leaned over placing his elbows on his knees and exhaled.

“Why haven’t you told me!” She asked; putting her arm around his shoulder. She rested her head back on his shoulder and gave him a loving squeeze.

“The memories didn’t resurface until I got here. Things started to emerge back at Omega when I put two and two together and saw them pairing up. I knew then what was going to happen.” He said, wiping more tears away.

“Jack I’m sorry.” She replied.

“If Red hadn’t beat me into the cabin, I would have blown Moon’s fucking head off.” He said, looking back at her.

They both sat there for nearly half an hour, without saying a word. “You good?” Jack finally said, breaking the silence.

“Yeah, I’m kind of hungry.” She said as she stood up.

“You know they’ve got pizza in there.” He said, looking up at her.

# Chapter Eight

# Let the Questioning Begin

After an hour and a half, Shay had calmed down and had her fill of Pizza. It was time to get back to work.

Shay walked over to Dana sitting on the couch. "Are you ok?" Dana asked; as Shay walked up.

"I'll be fine. Sorry for the little meltdown." Shay said, giving Dana a smile.

Dana looked up at her, "I was worried about you."

"You ready to get back to work?" Shay asked, glancing over at the monitor that displayed the room where Amy sat.

They both walked into the room where Amy had been sitting. "Sorry for the long wait. But we had some other matters to attend to." Dana said as they both took a seat.

"Can we get you something?" Shay asked.

"No, I'm fine. How is Jacob?" Amy asked.

"He's fine; playing some video games." Dana replied. "We have a few more questions for you."

"I don't know what else I can tell you." Amy replied.

"Tell us about the other kids here. How well do you know them?" Dana asked.

"Don't know much at all about Jackson. He's new, I think. This is the first time I've seen him." Amy replied.

"And Robert and Thomas, how about them?" Shay asked, leaning forward a little.

"I've seen them off and on for a few years. Robert is the oldest of the group. I guess he will be the next to disappear and then maybe me after that." Amy said; looking down at her hands resting in her lap.

"What do you mean disappear?" Dana asked, cocking her head slightly to one side.

"Once we reach a certain age." Amy paused, "Then you disappear."

"Disappear where?" Shay asked; looking at Amy with a questioning look on her face.

"Back to the streets, foster care, maybe. I don't know." Amy replied.

"But Amy you were not adopted. Why do you think you'll disappear?" Shay asked.

Amy looked at Shay with a confused look, "I don't know; isn't that how it works?"

Shay and Dana sat there in silence for a couple of minutes; trying to understand the depth of the trauma these kids have suffered.

"Tell us about Robert." Dana finally asked.

"There's not much to tell. I don't see him that much. Maybe two or three times a year." She replied.

"Robert seemed to resist when we tried to rescue him. He attacked one of our guys with a knife." Shay said in a not-so-subtle tone.

"He has changed a lot since last year. He's more accepting of the situation than he was before." Amy said.

"What do you mean?" Dana asked.

"He seems to.... I don't know. It's like he's enjoying it." She replied, in a puzzled tone. "The last time we were together I said something about running away."

"And what was his response?" Dana asked, looking very curious.

"He called me a bitch, and for me to grow-up and accept it." Amy replied, this time with more anger in her voice. "And this trip, he hung out with the men instead of with us. It was like, he was one of them."

"Amy, do you know a Jordan McCree?" Shay asked.

"I know a Jordan. I don't know her last name. I heard some of the men talking about a Jordan and her father was supposed to be here, but never made it." Amy replied. "You think that's her?"

"We don't know right now. We're still trying to put all the pieces together." Shay replied.

Dana looked at Shay and Back at Amy. "I think that's all the questions we have right now. Do you have any questions you'd like to ask us?"

"What is going to happen to us?" Amy asked, softly.

"First of all, you kids have done nothing wrong. I want you to understand that. I'm sure you'll be talking to more people soon. But for right now we need you to go back and take care of the other kids. You need to try and be strong in front of the others." Dana said and a comforting voice.

"And my dad?" Amy asked.

"Amy, your dad, and the other men have done some terrible things. I'm not sure what is going to happen to them. But be sure it's not your fault." Dana said, trying to reassure Amy.

"I know, my dad is in a lot of trouble. I understand." Amy replied as she lowered her head and tears started running down her face again.

"Amy, take your time, I'll be back in a few minutes to take you back to your brother." Dana said, as her and Shay stood up to leave.

Dana and Shay walked out into the hallway and closed the door behind them. They quietly walked towards the living room where the others were sitting.

"You guys did a great job with Amy." Jack said, as Shay and Dana entered.

"Well except for when I went ape shit on Mason." Shay replied, with a smile.

"I would have done the same thing." Kevin replied, if I had heard everything she was saying.

"Yes, don't beat yourself up Shay. You did what any normal person would have done." Nicholas added.

"Well... I don't know about 'Normal'." Jack said, using air-quotes around the word normal.

"Aye, referring to Shay as 'normal' is a wee bit of a stretch." Red said, with a grin. "Or any of us for that matter." He added. With that the entire group broke out into laughter.

"What's next?" Dana asked, looking at Jack and then to Dr. Wilson.

"Well next, Dr. Wilson will apply his expertise and see what information we can find out from the four guys." Jack replied; looking over at Wilson and giving him a thumbs-up.

"That's wonderful, can I help?" Dana asked enthusiastically.

"Sure. I think that would be a very eye-opening experience for you. And you can add some of what you learn to your future questioning." Jack replied as he leaned back in his chair.

"Who do we start with?" Dana asked, looking over at Wilson.

"Let's look in on Mr. Payne again." Wilson replied, as he stood and started walking down the hallway. "Please grab my bag, Dana."

They stopped before entering the room where Payne was being held. Wilson turned to Dana. "Are you ready?"

"Quick question. They gave you the cover name of Dr. Thanatos, does that have any meaning?" Dana asked.

“It’s the Greek name for, He who brings death.” Wilson replied as he opened the door and entered the room. Dana paused for a second with a shocked look on her face and slowly entered the room behind him; closing the door.

“Good evening Mr. Payne; how are you doing and how does that dog bite feel? We’re here to ask you some questions.” Wilson said; walking over to Payne’s side.

Payne tried to reply, but was not able to with the gag still covering his mouth.

“I’m sorry, allow me to remove this dreadful thing. There now, what were you saying?” Wilson asked.

“I said, I want a lawyer.” Payne replied, in a harsh tone.

“But Mr. Payne, when we talked before, you said you wanted me to question you.”

“I’ve changed my mind. I want a lawyer.... NOW!” Payne barked.

“We are not a law enforcement agency, nor are we part of any government Mr. Payne, so a lawyer will not do you any good.” Wilson replied; removing the blindfold from around Payne’s eyes.

“Then who the hell are you?” Payne asked.

“We are just concerned citizens.” Wilson replied; turning towards his bag that Dana was holding.

“You have no right to hold me! Now let me go!” Payne demanded; looking at Wilson and then at Dana.

“You gave up your rights as soon as you molested the first child, Mr. Payne.” Wilson replied as he pulled out a tourniquet out of the bag Dana was holding.

Dana placed his bag down on the dresser across from the chair that Payne was sitting in. She looked at Wilson with puzzlement on her face.

“What are you going to do with that?” Payne asked, looking at the tourniquet in Wilson’s hand.

“I’m going to apply it to your right arm a couple of inches above where you got bit.” Wilson replied, as he was preparing the device.

"What for?" Payne asked, looking down at the tourniquet, and back up at Wilson.

"It will help you answer my questions." He replied, looking down at Payne.

"I don't have to answer any of your questions. Now let me go!" Payne demanded.

"In due time. But first, tell me about this club you have here." Wilson asked.

"It's a hunting club. We get together and hunt deer, rabbits, and stuff like that." Payne said; looking back and forth from Wilson and Dana.

"And don't forget the children. The things you do with the children." Dana added, with a disgusting look on her face.

Payne looked at Dana, "Don't know what you're talking about."

"We have it all on video, asshole." Dana replied harshly.

"I'm not going to answer any of your questions." Payne said.

"That is totally up to you." Wilson replied as he placed the tourniquet around Payne's right upper arm.

"Get that fucking thing off my arm!" Payne said, looking down at his right arm and then to Wilson as he took up the slack.

"Mr. Payne, have you ever had a tourniquet applied to an arm or a leg?" Wilson asked.

"NO!" Payne replied, trying to struggle against his bindings.

"It is very painful. As it tightens down, your arm with start to throb and tingle. Soon after that the pressure of the blood will cause excruciating pain. Your arm will turn a nice dark shade of purple as the pain increases. If it's left on long enough, your arm will soon build up toxicants and will start to decay. Then sadly, you'll have to have your arm amputated." Wilson explained, standing next to the bed with both arms crossed.

"I'm not saying anything." Payne said, defiantly.

"Very well." Wilson replied, as he tightened down the tourniquet just enough to cause his arm to start to tingle and change color a little. "We'll be back shortly.

While we're gone, think about if you want to answer our questions or not." Wilson replaced the gag over Payne's mouth and blindfold over his eyes.

Dana stood there for a second with her mouth half open. She was shocked to see what Wilson had done.

"Are you coming my dear?" Wilson asked, as he walked to the door and opened it. "Don't forget to grab my bag on the way out."

Without saying a word, Dana grabbed his bag, turned towards the door, and followed Wilson out of the room. Once the door closed, she said to him, "I thought doctors took an oath to do no harm?"

"True. But I'm officially not a doctor anymore." He replied as they walked down the hallway.

"What do you mean?" she asked; looking at him with a shocked look on her face.

"My former employer didn't totally agree with my methods." He replied, not slowing his step.

They walked into the living room and Dana stopped at the doorway. Wilson continued into the living room and picked up a file folder. "I'll be right back Ms. Dana. I need to grab a bite to eat and then I'll be ready to talk with our next individual." Wilson exited the living room and walked into the kitchen.

"Did you see what he did?" Dana asked, as she pointed toward the door that Wilson went through.

"What?" Nicholas replied, looking up from one of the monitors.

"He put a damn tourniquet on Payne's arm for no reason." Dana exclaimed; looking right at Nicholas.

"Oh that, I hear he does a lot worse." Nicholas replied, looking over at Dana.

"Just wait till he gets in the groove." Kevin added, with a smile.

"What are you talking about?" Dana insisted.

"You guys didn't see him use the Ten's machine." Kevin said, looking over at Red and Nicholas.

"No but we heard about it." Red said. "And I hear that Shay had her turn at the machine too."

"That was cool." Shay replied, giving Red a thumbs-up; not looking up from her word search book.

"What is ten's machine?" Dana inquired, looking at each of the team members.

"It's a little device that delivers a mild shock to your body, usually your shoulder. It's very relaxing." Ray replied over the speaker next to the monitors. Vicky, Ray, and Tony had been monitoring the questioning and team from Omega headquarters.

"Well, it maybe relaxing if it's applied to your shoulders." Robert said, as he started to laugh.

"But not your balls!" Shay said, looking up from her book.

"I still don't understand. Does it massage you?" Dana asked to the laughter of the group.

"Dana, have you ever accidently touched a live electrical wire or maybe an electric fence." Nicholas asked.

"Yes, when I was a kid, my uncle had a farm and had an electric wire around the fence to shock the cows if they brushed up against it." She replied.

"At a low voltage, it's more of a stimulating shock to sore muscles." Robert added.

"But imagine turning the voltage up and connecting it to your nutsack." Jack said; looking over at Dana. "Sorry, bad example." He added.

"I get the picture." Dana said, with a shocked look on her face.

"Tell her about the rats." Kevin said, looking over at Jack.

"Jack, I hate to breakup your little shoptalk. Is Doctor Wilson there?" Vicky asked over the speaker and her picture popped up on one of the monitors.

"I'm here, Ms. Vicky." Wilson replied as he walked into the room. "How may I be of service?" he added, with a smile.

“You’re not going to question Jamerson Junior are you?” Vicky inquired, with a concerned tone in her voice.

“Heavens no. I’m afraid my methods would not have the results we are looking for. Mr. Jamerson Junior is going to need months of psychiatric treatment, to bring him back from where he is now.” He said.

“OK good, Tony’s still working on an exit plan.” Vicky replied. “He’s almost got it in place.”

Wilson nodded, “Very good. Dana and I will get to work on the others.”

“Ray.” Jack said.

“Yes Jack, I’m here.”

“Can you get some information on Susan Jamerson and Judy Mason?” he asked.

“Sure thing. Give me about an hour and I’ll send you what I get.” Ray replied.

Wilson looked over at Dana, “Shall we look in on Mr. Mason?”

“Sure.” she replied.

They reached the room that held Mason and they entered. “Mr. Mason, I’m Dr. Thanatos and my assistant here is Jane.” Wilson said as he walked up to Mason.

“I demand you let me go this instant!” Mason demanded.

“I’m sorry Mr. Mason, you’re in no position to demand anything.” Wilson replied as he looked down on Mason sitting in the chair.

“I’m a District Attorney; I know my rights.” Mason said, defiantly.

“Mr. Mason, you have no rights. You gave up those rights the moment you molested those children.” Wilson replied with a devilish smile.

“I don’t know what you are talking about.” Mason replied.

Dana looked at Mason with a disgusted look on her face, “We have you on video with young Robert Jamerson Jr., you know the fourteen-year-old we caught you with. Also, we know about your work with the adoption agency.”

“I don’t know anything about any adoption agency.” Mason declared.

Wilson opened a file folder that he had brought in with him and flipped over a couple of pages. "I sure you know Marcus and Alex Kovenski." Wilson said without looking up from the folder.

"Never heard of them." Mason replied, but with some concern in his voice.

"That's funny, they know you very well." Wilson said, although Wilson was not being totally honest. All Omega had at the time, was the two names, but Mason did not know that.

Mason sat there not saying a word until he finally asked. "I want to make a deal." Mason said, as he looked at both Wilson and Dana.

"The deal is, Mr. Mason, whoever talks first wins." Wilson replied.

"And what will I get if I don't talk?" Mason asked, weighing his options.

Wilson leaned forward and placed his hands, one on each side of Mason. Wilson's face was just six inches from Mason's, "Pain, Mr. Mason. More pain than you could ever imagine."

Mason looked at Wilson for a second or two and smiled. "You're bluffing."

"Very well Mr. Mason." Wilson replied as he stood upright. Wilson looked over at the camera, "Can someone bring me my foldup table sitting next to my red bag?"

"I'll take it to him." Shay said, as she stood up and retrieved the table from the corner of the room. Half a minute later Shay entered the room carrying the table that Wilson had requested.

"Remember me?" Shay asked, as she placed the table next to Mason.

"You're the crazy bitch that beat me earlier." Mason replied, with a hint of fear in his voice.

"I'd love to untie you. You and I could have some alone time together. With no interruptions this time. But I'll leave you with these two." Shay smiled and walked towards the door. Just before the door closed completely behind her, Shay looked back at Mason, "Have fun... Bitch." She said and slowly closed the door shut.

"Let me see." Wilson said, looking down at Mason. "I believe you are right-handed?"

"So." Mason replied, looking up at Wilson.

"Jane, could you be so kind as to move the table over to Mr. Mason's right side, next to his arm." Wilson said, as he walked over to his bag.

"What are you going to do, shoot me full of truth serum, to make me talk?" Mason asked, as he watched Dana position the small table.

"No Mr. Mason, that's nowhere near as enjoyable as what I plan on doing." Wilson replied without turning around, "Besides, those drugs don't really work like they do in the movies. I prefer my own methods of getting the truth out of people. While I'm getting things together, can you tell us about this property that you and Mr. Payne own together?" Wilson asked; retrieving things from his bag.

"It's a hunting club. We get together and hunt." Mason replied.

"And molest children." Dana said, as she stood next to Mason.

"I'm sure the Bar Association will not look kindly on you not disclosing your relationship with Mr. Payne and not excusing him from the Jamerson jury." Wilson said while looking back over his shoulder at Mason.

"So what. I'll get a slap on the wrist and maybe have to pay a fine." Mason replied.

"Mr. Mason, do you smoke?" Wilson asked as he turned toward Mason. Wilson had a Dominican Arturo Fuente cigar in his mouth and walked over to where Mason was seated.

"No, those things will kill you." Mason replied as he watched Wilson approach.

"We all must die sometime, Mr. Mason. Sometimes we have a choice on how we do it." Wilson said with a smile. Wilson retrieved a syringe of Etorphine M99 tranquilizer from his pocket and gave Mason a small dose in the side of the neck. The sedative would work almost instantly, rendering Mason immobile and unconscious within a couple of seconds, and lasting for several hours.

"Dana would you be so kind as to untie his right arm. Strap his arm down on the table, using the Velcro straps that are attached to the table?" Wilson asked, as he turned back towards his bag.

"What did you give him?" Dana asked, as she worked to untie his arm from the chair.

"Just a small dose of Etorphine. It is a semi-synthetic opioid having an analgesic potency approximately 1,000-3,000 times that of morphine. It's normally used to immobilize elephants and other large mammals.

But in exceedingly small doses, it will render a person unconscious in a matter of seconds as you see." Wilson explained as he closed his bag.

Dana looked down at Mason who was already out cold.

"We should look in on Mr. Payne and see how he's doing." Wilson said as he walked towards the door. "We'll come back to Mr. Mason in a little while."

"PaPa down and out!" Shay laughed, as she watched Wilson give Mason the shot of M99, over the monitor.

"What?" Robert said, looking over at Shay.

"She refers to Perverts and Pedophiles sometimes using the military alphabet Papa for P." Jack said, not looking up from the magazine he was reading.

"Oh." Robert replied and went back to what he was doing.

"I know, weird." Jack said.

The door opened into Payne's room and in walked Wilson followed by a very hesitant Dana.

"Jane, will you please remove the gag and blindfold from Mr. Payne." Wilson said; looking at Payne sitting in the chair.

"Yes sir." Dana replied, as she walked around Wilson and over to Payne.

"Mr. Payne." Wilson said loudly. "You ready to talk?"

"I have nothing to say." Payne replied, with some discomfort in his voice.

"Very well. Your partner Mr. Mason, has been more than happy to cooperate with us." Wilson said as he walked up next to Payne.

"Then you don't need me anymore, so take this fucking thing off my arm!" Mason replied, glancing down at the tourniquet on his right arm.

"Oh Mr. Payne, we're not finished with you quite yet." Wilson replied as he reached down to check the pulse in Payne's right wrist. "Ok, Mr. Payne, you still have blood flowing into your lower right arm. Although it's somewhat restricted, it's still getting blood flow.... For now."

Payne looked up from the tourniquet and at Wilson. "Take it off." Payne demanded.

Wilson looked down at Payne, "Now, now Mr. Payne. As I said, I have a few more questions to ask you."

"What do you want to know?" Payne asked; looking at Wilson and then at Dana.

"Very good Mr. Payne. Here are the rules." Wilson said; smiling at Payne.

"Rules? If I answer your questions, then you take this thing off my arm." Payne said defiantly.

"No, no, here are the rules of the game. I ask a question and you answer. If you refuse or answer falsely, then I tighten the tourniquet one turn."

Payne looked down at the tourniquet and back up at Wilson, "What do you want to know?"

"Who owns the property here?" Wilson asked.

"Me and Mason. But I think you already know that." Payne replied.

Wilson smiled and gave a slight nod, "Very good start. Now, you made a comment to Thomas Jamerson, just before you started molesting him. That you didn't come here and pay money to just sleep. Please explain."

"We have to pay a fee to spend time with someone." Payne replied; still looking at Wilson.

"Someone? You are referring to one of the children?" Wilson asked, cocking his head to one side.

"Yes. We must pay a price for each child." Payne replied, as he lowered his head and looked down at the floor.

"Who gets the money?" Wilson asked.

"I don't know, it's deposited into an account." He replied, looking up at Dana and then back to Wilson.

Wilson pulled up a chair next to Payne, "Tell us about that account."

"What do you want to know?" Payne replied.

"Who manages the account, where the account is, anything you know about the account and the money." Dana asked and looked over at Wilson for approval.

"The Wells Fargo bank in town. The name on the account is Small Shots Hunting." Payne replied. "Mason and I opened the account right after we bought the property."

"You use the money for what?" Dana asked.

"We don't use the money." He replied, looking at Dana.

"What do you mean, you don't use the money?" She asked, with a somewhat puzzled look.

"Soon after we deposit the money, it's transferred out. To where I don't know." Payne replied, in a nervous voice.

"I'm on it!" Ray said, looking over at Vicky. They had been watching the questioning from Omega.

"How many other groups like this are in existence?" Wilson asked.

"Groups? You mean like this hunting club?" Payne asked.

"Yes, like this club that uses children as sex toys." Dana snapped.

Payne looked over at Dana and said, "Three others that I know of."

"Are they all setup like this one, with the accounts?" Wilson asked.

"Yes." Payne replied.

"We need the names, locations and members of each one of these clubs." Dana said.

"Yes of course. Just please take this thing off my arm." He said, looking over at Wilson.

"Jane, will you get Mr. Payne a sheet of paper and something to wright with." Wilson said, looking over at Dana. "There should be something in my bag."

Dana retrieved some paper and a felt-tipped marker from the bag and placed it on Payne's lap.

"How am I going to write with my arms tied down?" Payne asked looking down at the paper and then over at Wilson.

"I'm going to untie your right arm so you can write. However, if you try and untie your other arm and legs, you will vastly regret that. Do I make myself clear Mr. Payne?" Wilson asked, with a serious look on his face.

"Ok, no problem. What about the tourniquet?" Payne asked, looking down at his arm as Wilson untied the strap.

"No Mr. Payne, the tourniquet stays on until we verify your information. The rules still apply, if any of your answers are false, then I'll return, and the tourniquet gets tightened." He replied, as he then loosened the pressure on the tourniquet so Payne could write.

"Thank you." Payne replied.

"Before we leave, would you like to add to, or change any of your answers?" Wilson asked, as he stood up.

"No." Payne replied.

Wilson and Dana walked towards the door. Dana opened it and stepped out into the hallway. Before Wilson closed the door behind him, he looked back at Payne.

"When you're finished; just let us know. We'll be watching you with the camera. So don't make me come back in here. Do you understand?" Wilson said, and Payne nodded his head.

Wilson slowly started closing the door. Just before the door completely closed, he reopened it about halfway.

"One more question, do you know a Peter McCree?" Wilson asked, looking into the room at Payne.

"I met him through Robert Jamerson, but don't know anything about him. I think he was supposed to be here this weekend, but he never showed." Payne replied, looking at Wilson as the door closed behind.

Once the door closed; Wilson and Dana walked down the hall towards Jeffery Moon's room.

"You didn't ask him about the Loving Arms adoption agency." Dana said, as Wilson reached for the doorknob to Moon's room.

"We need to get more information before we ask. He seems to be cooperating so far, and I want to make sure he continues." He said, as he turned the doorknob.

"Mr. Moon; tell me what kind of State Speaker of the House molests children?" Wilson asked as he walked through the door.

"I told you, I'm not saying a word." Moon replied through his swollen lips.

"We don't need you to tell us. We have it all on video." Dana said, as she walked over next to the bed.

"Then why do you bother asking?" Moon asked.

"If you answer our questions; things will go much easier for you." Wilson said, placing his bag on the side of the bed.

"Look, turn me loose and I won't press charges." Moon said; looking over at Wilson.

"Charges? What kind of charges do you think you're going to file?" Wilson asked, with a chuckle.

"Assault and kidnapping to start." Moon shot back, the best he could.

This caused Wilson to laugh aloud. "Mr. Moon; the story is that you fell out of your bunkbed. And as far as being kidnapped; you're free to leave anytime you wish."

Moon struggled against the pain and sat up in the bed. He painfully moved his feet onto the floor. He sat there for a few seconds trying to catch his breath and trying to ignore the pain. He looked up at Wilson, who had taken a couple of steps back. "Then I'm free to leave." Moon said.

"Sure, there's the door." Wilson said, motioning towards the door.

"Fine, you've not heard the end of this." Moon exclaimed, as he struggled to stand.

"However, if you leave Mr. Moon; a video of you will be sent to every news agency in the country showing you having sex with a young boy." Wilson said, with a smile.

"I've got some very powerful friends." Moon replied, looking at Wilson and then at Dana.

"Your friends will run from you like roaches when the lights have been turned on." Wilson said. "You think they are going to support you when they see the video? Are they going to come to your aid once they learn that you are part of a child sex group?" Wilson added, now looking profoundly serious.

Moon slowly sat back down on the edge of the bed. He looked down at the ground and then looked up at Wilson.

"Mr. Moon; your so-called friends will turn on you like a pack of wild dogs." Wilson said, as he took a couple of steps towards Moon.

Moon sat there without saying a word. He was thinking back to when he was State Speaker of the House, and how he was able to broker deals and always came out ahead. But what did he have to offer? *"Money!" Everyone has a price."* He said to himself.

"What do you want?" Moon finally asked.

"Information Mr. Moon, information." Wilson replied; giving Moon a cold stare.

"I have money. I can pay you. Just give me my phone and I'll transfer everything." Moon pleaded.

Wilson motioned for Dana to get Moon's phone. She left the room and in a couple of minutes she returned to hand Moon his phone.

Moon took his phone; entered the password to his phone and signed into his bank account. "Here!" Moon said as he handed Dana the phone back. "Take all the money and transfer it into your account. Take it all!" Moon looked over at Wilson and then back at Dana; who was looking at his phone.

"All of it Mr. Moon?" Dana asked, looking at Moon.

"Yes!" Moon replied, nodding his head.

"All fifty dollars and sixty-nine cents?" Dana exclaimed. "You are far too generous."

"What!" Moon exclaimed with a more than shocked look on his face. "Give me my phone."

Moon took his phone and looked at it in bewilderment. "Wait. There was more than three million dollars there a couple of days ago. There must be some mistake." He said; looking at both Dana and Wilson with an expression of total shock

Dana smiled, "You should manage your money more wisely."

"But it was there." Moon said in a frantic voice. He punched some numbers on his cell phone and looked up at Dana. "My brokerage account.... It's empty. There was close to ninety million dollars in those accounts! What's going on?"

"Aye, looks like Robin Hood has struck again." Red said, looking up from the monitor. "I could buy me some good Scotch with that lot." He added with a grin and leaned back in his chair.

"What's going on?" Robert asked, looking over at Red.

Red looked over at Robert, "Ray just relieved Moon of all his hard-earned money."

Robert looked back at the television program he had been watching. "I'm sure most of it was money taken under the table."

"Aye." Red replied, turning his attention back to the monitor.

"Mr. Moon, fifty dollars might feel generous to some. But it's not going to buy your way out of this mess you're in." Wilson replied, shaking his head slowly as Moon looked at him.

"I don't understand." Moon said in a shocked nervous voice.

"All you have now is information." Wilson replied, as he pulled up a chair next to the bed.

"I don't have any information." Moon pleaded.

Wilson leaned back in his chair and crossed his legs, "Oh, but a man of your power, connections, and wealth.... Well maybe not wealth, knows many things."

"Like what?" Moon asked, looking at Wilson.

"Tell us everything you know about this club, the money, the Loving Arms Adoption agency and who heads up the operation." Wilson said with a pleasant tone.

"If I tell you, will you let me go?" Moon asked.

"Mr. Moon, if you tell us and everything checks out. I promise you'll never hear from us again." Wilson replied with a smile.

"Never heard of that Loving Arms place. The club? I've only been to this one. I've heard of maybe two others, but I can't tell you anything about them." Moon paused and looked at both Wilson and Dana.

"What about the money?" Wilson asked. "We know you have to pay to visit the clubs and the money is deposited into a bank in town."

Moon looked at Wilson, "Yes, that is correct."

"Where does the money go from there?" Wilson asked.

"Some guy in the Middle East. From Qatar I think." Moon replied.

"Do you have a name?" Dana asked, as she took a seat on the edge of the bed.

"Nasir Al-Hadid. I think I pronounced his name correctly." Moon said, looking away slightly.

"Got it." Ray yelled out from behind his monitor at Omega.

"Ray you on this?" Jack asked through the speaker.

"Yes, I'll pull everything I can on this dude and get back at you ASAP!" Ray replied over the speaker.

"Jack." Tony said, as he sat next to Ray. "I'll dig around with some of my contacts as well and see what I can find out."

"Where's Vicky?" Jack asked.

"She went home to get some rest. I'll fill her in when she calls." Ray replied.

"Ok, later dude." Jack replied and turned his attention back to the monitor showing Moon's room.

"Tell us what you know about this Nasir Al-Hadid." Wilson said, leaning forward now in his chair.

"You need to ask Mason and Jamerson about him. I only know of him through them." Moon replied.

"You've never met this Nasir Al-Hadid?" Dana asked.

"No just have heard Mason and Jamerson talking about him after they had a few drinks." Moon said, looking over at Dana. "They didn't know I was listening. I was in the living room here and they were talking in the kitchen." Moon replied. His words were starting to come out better through his swollen lips.

"What did they say?" Dana asked, leaning forward a little.

He looked at Wilson and back at Dana, "They were talking about Mason's meeting with Nasir Al-Hadid and how he wanted to open-up some more clubs in the U.S."

"What else?" Wilson asked.

"Jamerson asked Mason how Nasir liked the young Ukrainian girl his friends hooked him up with." Moon replied.

"Who's friends?" Wilson asked.

"Jamerson's friends." Moon replied.

"WHAT UKRAINIAN GIRL!" Dana yelled as she stood-up.

The sudden outburst startled both Moon and Wilson. Moon groaned out in pain as he suddenly turned towards Dana.

"Ray, are you getting this Bro?" Jack said over the monitor.

"Got it." Ray replied in a hurried voice.

"This is starting to get very interesting." Shay said, as she pulled up a chair next to Red and Jack.

"Aye that it is. I think Dana is about to go Shay on him." Red said, with a laugh.

Shay looked over at Red and slapped him on the arm with the back of her hand.

"Ouch missy that stung." Red said, laughing and rubbing his arm.

"Jack, I think we need to get Dana out, before she." Shay was saying before Jack cut her off.

"Before she goes Shay on him?" Jack said, laughing and leaned away from the backhand that he was expecting from Shay.

Robert looked over from his television program, "I say let her loose on Moon."

"It's not Moon I'm worried about. It's Mason and Jamerson. She doesn't need to go in there before Wilson is ready." Jack said, looking back at Robert.

"Wilson, Dana. Let's take a break." Jack said over their earpieces.

Wilson stood up and started for the door. "Jane, are you coming?" he asked, pausing, and looking back at Dana.

Dana stood there for a few seconds looking at Moon before she turned and walked out. Shay met her in the hallway.

"Let's take a walk." Shay said, as Dana approached. They both turned and walked out the back door of the house.

"What's going on?" Wilson asked as he entered the living room.

"Dana's little sister was taken and she.... We suspect that Jamerson had something to do with it." Jack replied.

"Aye, that's sort of how we ran into Dana. Or how Jack ran into her." Red said, looking over at Wilson.

"I see now. She's the one who." Wilson started, before being cutoff.

"YES! She's the one. Can we get back to this Al-Hadid guy?" Jack blurted out.

"You sure its ok for Shay to try and talk to Dana? That's like trying to put out a fire with a can of gasoline." Robert said, standing and walking over towards the kitchen. "You guys need anything?"

Jack threw his hands up in the air. "I don't know. We have three stubborn head-strong over-reacting women to deal with. How in the hell do I know?"

"I heard that, Jack." Vicky said over the monitor.

"Oh, hey Vicky." Jack said in an apologizing tone. Jack leaned over towards Red and whispered, "Shit."

Ray said, with a bit of amusement in his voice, "I forgot to tell you that Vicky is here."

"Not to over-react Jack. But I hear we may have come across the head of this organization?" Vicky said in a smug but playful voice.

Red leaned over to one side away from Jack and slightly turned his body towards him and placed his right hand under his chin. "*Ye'v git yersel' intae some trioblaid lad*." (You've got yourself into some trouble young man.) Red said with a smile.

Jack looking over at Red and squinted his eyes, "What?"

"I think he said, you fucked-up." Robert said as he walked back into the room from the kitchen.

"Λye, close enough." Red replied.

"God, I need a drink." Jack said, as he lowered his head and slowly shook it.

Red reached over to his backpack, that was sitting next to him, and pulled out a half empty bottle of Scotch whiskey. "Here, enjoy." Red said, handing the bottle to Jack.

## Chapter Nine

# Welcome to the Dark Side

Shay and Dana walked outside to the firepit and sat down. They both sat there for a few seconds without saying a word.

"The last time we were out here it was me that had lost it." Shay said looking down at the ground.

"He knows something about Katryna." Dana replied, as she looked up into the sky, trying to hold it together.

"We'll find out what he knows." Shay assured her.

Dana looked over at Shay, "How?"

"Wilson has his ways." Shay said, looking at Dana.

"How, with that 10-box thing?" Dana asked, in a noticeable upset voice.

"Tens Unit." Shay replied.

"Whatever." Dana replied as she looked away. "I'm never going to see Katryna again."

"Don't say that. We're going to do everything we can to find her and get her back." Shay assured.

"What is Dr. Wilson going to do? Torture them to get them to talk?" Dana asked, cautiously.

Shay leaned back, “If that is what it takes.” and took Dana’s hand.

Dana looked at Shay, “I don’t know if I agree with that.”

“I’m surprised.” Shay said.

“Why that is?” Dana replied, shifting her body slightly towards Shay.

“Didn’t you just try and kill Jamerson, just a short time ago?”

“Yes, but.” Dana stopped and looked down at the ground.

“Let Wilson do his thing. Don’t you want to get your sister back?”

“Yes of course I do.” Dana replied, looking at Shay.

Shay stood, “Then let Wilson do what Wilson does best.”

“What? Torture them?” Dana replied, looking up at Shay.

“Look. If these guys know where your sister is; don’t you want to know?”

“Of course, I do. What kind of question is that?” Dana asked, harshly.

“If they know something and they are not willing to say; do you want us to just cut them loose?” Shay asked, standing there with her hands on her hips.

“NO! I want to know where my sister is.” Dana exclaimed, still looking up at Shay.

“Then let Wilson do his thing. It could result in getting your sister back or not getting her back.” Shay explained.

“Ok.” Dana said softly.

“Think of the pain these guys have inflicted on these children. They deserve what Wilson does to them. If not more... Ok, come on Dana, let’s head back in and get to work finding out where your sister is.” She reached down with her hand to help Dana up.

“But getting information by way of torture is not reliable.” Dana said as she stood.

“Getting someone to agree to being guilty of something by way of torture can be questionable. But if it’s detailed information and we can verify it, then it’s much more reliable.” Shay said, as the two turned and walked towards the house. They entered the house and walked into the living room where the others were sitting.

"What's up guys did we miss anything?" Shay asked; looking over at Robert and Red.

Robert looked back at Shay, "Jamerson got a text message a few minutes ago."

"Junior or Senior? Dana asked. walking over to Red and Robert and looking at the monitors.

"Senior." Robert replied.

"From who?" Dana asked, leaning over, and looking at the message on the phone.

"Looks like it's from the wife, Susan." Robert said, looking up at Dana.

"Did Ray ever dig up anything on Susan Jamerson?" Shay asked, looking back at Jack who was on the phone.

"Jack is talking with Vicky and Ray right now." Robert replied, looking back down at the monitors.

Once Jack got off the phone he walked over to where the others were.

"What did you find out?" Kevin asked.

"Ray hacked into Jamerson's phone to look back on the text history with Susan. Vicky thinks we should use this opportunity to get Susan to come here." Jack said, looking at Dana and Shay.

"Looks like Susan Jamerson is just as guilty as the others." Jack said. "Ray just filled me in on what he found."

"Aye, do tell us." Red said, who was sitting over in the corner trying to catch some shut eye.

"Looks like Susan is a Child and Family social worker." Jack began. "She also works with our other two, at Loving Arms Adoption Agency. Susan was asking how things were going here at the camp. "Vicky wants us to reply and bait her into coming."

"Well let's do it." Dana said; looking a little excited. "What are we going to say?" Dana asked, looking at Jack and down at the phone sitting on the table.

"I don't know." Jack replied looking perplexed.

"I know." Shay said. "Tell her that Thomas is sick, and she needs to come get him." Shay said with a grin. "I used that excuse to get Vicky to come and get me out of school several times."

"Sounds good. How does that sound to you Vicky?" Jack said, leaning over towards the speaker.

"Sounds good. And Shay; you never fooled me with that excuse." Vicky said, with a little humor in her voice.

Jack picked up the cell phone and started typing. '*Sorry for the delay. Just got back from the woods. Thomas not feeling good, could you come and get him?*' Before jack pressed the send button, he showed the other what he had typed.

"Looks good." Dana said.

A few minutes later, a reply came, '*What's wrong with Thomas?*'

"Hell, what do I say?" Jack stood there looking around.

"Tell her a stomachache." Dana replied, looking at Jack.

"Good idea." Jack said and entered the reply on the texted screen and pressed send.

A few minutes later the reply came. '*Did Payne give Thomas too much candy again? He did that the last time you guys got together.*'

"When you end it make sure you end with XXOO. That's how he ends his text messages with her." Ray said.

"Got you." Jack replied and typed in the next text reply, '*I'll see you in a couple of hours. XXOO.*' And pressed send.

Susan replied with, '*See you in couple hours. Have Thomas ready when I get there. OOXX*' in her reply.

"I hope that works." Kevin said, as he walked out of the room into the kitchen.

"We'll find out in a couple of hours." Shay said, looking over at Kevin.

"We need a room to put her in. They are all full right now." Jack said, looking at Dana.

"Why don't we take the kids and move them to one of the cabins?" Nicholas replied, "We can take turns watching them. We still have the cameras, so we can also see inside."

"No, I don't want to do that. Those kids have bad memories of those cabins." Jack said, shaking his head.

"May I make a suggestion?" Wilson said, as he had been sitting over on the couch reading the local newspaper.

"Sure thing, what is it?" Jack asked, turning, and looking at Wilson.

"We can put Payne and Moon together in one room and I can sedate them. I believe we have all the information out of them that we're going to get. If we need to question them more, we can wake them up." He said, looking over the top of his newspaper.

Jack looked over at Nicholas. "Great, let's get that taken care of now. We don't know when Susan will be here. Nicholas: how about you stand watch outside, close to the road and let us know when she arrives."

Jack looked over at Wilson, "Wilson; after you get those two settled and sedated, how about getting one of your sleep juices ready for Susan when she arrives. Here's what we'll do..."

After about two hours; the radio sounded with the voice of Nicholas as he reported in, "She's pulling in now."

"Copy." Red replied. He looked over toward Jack and Shay as they played cards over on the couch.

"Let's get ready." Shay said, tossing her cards down.

"Wilson, it's show time." Jack yelled out to Wilson who was sitting in the kitchen with Robert and Jim. The three of them stood up together.

"She's coming in through the back door." Nicholas relayed over the radio.

Jim, Robert, and Wilson stepped around the corner into the dimly lit hallway as Susan entered through the kitchen door.

"Robert, Thomas I'm here. Where are you guys?" Susan yelled out as she walked through the kitchen and into the living room.

Susan stopped in her tracks, "WHO THE HELL ARE YOU?" she shouted out as she stood face to face with several masked figures. She didn't notice the three silently coming up behind her including Wilson; who had a nice shot for her. Within seconds, she was out cold and carried by Jim and Robert to the room.

"She's locked up and resting." Jim said, as he walked back into the living room.

"Won't be the last time she'll be in lockup." Shay said, looking down at the cards in her hand. She and Jack had resumed their card game, which was interrupted by Susan's arrival.

"What are we going to do with Susan?" Dana asked, looking at Jack.

"What do you mean?" Jack replied, as he dealt out the cards to Shay and himself.

"As far as the questioning and things." Dana replied, leaning against the doorway.

"You and Wilson will be handling the questioning and stuff like the others." Jack replied, glancing over at her.

Dana looked down at the floor, "Does that mean torture too?" she asked, with a not so sure tone.

"She is one of the major players in this sex trafficking ring. So, what do you think?" Jack replied in a matter-of-fact voice.

"That's up to you and Wilson as to how you get the answers. If it were up to me, I'd torture the shit out of all of them and leave them to the rats." Shay said, looking over at Dana.

The rest of the team, also agreed with what Shay had said, along with putting their own spin on how they would gladly deal with them.

"I don't know." Dana replied softly while looking up at the ceiling.

"Don't you remember what I said earlier? Shay said. "About if someone knew where your little sister was being held?"

"Yes." Dana replied.

"Well, she knows where someone's little sister or brother is. Not yours, but someone else's." Shay said, leaning back slightly in her chair and addressed Dana in a stern voice.

Dana bit her lower lip slightly and cut her eyes over towards Shay, "I know, sorry." Dana replied.

"We do what we must do to save these children and the lives of future children from suffering. And if it means some of these perverts must suffer some, then so be it." Jack added, also letting Dana know the importance in the matter.

"Aye, and the more suffering the better." Red added, with a grin.

Dana turned and hadn't noticed that Wilson had walked up behind her. "Crap! You scared the hell out of me." Dana said, looking at Wilson who was just inches from her.

Wilson smiled, "Are you ready to get started Dana?"

"Sure." She said as she took a couple steps back.

Wilson turned and started down the hallway. "I've already collected the names and locations from our Mr. Payne. Who would you like to start with?" He asked.

Dana fell in behind Wilson, "Can we start with Jamerson Jr.?"

"If you wish. I'm afraid he may feel a little uncomfortable with me in the room, but I'm happy to observe if you like." Wilson said, pausing outside the door.

"Uh. Ok. But no torturing." Dana said; pointing her finger at Wilson.

Wilson smiled, "Very well. He's all yours." Wilson replied and opened the door.

The two entered the room and Dana walked over to the chair that Robert Jr. was strapped to. Dana reached over and removed the blindfold. She immediately saw the hate in his eyes as Robert Jr. looked at her. Dana paused for a second and reached and pulled down the gag that was covering his mouth.

"Let me go BITCH!" Robert Jr. yelled, as he struggled to get free. This caused Dana to take a half step back.

Dana looked over at Wilson, who was leaning against the wall, with his arms folded across his chest. Wilson didn't flinch or change his expression at the outburst. He just continued to look at Robert Jr.

"Hey guys you need to watch this." Kevin said, as he watched everything on the monitor.

Robert Jr. looked over at Wilson and then back at Dana with a mean and threating look. Dana just stood there matching his glaze.

"This is like an old western gun fight. Waiting to see who draws first." Kevin said, looking up at Shay who was standing behind him.

"We'll see now how she handles some hostile person." Nicholas said, taking a swig from his water bottle.

"Maybe she'll go all out Shay on him." Jack replied with a laugh. Shay immediately punched Jack on the arm, which caused the others to laugh too.

"Let me go!" Robert Jr. demanded, not taking his eyes off Dana.

"No." Dana finally said, without looking away and maintaining eye contact with Robert Jr.

"I've not done anything wrong, so let me go!" he demanded again.

"You've got to earn your freedom." Dana said calmly.

"I don't have to earn shit." He shot back, as he tried again to struggle to get free.

"We're trying to help you, Robert." Dana calmly said.

"You can help by letting me go, I've done nothing wrong. Now let me go!" he said, but this time in a calmer tone.

"You tried to stab one of our team members." She replied. "Don't you remember?"

"What would you have done if someone come barging in with guns and wearing masks?" he replied glancing from Dana over to Wilson. "Why are you wearing a mask and that old dude is not?" motioning with his head towards Wilson.

Dana pulled up a chair close to where Robert was sitting. "Robert, tell us why you came here to this place."

"To hunt. Why else would we come to a hunting club?" he replied, putting emphasis on the words hunting club.

"What else do you do?" she asked, leaning forward a little in her chair.

"We cook hotdogs and marshmallows and sing campfire songs." He replied smartly and smiled at Dana.

"And having sex with adult men?" Dana said, looking at any type of reaction from him to indicate how he stood. "We have you on video, having sex with Bill Mason."

"I'm not some faggot!" he shouted out, and again struggled to free himself.

"No one is saying you are. We are not here to judge you. We're here to help you." Dana tried to explain.

"Sounds to me like you're calling me a homo or something." He said defensibly.

"Robert, we are not judging you in anyway." She replied, trying to reassure him.

"Look lady, I like girls. Last summer I nailed several girls." He said, looking over at Wilson, who had not moved or said a word.

"Robert, you have done nothing wrong. An adult having sex with a minor, whether it's consensual or not, is against the law." She tried to explain.

"I bet that little bitch Amy, told on us, didn't she? DIDN'T SHE!" Robert yelled, leaning towards Dana and with spit flying out of his mouth.

"How about we take a break." Dana said, as she stood.

"I don't care what the fuck you do lady." He replied, as Dana started to walk away. She stopped and turned around and looked down at him.

“She’s about to go Shay on him.” Robert said excitedly.

“I’m going to go Shay on all your asses if you don’t stop.” Shay said, not looking away from the monitor.

Dana slowly walked over next to Robert Jr. and stopped and looked down at him.

“Here it comes.” Kevin said, sounding excited.

Dana leaned over close and whispered into his ear. “Fine.” Then she pulled his gag back over his mouth and placed the blindfold back over his eyes. “Maybe that will shut your fat little mouth.” She turned, and walked out of the room, followed by an amused Wilson.

As the two of them walked out of the room, all the guys that had been watching the drama play out, scattered.

Dana walked into the Living room and flopped down on the couch next to Nicholas. God that kid pisses me off.” She said, throwing her hands up in the air.

“What happened?” Kevin asked trying to look surprised.

“Guy’s grow up.” Shay said, leaning against the table that the monitors were sitting. “We watched the whole thing. What do you think?”

“He’s definitely suffering from some level of Stockholm Syndrome.” Dana replied, placing the back of her hands over her eyes.

“You did an excellent job Dana.” Wilson said, as he stood in the doorway.

“Aye, I would have gone total Shaaaaa....” Red stopped in mid-sentence, as he saw Shay giving him the stink-eye.

“I’m sorry Red, what did you say?” Dana asked, clasping her hands behind her head.

“Never mind, ye did a great job not getting ye hackles up.” Red replied, with a glance at Shay.

“Dana, would you like to look in on Mr. Mason and see if he’s ready to answer some questions?” Wilson asked.

“Sure, why not.” She replied and stood up from the couch.

The two of them entered the room that held Mason. They both walked over to him, “Are you ready to answer some questions?” Wilson asked.

“I still don’t know anything about any adoption agency or that Marcus and Alex Kovenski.” Mason said.

“We already know your involvement with them Mr. Mason. You may as well tell us everything.” Dana said, looking down at him and at his arm, that was strapped down to the small table next to him on the other side.

“You don’t know Jack shit.” Mason shot back.

“We know that you handled the adoptions for the agency. That makes you part of the sex trafficking ring.” Wilson replied, standing next to the small table that held Mason’s right arm.

Mason just looked up at Wilson and then at Dana.

“This makes you even more of a guilty scumbag. Along with molesting Robert Jamerson Jr. and the many others that you have molested.” Dana said in a disgusting voice.

Mason just looked at Dana without showing any emotions.

“Last chance Mr. Mason, tell us what you know about the adoption agency.” Wilson said, as he reached into his pocket.

Mason just looked straight ahead and said nothing.

Wilson pulled out a Cigar cutter, or some refer to it as a Straight Cutter. He grabbed Mason’s right hand and held it firmly down on the small table. Mason looked sharply down at his hand and then at the cutter in Wilson’s hand. Wilson placed the cutter around Mason’s right little finger and quickly cut Mason’s finger off just above the hand.

Mason let out a scream that would have awaken the dead, as his little finger laid there about an inch from his hand. Dana turned away placing her hand over her mouth trying not to throw-up.

“Now Mr. Mason, you have nine more chances to tell us what we want to know.” Wilson said, as he placed the cutter on his ring finger. “Tell us about the adoption agency.” He added, in a very calm voice.

Jim pushed himself away from the monitor and looked back at the others, "DAMN! Did you see that? He just cut Mason's little finger off."

"What did Dana do?" Jack asked, looking over from the couch.

"She's doing her best not to lose her cookies." Jim said, looking back at the monitor.

Nicholas and Robert came walking in from the kitchen, "What's with all the screaming?" Robert asked as the two walked over and looked at the monitor.

"Wilson just chopped off Mason's little finger." Jim replied, still in disbelief.

Mason looked down at his right hand and then back up at Wilson. "I handle the legal paperwork for the adoption agency." Mason said, as tears rolled down his face.

"Very good. That wasn't so hard now, was it?" Wilson said, still holding the cutter around Mason's ring finger.

Dana finally got her composure back and turned back towards Mason.

"Tell us about the money in the Wells Fargo account." Wilson said, looking down at Mason, who was shaking.

"What money?" He asked in a whimpering voice. Wilson squeezed the cutter, just enough to cut Mason's finger and to make it bleed some.

"Ok, Ok. Payne and I manage an account that the club has." Mason said as he looked down at his hand.

"What is the money used for?" Wilson asked, still not removing the cutter from around his finger.

"IT GOES TO THIS GUY, NAMED NASIR AL-HADID!" He shouted out.

"I think we need to get Dana out. Wilson is getting too close to questions dealing with Dana's little sister. I'm not sure she needs to be in there." Shay said, looking over at Jack.

Jack clicked a button on the monitor that activated only Wilson's earpiece. "We're pulling Dana out. You're getting close to information that might pertain to her younger sister. I don't know how she'll react. Send her out to get something." Wilson, glanced over to the camera and gave it a slight nod.

"Jane, would you go get my blue bag. I seemed to have left it." He said, looking over at Dana.

"Ok, I'll be right back." Dana said and turned towards the door.

Dana walked into the Living room, "Where is Wilson's blue bag?"

"He doesn't have a blue bag." Jack replied; walking over to her.

"What's going on?" she asked; looking very confused.

"We don't want you in there right now. Here sit." Jack said, pushing a chair up in front of the monitor.

"I don't understand. Why can't I be in there?" she asked; looking at Jack and then over at Shay.

"He's about to ask questions that might be related to your sister. It's best that you stay out here." Shay replied. She then walked over to stand behind Dana as she took a seat.

"Tell me about this Nasir Al-Hadid person." Wilson asked; still holding the cutter on Mason's ring finger.

"Like what?" Mason asked as he looked over at Wilson, and then down at his bloodied hand.

"What is your relationship with this Nasir Al-Hadid?" Wilson asked.

"He runs things. All the money goes to him, minus some operating expenses for the upkeep of the clubs." Mason replied.

"You're referring to this club?" Wilson asked.

"Yes, and others." He replied; looking down at his hand.

"Have you ever met him?" Wilson asked.

"Yes. twice."

"What did you meet about?" Wilson asked.

"Expanding his operation here in the United States." Mason replied.

"More than the three camps?" Wilson asked.

"Three?" Mason replied with a laugh.

Wilson cocked his head to one side, "What's so funny?"

Mason laughed, "You think this is the only operation that Nasir Al-Hadid has here?"

"We are only a small fraction of what he's has here; not to mention over the entire world."

Wilson removed the cigar cutter from around his finger, "Tell me more."

"You'll have to ask Jamerson. He's one of his Lieutenants. And don't forget his wife, Susan. She is a real sadistic bitch." Mason replied.

"What do you mean?" Wilson asked, with a curious tone.

"She does all this bondage and sadomasochism crap with some of the kids. Look; I know what I do is wrong and perverted, but this lady takes things to a new level. I draw the line with just sex." Mason said.

"Really." Wilson said as he leaned back in his chair.

"Yes, I hooked up with her once at one of the house parties. Never again; she's way over the top. Never seen anything like it. But after sitting here, I think you and her would hit it off." He replied with a laugh.

"How is she involved?" Wilson asked.

"She's one of the major merchandise suppliers and trainers." He replied.

"Merchandise and trainer? Please explain." Wilson said.

"Kids." Mason said, looking at Wilson. "She works for one of those Child and Family Services groups."

"How exactly does that work?" Wilson asked.

"She gets a lead on a child that is being put up for adoption or is being abused. If there is an order for a child that meets the profile; she puts them into the system." Mason replied.

"What do you mean by 'The System'?" Wilson asked.

"The trafficking system. Nasir Al-Hadid's inventory." Mason said.

"And you handle the paperwork? You make it a legal adoption for someone who is looking for a sex slave?" Wilson asked.

"Yes. I'm not proud of what I do, but the DA position doesn't pay that well. I make three or four times the money doing the adoptions than I do serving as a DA." Mason said.

"Tell me about a Ukrainian girl that you and Jamerson had talked about." Wilson asked.

Dana looked back at Shay and slid a little closer to the monitor when Wilson asked about the Ukrainian girl. Shay gave Dana's shoulder a slight squeeze, which gave her some reassurance that she was behind her.

"Don't really know much about that one. Nasir had an order for a specific girl." Mason said.

"Specific girl?" Wilson asked.

"Yes, for his own personal use. But you'll have to asked Robert and Susan about that one."

"Did Susan make that arrangement?" Wilson asked.

"Not directly." He replied.

"What do you mean, 'not directly'?" Wilson asked.

"There was a high bounty on that one. Susan had some contacts in the Ukraine, and she sent them looking." Mason replied.

"How much are we talking about?" Wilson asked.

"He was willing to pay up to a Hundred thousand for this specific girl." Mason replied.

"Why did it have to be a specific type?" Wilson asked. "Why Ukrainian?"

"That you'll have to ask Nasir himself." Mason said.

"I hope someday I get the chance." Wilson replied.

"Good luck with that. He's surrounded by well-trained bodyguards. You'd have a better chance getting to the president." Mason said and laughed.

"Tell me about Robert Jr. and Thomas Jamerson." Wilson said. "Did you also handle the adoptions of those two?"

"Yes."

"What do you know about them?" Wilson asked.

"They came from different families." He replied.

"From different families? So, they are not brothers?" Wilson asked.

"They are not blood brothers. Susan wanted two children from an abusive family. She found Robert and Thomas. She put them into the system and she and Robert adopted them. I handled the paperwork for the adoption."

"Why did she want someone from an abusive family?" Wilson asked.

"So that part of her work was already done." He replied.

"Explain."

"They were already broken, as far as being abused. Physically that is. All she needed to do was to turn them into her submissive sex toys." Mason said.

"What about Jackson Payne?" Wilson asked.

"She worked with him some." Mason replied.

"Worked with him?"

Mason was starting to relax some as their conversation continued, "Yes. He wasn't really taking to the training like some of the others. She worked with several of the kids. Some learned faster than others."

"Worked with them in what way?"

"Sometimes the customers wanted their kids trained, so they didn't have to do it themselves. They would hire Susan to come in. She would then train their kids to whatever level they wanted." Mason replied.

"She would train them to become sexually submissive to their parents?" Wilson asked.

"Mostly, but some she would also train how to be a dominate." Mason replied.

"The children?" Wilson asked.

"Yes, but sometimes both the children and parents." Mason added.

"What about Robert Sr.?" Wilson asked.

Mason smiled, "He was the muscle and did the marketing of the kids. You know, pictures, sales, and delivery." He had the feeling that he was shifting the heat away from himself.

"Sounds like a nice little business they had going." Wilson said.

"A big money maker." Mason replied.

"Tell me more about Robert Jr. You were with him." Wilson said.

"He was both a Sub and Dom, but nowhere near as bad as Susan is. She likes pain and a lot of it." Mason said, shaking his head.

"I want to get my hands on that sick bitch! I'll show her what pain is." Dana yelled out.

Shay leaned over and whispered into her ear, "Welcome to the dark side."

Wilson stood up and walked towards the door, "I think that is enough for right now." Wilson opened the door and started out.

"Look, I know what we do is wrong, but it's a sickness. We can't help it." Mason pleaded with Wilson.

Wilson turned back toward Mason, "Yes, it is a sickness Mr. Mason, and we are the cure."

## Chapter Ten

# All in the Family

Wilson walked down the hallway and into the living room where the others were waiting. "Well, well. That was interesting." Wilson said, as he took a seat on the couch.

"Looks like Robert Sr. and Susan are the main sleazeballs." Kevin said.

"Talk about a dominate spouse." Jim said, with a smile.

"How are we going to handle this? Or should I say, how are you going to handle this?" Jack asked, looking over at Wilson.

"This is going to be a difficult one." Wilson replied, as he picked up a magazine off the end table.

"I'm going in with you." Dana said firmly, as she looked at Wilson.

"Of course, you will." Wilson replied with a smile. "Let's take a break and relax for an hour before we go in."

"Sounds good to me." Jack said as he stood and headed for the kitchen. "I'm going outside to get some fresh air." He said, as he walked out of the room.

Dana looked up at Shay who was standing behind her. "Please explain. What you mean by 'Welcome to the dark side'?" Dana said, with a questioning look on her face.

"Let's go outside and talk." Shay replied and squeezed Dana on the shoulder.

Dana stood up and followed Shay through the kitchen and out the backdoor. They walked over and took a seat next to the firepit, about ten feet away from where Jack was sitting.

"Please explain what you mean by 'Welcome to dark side'?" Dana again asked; looking at Shay who sat next to her.

Shay looked at Dana and then down at the ground, "How do I start? Well... child molesting is one of the darkest sides of the human nature. You're going to see; working with us, just how dark and evil a person can be." Shay said, looking back up at Dana.

"People like these men?" Dana asked.

"Yes, and women too." Shay added.

"This Susan, she is very evil." Dana said, shaking her head.

"Yes, she is. She crossed the line in many ways once she involved children into her world of sex and torture." Shay said.

"I had a former boyfriend who like that kind of stuff. But we didn't take it too far." Dana added, glancing over at Jack.

"What two consenting adults do behind closed doors is their business. As long as they are both in agreement and cool with things; they can get their kink on all they want as far as I'm concerned." Shay said.

Jack looked over at the two, leaned back and stretched both arms across the back of the bench he was sitting on. "There is another dark side." Jack said.

"What is that?" Dana asked, looking curious at him.

"Your dark side. Your own inner self." Jack replied, shifting himself on the bench to face Dana and Shay directly.

"My inner self?" Dana replied, cocking her head to one side.

"How far are you willing to go to save these children? Torture? Murder?" Jack said with an expressionless look on his face.

"I don't know." Dana replied, sorrowfully.

"How far will you go to get your sister back?" Shay asked, taking Dana's hand.

"But how far do you go?" Dana asked, looking at Shay and then at Jack.

"Into the depths of hell and back, if you need to in order to save these children." Jack replied. "But that's just my opinion."

Dana looked at Jack, "I think I understand. We do what we have to do to get the answers."

"We do it so that other children will not have to suffer in the future. If it means cutting someone's fingers off or..." Jack was saying.

"Shocking someone's balls off." Shay added.

"Yes, or shocking someone's ball's off, as she just said. Then so be it." Jack said, with a grin as he looked at Shay.

"And your limit?" Dana said looking at both Jack and Shay.

"I don't know. Each situation will test your limits." Shay replied with a glance over at Jack.

"I agree. No one really knows what their limit is until they have reached it." He added.

"And Dr. Wilson? Does he have a limit?" Dana asked.

Jack smiled, "I don't think he has a limit."

"That rat and peanut butter thing was a little over the top." Shay replied and shivered at the thought.

"If I remember correctly; you enjoyed using the ball shocker on that guy." Jack said, now laughing aloud.

Shay lowered her head a little and nodded, "I'd have to admit. I did enjoy it just a little bit."

"Bull shit. You loved it and you know it." Jack replied, as Shay nodded her head again in agreement.

"As for Wilson though, I think he's reached his dark side long ago and he lives there permanently." Shay replied.

"You Shay, how far have you gone?" Dana asked, looking at Shay and leaning forward towards her.

"Are you talking torture?" Shay asked.

"Yes." Dana replied.

"I guess it would be the ball tingler." She said, looking up and tapping her index finger to her chin in thought.

"And you Jack?" Dana turned and asked.

"It would have to be the gun shots to the feet." He replied.

"You shot someone in the feet?" Dana exclaimed in total surprise.

"Yes, once." He replied, as he stood and stretched.

Shay looked up at him, "And he died too."

Jack playfully shook his index finger at her and said, "Minor detail, and in my defense; I didn't know he had a bad heart."

The three slowly walked back towards the house and into the kitchen. Wilson was in there pouring himself a cup of coffee. "Are you ready Dana?" Wilson asked, as he blew into his cup to try and cool the coffee some.

"Sure, what's the plan?" she asked.

"I think we'll look in on Mr. Jamerson Sr., I don't want him to feel neglected." Wilson replied, after taking a sip of coffee. "By the way, how long has he been tied-up?" he asked, looking over at Jack who had pulled opened the refrigerator.

"Two days maybe. I don't even remember how long we've been here." Jack replied in thought.

"I hope you've given him a bathroom break and some food." Wilson said as he placed his cup on the counter.

"They have all been fed and given a chance to go to the bathroom. We're not savages you know." Jack replied.

"That's good. I would not want him to soil himself prematurely. And to have to sit in your own waste. That would be pure torture and I wouldn't want that." Wilson replied and gave them a wink.

They stood there in the kitchen for a few minutes as they prepared themselves a snack before getting back to work.

"What condition will I find Mr. Jamerson in?" Wilson asked, looking at Jack.

Jack held up a finger, as he tried to swallow the mouth full of pizza before answering. "He's fine. His feet are a little cutup from his walk here from his cabin. Other than that, no visible injuries." Jack finally said.

"He only has on his underwear." Dana replied, throwing her napkin into the trash.

"Oh, and keep an eye on Dana, she's already tried to kill him once already." Shay said, giving Dana a wink.

Wilson looked at Dana, "And why in pray tell would you do that?"

"She thought he knew something about the disappearance of her younger sister." Jack said, taking a drink of water.

"Well, we've confirmed that he did possibly play a role in the young Ukrainian girls kidnapping. Shall we find out Dana if it is in fact your sister?" Wilson asked.

Wilson and Dana walked out of the kitchen and down the hallway towards Jamerson's room.

"Watch out, she bites." Jack yelled down the hall.

"Yes, I know. Zeus told me about the entire story on how you and her first met." Wilson replied as he walked down the hall.

Jack threw his hands up in the air and just shook his head. When he walked into the living room, he saw Nicholas sitting there with a big smile on his face. "I'm going to get you." Jack said and tossed the crumpled-up napkin in his hand at him.

Wilson and Dana entered the room; startling the blindfolded Jamerson Sr., "How are you doing Mr. Jamerson, my name is Dr. Thanatos, and this is my assistant Jane."

The two walked over to the dresser and Wilson placed his bag down on top of it. Dana turned and leaned against the table. She stared at the bound Jamerson sitting in the middle of the room with pure hatred in her eyes.

"Allow me to remove your blindfold and gag Mr. Jamerson." Wilson said, as he walked over to Jamerson and proceeded to do so.

Jamerson blinked several times, allowing his eyes to adjust to the bright light in the room. He looked up at Wilson and then over at Dana.

"What do you want?" Jamerson asked, looking back up at Wilson.

"Information Mr. Jamerson." Wilson said, "Answer our questions and we'll all be able to go about our business."

"I have nothing to say." Jamerson blurted out.

"Then we're going to have a long day ahead of us." Wilson replied, as he turned towards the dresser. Wilson reached into his bag and pulled out a roll of three-inch-wide tape.

"Jane would you be so kind as to take this tape and seal off the heat vents." Wilson asked as he handed the tape to Dana. Dana took the tape and proceeded to seal off the only vent in the room located on the floor behind Jamerson.

Wilson walked over to the window and opened it about six inches. "There now, fresh air." Wilson said, turning back towards Jamerson.

It was in the low forties and as the sun went down it was expected to reach the mid to low thirties by midnight. Jamerson had remained dressed only in his underwear, since he was taken from the cabin.

"Would you like something to drink?" Wilson asked Jamerson as he reached into his bag and pulled out two water bottles.

"Sure." Jamerson replied; looking at the two bottles in Wilson's hand.

Wilson removed the caps from each of the bottles and walked over next to Jamerson.

"You'll have to untie me." Jamerson said, looking up at Wilson who was standing over him.

Wilson took the first bottle and poured it over the top of Jamerson's head and repeated it with the second bottle.

"There now, do you feel better?" Wilson asked.

"WHAT THE HELL DID YOU DO THAT FOR?" Jamerson shouted out.

"Jane, would you please turn on the ceiling fan? Make sure you set it on high." Wilson said, looking over at Dana. Dana walked over and flipped the switch on the fan and turned it on the maximum speed. She returned to the dresser and leaned back again, not saying a word.

Jamerson's hair and face were dripping with icy water and most of it had puddled down between his legs and his crotch. After a few seconds of frigid air coming in from the outside. With the addition of the ceiling fan blowing right on top of Jamerson's head; he started shivering from the wet and cold.

"Mr. Jamerson are you ready to answer some of our questions?" Wilson asked.

"Go to hell. My wife has done far worse to me than this." He replied through chattering teeth.

"I'm sure she has. However, we have no safe word to stop once you've reached your limit. The only thing that will save you is to answer our questions." Wilson said, smiling slightly.

Wilson walked over to the front of the chair and leaned over, placing one hand on each arm of the chair that Jamerson was tied to. Wilson leaned over just inches from Jamerson's face and said. "There will be no sexual satisfaction that you'll receive from our little play session, like you get from your wife."

Jamerson just sat there staring back at Wilson as his teeth continued to chatter.

"Tell us about this Nasir Al-Hadid friend of yours." Wilson asked.

"Never heard of him." Jamerson replied.

"Now Mr. Jamerson, your friends here have already told us many things about your involvement with this sex trafficking organization. It would be in your best interest to tell us everything you know." Wilson said.

"Tell us about the Ukrainian girl you sold to Nasir!" Dana shouted as she took a couple of steps towards Jamerson.

Robert had been watching the interview with Jamerson over the monitor in the living room when he heard Dana ask Jamerson about the Ukrainian girl, "Hey guys; Dana has just walked up to the edge of the rabbit hole." Robert said, looking over his shoulder.

Jamerson looked up at her and laughed. "I don't know anything about some little Ukrainian bitch." He replied with a smiled.

Dana pulled out a picture of her sister and showed it to Jamerson. "*Skazhy meni, de vona, svynya. Skazhy meni, a to ya tebe do layna pob'yu!*" (Tell me where she is, you pig. Tell me or I'll beat the shit out of you!) Dana blurted out in her native Ukrainian language.

Jamerson looked up at Dana and laughed aloud. "Lady, I didn't understand a word you said." He looked her straight in the eyes. "Maybe you should speak fucking English, you commie bitch."

"Tell...Me... Where...she is, you pig. Tell me or I'll beat the shit out of you! Is that better?" Dana replied as she grabbed Jamerson's throat with her right hand. "Did you understand that?"

"Dana just took a swan dive into the rabbit hole." Robert said, not looking away from the monitor this time.

"I don't think either one of the Jamerson's are going to give up much if any information." Kevin said from the couch.

"Nope." Nicholas added, "They both know what deep shit they are in. Anything they say is just going to put them deeper in the hole."

"You think you scare me?" Jamerson shot back with a smile. "I can take anything you dish out. All you're going to do is get me aroused."

"Mr. Jamerson, it would be to your best interest if you answer our questions." Wilson said, as he leaned against the wall with his arms folded in front of him.

"Well, it would be to my best interest if the two of you go fuck yourselves." Jamerson replied with a laugh.

Dana walked over to the dresser and stood there for a few seconds looking down at her sister's picture. She placed the picture down on the dresser and closed her eyes for a brief moment.

"She's about to go Shay on his ass." Robert said, finally looking back at Kevin and Nicholas.

"I heard that." Shay's voice came from the kitchen. Robert ducked his head slightly and smiled, as Kevin and Nicholas laughed.

"Do we need to pull her?" Kevin asked.

"Jack and Shay came walking into the living room from the kitchen. "No, let her be. Jamerson is of no use to us." He said, as he walked around and looked at the monitor.

Dana slowly turned and leaned against the dresser and looked at Jamerson.

"Ok, what's next? You going to flog me?" Jamerson said with a dirty look on his face.

Wilson looked over at Dana and then back at Jamerson. He walked over to where Jamerson was seated and pulled out his pocketknife.

"What are you going to do with that little knife of yours... Cut me?" Jamerson said, looking down at the knife in Wilson's hand.

Wilson reached down and grabbed the right side of Jamerson's underwear, above the leg hole, and cut. He repeated on the left side, and fully exposed Jamerson's genital area.

"Now we're talking." Jamerson said and looked over at Dana. "Come on over here and be a nice little servant and make me happy."

Wilson turned and walked over to his black bag sitting on the dresser. "Jane, would you like to assist me?" Wilson said and he pulled something out of his bag.

Dana looked at the object in his hand and said, "Is that a..." Wilson cut her off, "Yes, have you ever seen one before?" he asked and looked over at Dana.

"Yes, my uncle used one on his farm." She replied.

"What is that in Wilson's hand?" Robert asked, leaning forward to take a closer look at the monitor.

"Can't tell from this angle." Jack replied, as he too leaned forward.

"May I?" Dana asked, as she reached for the item in his hand.

"But of course, my dear, be my guest." He replied and handed it over to Dana.

Wilson retrieved a ball gag from his bag. "Well!" Dana exclaimed, "Looks like you and the Jamerson's have something in common after all." She added with a smile.

"I fine some of their toys to be especially useful in my line of work." Wilson replied and turned and face Jamerson.

"Now we're talking." Jamerson said, when he saw the ball gag in Wilson's hand.

Dana was facing away, working on the device that Wilson had given her. Once she was ready, she turned and faced Jamerson, but kept the device behind her back. She smiled and slowly walked towards Jamerson.

"What is that in her hand?" Kevin asked, mostly to himself.

"Whatever it is, Jamerson's not going to like it." Nicholas replied, as he stood behind Robert.

Jim walked in from outside and stopped in the kitchen to grab a bite to eat. He heard the others talking in the next room and walked in. "What are you guys looking at?" Jim asked as he entered the living room.

"We're about to see what Dana's going to do to Jamerson." Jack replied, looking over his shoulder back at Jim.

"Jack." Came Vicky's voice over the speaker.

"Yes, Vicky." Jack replied, without taking his eyes off the monitor.

"What are they doing?" Vicky asked.

"I think Wilson and Dana have gotten all the useful information from Jamerson. I guess they don't see any use in continuing." Jack replied.

"What are they about to do to him?" Vicky asked, with an overly concerned and curious tone.

"Your guess is as good as mine. Besides this is Wilson's area." Jack said.

"But Jack...." Vicky started and was cut off by Jack.

"But nothing. The last time I tried to stop Dana from doing something to Jamerson...." Jack was saying before being interrupted by Shay.

"You had your ass handed to you." Shay said, smiling.

"Red, you go in there." Vicky said, in a soft but wishful voice.

"Sorry missy, I must have slept wrong on me back. It's giving me a wee bit of trouble today." Red replied, as he grabbed his back.

"I'm sure it is. And I guess the others have something hurting them too." Vicky said in a not so convincing tone. "Well Jack, you're going to clean up the mess."

"Why me?" he asked.

"You're in charge." Vicky replied.

Their attention went back to the monitor, as they watched Wilson step around behind Jamerson, with the Ball gag. Dana slowly walked over to the front of the seated Jamerson and dropped down to her knees between Jamerson's spread bound legs.

"Now we're talking. Be gentle with me darling." Jamerson said as he gave Dana a big smile.

Dana reached up with her left hand and slowly caressed his balls and penis in her hand. She smiled and winked at him, and then gave Wilson a slight nod.

"Open up Mr. Jamerson." Wilson said, as he placed the ball gag into Jamerson's mouth.

"What is going on?" Jim asked, as the team watched intently on the monitor.

"I don't know, but I'll bet twenty dollars that after today, Jamerson is going to have to check other on the box when asked what sex he is." Kevin replied to a quiet room.

"Close your eyes, Robert." Dana said in a sexy voice.

Once he closed his eyes, Dana pulled the device from around her back and placed it around Jamerson's testicles and penis. As soon as he felt the cold steel touch the side of his leg, Jamerson opened his eyes.

He looked down and saw what she had done. His eyes widened and he started to struggle. But it was no use, he was tightly strapped down to the chair. He tried to scream, but the ball gag did not allow it. He looked down at Dana with terror in his eyes.

"This is for all the little children that you raped, sold, and victimized. And it is for my little sister, Katryna Kovalenko. I want you to never forget her name!" Dana screamed and released the band.

"Holy shit!" Jim yelled out, "What in the hell is that?" he added as he pushed himself away from the table.

"That is a bull castration device." Kevin replied, as he too was in shock at what just happened.

"Damn!" Jack said, as he turned and looked at Shay.

"I was NOT expecting that." Shay said as she folded her arms across her chest.

"Me shooting that guy in the feet isn't looking so bad now, is it?" Jack said and looked over at Shay.

"Nope." Shay replied.

"I think she gets an A+." Jack said, shaking his head.

"You're OK with this?" Nicholas said, looking at Jack and then at Shay.

"As a child, have you ever been repeatedly raped by someone twice your size? Have you ever been forced to have oral sex with someone?" Jack snapped back at him.

"No." Nicholas replied.

Jack looked over at Nicholas, "Then you can't know the pain that is carried by someone who has." Jack said, calmly and without emotion. "And I'm not talking about physical pain. That eventually goes away. I'm talking about the emotional pain that a child will have to carry with them the rest of their life."

"Sorry man." Nicholas replied.

"You don't know how many times I've dreamed of cutting the balls and dicks off my stepfather and his friends. But I settled for a bullet to the back of his head." Jack replied coldly.

Dana stood up and looked down at Jamerson. He was trying to scream, but the ball gag muffled any screams he tried. He struggled as hard has he could against his restraints, but it was no use. Dana leaned over and spit at Jamerson, then she turned and walked out the door. She stormed into the kitchen where she immediately washed her hands in the sink. After several seconds of scrubbing her hands, she turned the water off and walked into the living room where the others were.

As she entered the living room, Jack put his hand up to give her a high-five. But she walked right past him and flopped down hard on the couch.

"Maybe not." Jack said sheepishly as he dropped his hand down to his side.

*"KHIBA! VIN NIKOLY BIL'SHE NE Z·HVALTUYE ZHODNU DYTYNU! YA SPODIVAYUSYA, SHCHO YOHO CHAS VIDPADE!"* (FUCKING SHIT! HE'LL NEVER RAPE ANOTHER CHILD AGAIN. I HOPE HIS DICK ROTS OFF!) Dana yelled out.

Shay walked over, sat down next to Dana, and put her arm around Dana's shoulder. Dana laid her head over on Shay's shoulder and started to cry.

"Have I... How did you say it, crossed over to the dark side?" Dana asked, as tears rolled down her face. Shay turned her face towards Dana and kissed her on top of her head. "Don't worry about it Dana, we do what we have to do to get justice for these children."

The others in the room tried to go about their business as if nothing had happened. Then Jack's cellphone started to ring. Jack looked at the screen and saw that it was Vicky.

Jack turned and walked outside before answering it. "Yes Vicky." Jack finally said.

"Jack you're not going to leave that thing on Jamerson are you?" she asked.

"What thing?" Jack replied.

"You know damn well what thing I'm talking about. That castration rubber band." She replied.

"Oh, that thing. I'm sure Dana or Wilson will take it off soon. If it doesn't fall off first." He replied, sarcastically.

"Look Jack, when we turn over these people to the authorities, they need to have all their parts attached." Vicky said.

"What and let Robert and Susan get off on some technicality? Or serve two or three years in prison and then they are right back at it again." Jack replied in an angry tone.

"Jack, I understand where you're coming from." Vicky replied.

"Do you?" Jack shot back.

"Sorry Jack. I can never know how you feel. I should not have said it." She said very apologetically.

"These two are high up on the sex trafficking food chain. They are not just some sex perverts that get their kicks out of molesting children." Jack said, now in a calmer tone.

"What did you do with Sutton? Didn't you dress him up like some FBI or DEA undercover agent and drop him in the laps of the Mexican drug cartel?" Jack politely asked

"Ok fine Jack. This is your operation. If you want to fly them out over the Pacific and drop them in, then that's fine. I'll support you either way."

"The Gulf." Jack replied.

"The Gulf? What are you talking about?" Vicky replied confused.

"The Gulf of Mexico is closer." Jack said with a chuckle. "Well, the Atlantic is, but either one will do."

"Ok fine Jack. Do with them as you please. Just make sure you have all your bases covered." She replied, in a defeated voice. "What are you going to do with Susan Jamerson?" she asked.

"What do you mean?" he replied.

"That castration thing is not going to work on her, now, is it?" she said, trying to ease the tension more.

"Maybe I'll ask her if she can swim." He replied, with a serious tone.

"Goodbye Jack." She said and ended the call.

Jack walked back inside and into the living room. He looked over at the monitor and saw Wilson reading a magazine while Jamerson was still struggling.

"How long are you going to leave that band around Jamerson's junk?" Jack asked, looking at Dana.

"Until his nads and wanker falls off me hopes." Red replied.

"Like Red just said, I think." Dana looked over at Red with a questioning look on her face. "I'll go and ask Wilson." She replied, glancing at Jack.

Dana got up and slowly walked down the hall and into Jamerson's room. Wilson was sitting in a chair in the corner of the room looking at a magazine. Jamerson was still retching from the pain from the castration band. Struggling and fighting to try and reach the band, that was tight around his genitals. The band was rapidly causing his genitals to swell, turn black and soon start to die.

"How long until they fall off?" Dana asked, referring to Jamerson's swollen parts.

"In about four to six hours, they will have died and eventually have to be removed." He replied, not looking up from his magazine. "After about an hour the discomfort becomes excruciating and most likely an infection will occur. Testicular necrosis occurs, and the testicles shrink, soften, and eventually deteriorate completely."

"How long has it been?" Dana asked.

Wilson looked at his watch, "About 35 minutes. Give or take a few." He replied, returning to his reading. "Mr. Jamerson, you ready to talk?" Wilson asked.

Jamerson was still struggling but was rapidly tiring. The adrenaline from the pain of the castration band, was the only thing that gave him energy to struggle.

"Shall we go and look in on the wife?" Wilson asked, as he stood and walked towards the door.

"Sure, looking forward to it." Dana replied, following Wilson into Susan Jamerson's room. She stopped at the foot of the bed where Susan was sitting.

Susan had her left hand handcuffed to the headboard of the bed. Her right hand was free, and she was allowed to move as far as the handcuff would allow.

"You think being handcuffed to a bed is going to make me talk?" Susan said, with a laugh.

"Not in the least." Wilson replied, as he walked in and stood next to Dana

"I'm sure you enjoy being cuffed to the bed." Dana replied.

"I'm usually the one cuffing the other person, but I've spent my time being cuffed to a bed too. Susan replied, with a smile.

"We have some questions for you." Wilson said, stepping around to the side of the bed.

"Are you going to torture me too? I heard Robert screaming, although his screams were muffled, I could tell he was in excruciating pain." Susan said with a wink and a smile.

"I don't think you're going to have any intimate relations with him anymore, with him being castrated now." Dana said.

"Que sera, sera. There are plenty others out there that can satisfy me. I was getting tired of him anyway."

Dana cocked her head to one side. "What about Robert Jr. and Thomas, your children?"

"They are a dime a dozen. Do with them as you please.

Dana pulled out the picture of her younger sister and showed it to Susan. "Do you recognize her?"

Susan looked at the picture and up at Dana, "Yes, I do, Katryna Kovalenko, she was a good find. I made a lot of money off her. Nasir was very pleased with the little bitch. She'll give him many children."

Dana ripped off her mask and got inches from Susan's face, "WHERE IS SHE!" Dana demanded.

"Ah yes, I see the resemblance, your younger sister. You must be Bohdana Kovalenko."

"Jack.... JACK! This is going downhill fast." Vicky's voice screaming out of the monitor.

Jack leaned over and called both Dana and Wilson on their earpieces, "Ok guys, let's take a break."

Dana reached up to her ear and ripped her earpiece out of her ear and tossed it across the room.

"SHIT! WILSON, GET HER OUT OF THERE!" Jack said to Wilson. But Wilson didn't respond, he just stood there watching.

Susan leaned as close as she could to Dana, "I took special pleasure in breaking her. I rode her with my strap-on like the bitch dog that she is."

"Jack! You get in there and get her out!" Vicky said.

"I'm not going in there. I already grabbed the wrong end of that she-devil." Jack replied, pushing back away from the monitor.

Dana backhanded Susan hard across the side of the face, busting her lip. As a trickle of blood rolled down Susan's chin, Susan took her finger and wiped some of the blood off. She stuck the bloody finger into her mouth and smiled. "I love the taste of my blood. But you're going to have to do better than that." Susan said.

"RED, NICHOLAS, KEVIN hell all of you get in there!" Vicky screamed.

Dana grabbed Susan's hair on each side of her head and started pounding the back of Susan's head against the headboard of the bed. Blood started running down the headboard as Red, Nicholas, and Kevin came busting into the room. They grabbed Dana under each of her arms and pulled her out of the room and into the hallway.

"I wasn't anywhere near that bad with Mason." Shay said as she stood behind Jack watching everything on the monitor.

Wilson stood there and watch as Susan started laughing as blood was oozing from the back of her head and blood was pouring from her nose and mouth.

"Is that all you've got Bohdana Kovalenko. Your sister fought harder when I was fucking her in the ass."

Wilson stood there watching and studying her. After about a minute he turned and walked out the door.

The three brought Dana down the hall and into the living room. "What do you want us to do with her boss?" Kevin said, holding onto one of Dana's arms.

"Sit her down on the couch." Jack said, pointing over to the couch. They walked her over and she sat down and crossed her arms in front of her." Jack began rubbing his forehead with his right hand, "WOMEN!" he said as he shook his head.

"Excuse me!" Shay said as she looked directly at Jack with a look that could kill.

Shay walked over and sat down beside her, "Are you ok?"

"No!" Dana replied softly.

Wilson entered the room with the others and leaned against the doorway, "I'm afraid that Ms. Jamerson displays signs of being a classic Psychopath and also suffers from CIPA." Wilson said in a puzzled tone.

"I don't understand." Jack replied, cocking his head slightly.

"That makes two of us." Robert added, and the others also showed their interest in knowing what that meant.

Jack looked around at the others and back at Wilson, "Please explain."

"Well, a psychopath doesn't have a conscience. They can lie, steal, harm someone and not feel any moral qualms about it. And someone with, Congenital Insensitivity to Pain and Anhydrosis (CIPA), this person is not able to feel pain or sweat." Wilson paused for a second. "Ms. Jamerson suffers from both."

"And what does that mean as far as getting any information out of her?" Vicky asked.

"In short, my dear Vicky. Anything I do to her, short of killing her, will not have the desired results."

## Chapter Eleven

# Who Are These People?

It was cold later that evening and Dana sat alone around the firepit. The fire was blazing and illuminated the area around. As the light faded in the distance, it cast an eerie shadow on the tree line behind her. She was thinking about the encounter with Susan Jamerson and her sister.

The woods had started their evening music of crickets, owls hooting and an occasional cry of some unknow animal out in the shadows.

Dana had a lot on her mind, her number one priority was to find her younger sister. Also, the question as to who are these people that she has joined up with and what had she become. She realized she really didn't know anything about them. She knew that they were extremely focused on their job of freeing children. But other than that, she knew very little about them.

As she sat contemplating her options, she would toss a small rock that lined the pit area into the fire, causing sparks to fly up from the fire. She saw a shadowy figure exit the backdoor of the house and slowly walk towards her.

"Hey Dana, whatcha doing out here all by yourself?" Shay asked, as she and Sam approached and became visible from the glow of the fire.

"Thinking." Dana replied, as she threw another rock into the firepit.

"About what?" Shay asked, stopping about ten feet away.

"My sister and other things." She replied, looking up at Shay.

"Would you like to talk about it?" Shay asked, still not approaching Dana.

Dana looked down and just shrugged her shoulders.

"Sometimes talking about it helps. Can I sit with you?" Shay asked, as she looked around into the darkness of the woods.

"Sure." She replied and motioned slightly with her hand for Shay to sit.

"*Sam, Bring.*" (Sam Fetch.) Shay said to Sam as she threw a tennis ball out towards the woods.

Shay took a seat next to Dana and they both sat there for several minutes without saying a work.

"You're thinking about your sister?" Shay asked, finally breaking the silence.

She replied with a slight nod of her head without looking over at Shay.

"You know we're going to do everything we can to help you find your sister and bring her home." Shay said, trying to comfort Dana.

Dana looked over at Shay, "You guys have been very kind to me. Even Jack has accepted me."

"It takes Jack awhile to accept things, but he normally comes around. He's just a little slow sometimes." Shay replied. This brought a smile to Dana's face. "You're part of the family." Shay added.

Dana looked back down at the ground, "Thank you."

"What else is bothering you?" Shay asked, leaning over slightly towards Dana.

"This is a strange group." Dana replied softly.

"What do you mean?" she asked, shifting her body more towards Dana.

"I know nothing about any of you, but I put my life in your hands." She said, looking again over at Shay.

"You are family now. We take care of family." Shay said and reached down to pick a small rock up off the ground.

"негідники та пильники." Dana replied in her native Ukrainian language.

"I'm sorry, I don't know what that is." Shay replied.

Dana thought for a few seconds, not knowing how Shay would take it, "Not sure of the words, but you would say, misfits and vigilantes."

Shay just smiled, "I guess you're right. We are a bunch of misfits now that you mentioned it." Shay replied and tossed a rock over into the fire.

"And the other thing?" Dana asked, leaning back, and looking directly at Shay.

"Vigilante?" Shay asked, as she picked another rock up and flipped it towards the fire.

"Yes." she replied.

Sam returned with the tennis ball in his mouth and dropped it at Shay's feet. She picked it up and held it for a few seconds, as Sam looked intently at the ball in her hand.

"I guess in a way, we are." She replied, looking over at Dana and then back at the fire.

"You are ok with that?" Dana asked.

Shay looked over towards the house, "We do what we do because the system has failed." She tossed the ball towards the house and watched as Sam took off after it.

"How has system... you say has failed?" Dana asked, with a curious look on her face.

Shay stopped and thought for a second. "Law enforcement agencies and courts have tried and have failed to stop sex trafficking. Sometimes it's up to the streets to hunt down and bring these perverts to justice."

"But isn't it illegal what we do?" Dana asked, trying to look for answers.

Shay took a deep breath, "Yes, it is. But when the authorities can't do anything, or these low life lawyers get their clients off due to some minor technicality; who else is going to rescue these abused children?" She said with a slight tone of justification.

"I know nothing about anyone here." Dana replied.

"I don't understand." Shay said, sounding unsure what Dana was asking.

"Why you do this?" Dana asked.

Shay looked at Dana, "I guess you don't know much about the backgrounds of the team members here."

"No, nothing."

Shay sat back and nodded her head, "What do you want to know? I'll do the best I can to fill you in."

"Please tell me about Omega. How did it start?" Dana asked.

"Well, I guess in a way it started because of me." Shay replied, sheepishly.

"You started Omega?" Dana said, with a surprised look on her face.

"No. No." Shay said with a laugh. "Because of me, not by me. My Aunt Vicky is the one who started it, because of what happened to me."

"What happened to you?" Dana asked, cocking her head slightly to the side.

"When I was eleven; I was out riding my horse Patches and these guys took me."

"They took you?" Dana replied in shock.

"Yes, they took me and killed my dog Midnight when he tried to save me." Shay said as she started to get misty-eyed.

"What about your parents?" Dana asked.

"They were killed in a car accident when I was eight. Vicky took me in and raised me." She replied, trying to regain her composure. Sam ran up to Shay and dropped his ball again at her feet. "*Platz.*" (Down) Shay said, as Sam laid down next to her feet. She reached down and gave him a couple of pats on his shoulder and rubbed his head. "*Braver Hund.*" (Good Dog)

"Wow! I'm sorry to hear that." Dana replied apologetically.

"Anyway, the kidnappers took me to Atlanta and held me there for eight days. I was able to escape, and I found this young couple nearby and they called the police." Shay said, more calmly now.

"And Vicky started Omega because of you getting taken?" Dana asked, as a shocked expression appeared on her face.

"Yes. She's the mother hen type and a little stubborn, but a very caring person." Shay replied.

"It takes lots of money to start something like this." Dana said, now getting increasingly interested.

"Vicky's father, my grandfather, was very wealthy. He started an international precious metals and Oil & Gas company shortly after college, called Vickers International. He left his estate to Vicky when he died of cancer. His wealth was in the billions. Vicky was his only surviving heir. My grandmother had passed away from heart failure. I think it was about a year or so before my grandfather died."

"Wow, that's fascinating." Dana said.

"Vicky also started a Private Investigation company called VPI, short for Vickers Private Investigation. That's where Robert and Jim came from."

"So, it was Vicky, Robert and Jim who started Omega?" Dana asked.

"No, No. Let me just tell you about everyone and when they started." She replied, leaning back in the chair.

"OK, I'm all ears." Dana said, leaning forward.

"Well, I told you about Vicky, next it was Hunter. She told him about this idea she had, about trying to stop what happened to me from ever happening to someone else.

"So, Vicky and Hunter started Omega?" Dana asked.

"Yes. Hunter was a little against it at first, but Vicky talked him into it."

"Hunter seems, how you say... Hard man, don't take shit from anyone." Dana replied.

"I guess you could say that about him. He's definitely a matter-of-fact kind of person." Shay replied, nodding her head. He's a retired Ranger 1st Sargent and part owner of Stockton's Guns and Ammo. Vicky put him as director of VPI when she started it. He's an old family friend and worked with my grandfather on some projects. He's sort of an older brother to Vicky."

"He's very protective and a little quick tempered, but he controls it very well. It's hard to tell when he's mad." Shay said.

"Good to know." Dana replied.

"When he has had it; he'll bite his lower lip slightly and start nodding his head slightly too. When he does that, it's time to shut up." Shay said.

"I see, and who came next?" She asked, showing increased interest in what Shay was saying.

"That would be Tony."

"But is he not also FBI?" Dana asked.

"Yes, he is. He worked on my case when I was kidnapped. He had expressed some disappointment in the system to Vicky. How ineffective the legal and court systems are in dealing with sex trafficking. He still works in the sex crimes unit out of the field office in Houston Texas. He's been able to help us track down information using his FBI resources."

"That is fascinating. He's been able to be an FBI man and a criminal at the same time." Dana replied with a surprised looked on her face.

"I hate to use the word criminal, but I guess technically it's correct." Shay said in a disappointed sounding voice. "He's also very laid back and easy going."

"Don't worry; where I come from, most government officials are also criminals too." Dana said with a smile.

"OK, and then Jack was brought into the group. Well, they both came in at the same time I guess." Shay said, glancing down at Sam who had fallen asleep.

"Please tell me about Jack." Dana asked, as her eyes widened with anticipation.

"Jack was abused by his stepfather and some of his stepfathers' friends when he was young."

"You mean sexually abused?" Dana asked, to clarify.

"Yes, him and his sister both. His sister committed suicide because of it, and it destroyed his mother. I never found out whatever happened to his mother.

Jack never talks about her." Shay said; looking down at the ground. "He ended up killing his stepfather a few years later." She said, as she looked up at Dana.

"I had no idea." Dana replied, softly and looked over towards the house.

"I just found out yesterday that he was also taken to places like this and abused." Shay said, looking down.

"That's why he's so emotional about this." Dana replied.

"Yes. But Jack is hard to read sometimes. He keeps a lot of stuff inside, but once you get to know him; he's a really nice person." Shay said with a half-smile.

"I don't think Jack likes me." Dana said.

"Don't worry about it. You hurt his male pride. It's not the first time and it's not going to be the last time." Shay said, now with a big smile on her face. "As you know, Jack can't fight worth shit." She said and they both laughed aloud, "But he tries."

"How you say, work in progress." Dana said, laughing.

"A lot of work." Shay added also laughing.

"Ok, Ok, who's next?" Dana asked.

"Guess that would be Ray." Shay replied, trying to remember how it went.

"Ray?" Dana said, with a puzzled look on her face.

"Yep, good ole Raymond Ray. We wouldn't be where we are today if it wasn't for Ray." Shay said, leaning back in her chair.

"How did he become part of this group. He doesn't seem the type."

"Hunter didn't give him much of a choice." Shay replied laughing slightly.

"How you mean?"

"Tony had arrested Ray for hacking into collages and altering student records." Shay said.

"That doesn't seem so bad." Dana said in a questioning tone and look.

"That's not all. He hacked into drug cartel accounts and transferred their money into several charitable organizations and his personal account too. He did that also to the Russian Mob."

"That will get you killed." Dana replied; now a little shocked.

"Yes, and that's what Hunter used to get Ray. He told him that if he didn't come and help, that he would let the cartel and mob know where he's at."

"Hunter blackmailed Ray into working. That doesn't sound particularly good." Dana replied, with a concerned look.

"He then told Ray that he could do anything he wanted to do, as far as building himself a computer system. And he would keep the FBI, cartel and Russian mob off him."

"I see, so Ray agreed?" Dana replied.

"Ray is very smart, he went to Texas A & M, and has an Electronic Systems Engineering Technology degree, along with a Cybersecurity and Computer Science degree. His father is a professor at Caltech in computers and his mother works for a robotics engineering firm. When it comes to computers and solving problems, Ray is your man."

"He does seem very smart." Dana added.

"Then Kevin joined. Or I should say, he confronted Vicky and Hunter about his suspicion about something going on."

"Really, so he had figured it out?" Dana said surprised.

"Not exactly. He knew something was going on, but he didn't know what. He's been with Vicky for a long time. Kevin is Vicky's personal pilot, driver, and unofficial bodyguard." Shay said.

"Really." Dana said.

"He says he can fly anything from fixed wing, to chopper, and most land vehicles. He flew Cobras for a while and then ended up flying the A-10 for about six years. Did four tours in Afghanistan." Shay said, as she reached down and gave Sam a rub on his head.

"What is Cobra and A-10?" Dana asked.

"The Cobra is a military attack helicopter, and the A-10 is a military jet that supports the ground troops mostly." Shay said, while looking down at Sam; who was enjoying the head rub.

"Impressive, I didn't know that. Who is next?" Dana asked.

"That would be me." Shay said, as she looked over at Dana and smiled.

"Oh, can't wait, tell me." Dana said as she moved to the edge of her seat closer to Shay.

"Vicky didn't want me in the group to start with." Shay said in a faint voice as if she was divulging some top-secret information.

"Really why?" Dana asked.

"She was afraid I would get hurt. You know how overprotective she can be." Shay said. "Anyway, I confronted her about what was going on and she finally had to tell me. We got into a big argument about it."

"She gave in?" Dana asked.

"She didn't have a choice. Besides, Hunter helped talk her into it." She said with a smile.

"Who taught you to fight?" Dana asked.

"After my parents were killed; Hunter hooked me up with Stan. And I took to the training like fish in water. I got obsessed with martial arts and couldn't get enough of it. I joined the Marines when I turned eighteen." Shay said, proudly.

"I took boxing and some Judo when I was growing up." Dana replied, also with a sense of pride.

"Stan taught me an Israeli form of martial arts called Krav Maga." Shay said.

"What is that?" Dana asked.

"It's mostly a striking martial art, created for the IDF, Israeli Defense Force. It has its roots in boxing, karate, and wrestling." Shay explained.

"Interesting." Dana replied.

"It is, I love it. It has been modified to include Muay Thai, Brazilian Jiu Jitsu, and various other arts. It's basically a militarized MMA style."

"You must teach me some." Dana said.

"I'll introduce you to Stan the next time we go to the gym. You've seen him there; he's usually in his office working on something."

"That would be great! Maybe he can teach me too. I never would have pictured you as a Marine." Dana said. "You're so small."

"I'm five foot one; thank you very much." Shay smiled and stuck her tongue out at Dana. "Well, I was a little small to carry all that crap. But when they found out how good I could fight; they made me one of the self-defense instructors."

"And how is Shay? I've seen your temper." Dana said.

"Who? Little ole me." Shay said and laughed aloud. "Everyone will tell you that I have a temper, and that I'm very independent and stubborn. But don't believe them."

"Never." Dana replied and they both laughed.

"Ok, back to the others." Shay said. "Next would be... Steve Wilson." She said, after giving it some thought.

"Now there's a very strange man." Dana replied. "Is he married?"

"Why; are you interested?" Shay asked, with a smile.

"Heavens no! Could you imagine being married to him. When he came home from work. Honeybun how was work today? Did you do anything interesting?" Dana said, fighting back the laughter. "No, same old thing. Cut off some fingers, shocked some guy's balls, you know just another day at the office." Dana added, wiping tears from her eyes.

"Hunter dug him up with help from Stan." Shay said, as she too was fighting back the tears and laughter.

"What do you know about him?" Dana asked, after regaining control of her emotions.

"He's a former ER doctor who served as an interrogator for MOSSAD, the Israeli intelligence, until they canned him for his extreme interrogation techniques." Shay replied, now more serious. "Apparently he was too extreme for the new more liberal government."

"I can see that." Dana said. "He's somewhat of a true Psychopath; who doesn't fear the consequences of their actions."

"He does have some unique ways of getting people to talk." Shay said. "I wouldn't want to be on his table."

"Me neither." Dana said in agreement. "Who's next?"

"That would be Jim and Robert. They both joined at the same time. Actually, they joined during our mission that saved you. There's really not much to say about them. They both started out working for VPI and then moved into Omega. Jim's a former Army Medic and Robert was a detective for the Houston PD before joining the team."

"And I guess that leaves us with Nicholas and Red." Dana said.

"Nicholas was a former Gold Medal Olympic shooter. He also helped in training military sharpshooters. He's an expert in long gun and long-distance shooting. Him and Christopher have been friends for many years. They are like brothers from another mother. They constantly bicker back and forth, but they are tight with each other." Shay said, as she picked up another rock and tossed it over into the fire.

"Christopher? Who is this?" Dana asked, puzzled to hear a name of someone she has never met.

Shay reached down and grabbed Sam's ball and tossed it towards the woods again. "*Sam Bring*. (Sam Fetch.) Oh, sorry, everyone calls him Red." Shay replied and watched Sam take off after the ball again.

"Oh Red. He's a funny man." Dana replied with a nod.

"He's more of an outdoors type person. He specializes in survival, hunting, small weapons, handgun, knife, crossbow, and longbow. He's also a tracker." Shay said, looking back to see where Sam was.

"Red doesn't talk a lot and mostly keeps to himself." Dana commented, as she too looked back towards the woods to look for Sam.

"Red is sort of like a big brother to me, we've done some training together." Shay said, "And he loves his whisky. He calls it the water of life. When he gets excited or very wound up you can't understand a word he says."

Sam finally came back into view. He stopped every few feet and looked back towards the woods. His ears would perk up at some of the sounds coming from different directions.

"Sam's not familiar with all these new sounds." Shay said to Dana, as she watched Sam slowly approach. "*Sam Hier.*" (Sam Come.) Shay called out and Sam looked over towards Shay and Dana and started running towards them.

"How long has Sam been a team member?" Dana asked, as Sam ran up and placed his ball at Shays feet.

"Just before you. He was a Military service dog, and his owner was killed by an IED." Shay said, rubbing Sam's neck with her hands.

"How did you end up with him?" Dana asked, as Sam looked over at her and down at his ball.

"Sam's handler was a good friend of mine. He had left word that if anything ever happened to him; he wanted Sam to go to me."

"Why didn't they just keep Sam and have someone else take over?" Dana asked.

"Sam was wounded also in the explosion. He was forced to retire." Shay said, then leaned over and kissed Sam on the top of his head.

Dana leaned back in her chair, "That answers a lot of questions that I had."

Shay looked over at Dana, "I've got one."

"What?" Dana replied.

"Tell me about Dana." Shay said, rubbing Sam on his neck.

"I grew up about one hundred kilometers from Kharkiv. Between Kharkiv and Sumy near Okhtyrka. It is the oil capital of Ukraine. My family raised cattle and sold part of their land to oil and gas company. Two older brothers and three cousins, little sister named Katryna. I attended, Kharkiv Karazin National University and majored in Psychology. But this you already know." Dana said, looking at Shay.

"How did you get hooked up with Sutton?" Shay asked.

"I was promised a modeling job. I dreamed of being model since I was little girl. Sutton said if I came to America, he would make sure that would happen." Dana replied, looking down at the ground.

"That's when he took you and tried to make you a sex slave." Shay asked.

"Yes. He lied just to get me to come to America. But you saved me and give me money." Dana said, gratefully.

"I'm glad we were there to help." Shay replied and tossed Sam's ball a few yards away. "*Sam Bleib.*" (Sam Stay.) Shay commanded. Sam remained still, as he looked at his ball, then back at Shay and again back at his ball.

"Whatever happened to Sutton?" Dana asked.

"He took a vacation down in South America somewhere, so I've been told." Shay replied. "*Sam Suchen.*" (Sam Seek.) Sam took off running a wide circle around where the two were sitting. Once Sam made his circle, he returned and sat down facing Shay. "*Sam Bring.*" (Sam fetch.) Sam turned and ran over to his ball and returned to where Shay was sitting.

"Sam is good dog." Dana commented as she watched Sam follow his commands.

"Yes, he is, but I can't take credit for all his training, the military and my friend did most of the work." Shay replied as she rubbed Sam's neck.

"What is our next move?" Dana asked; referring to the Omega group.

"Well.... We'll get together all the information that we have gathered here. Add it to whatever Ray and the others have dug up and come up with a plan." Shay said, leaning back in her chair and looking up at the stars.

"And my sister?" Dana asked.

"We'll keep looking for her and once we find out for sure where she is we will go and get her." Shay said, in a reassuring voice.

"Thank you." Dana replied with a big smile.

The two of them sat and spent the evening talking about Dana's hometown and Shay's time in the military. They took turns throwing Sam's ball in different direction to keep him entertained.

# Chapter Twelve

# THE SURPRISE

Shay threw the ball back towards the woods into the darkness. Sam jumped up and took off running after the ball. She watched as Sam disappeared into the darkness of the woods.

Suddenly there was a barely auditable pop sound followed by another from the darkness of the woods. As Shay felt a sharp pain on her back just to the right of her left shoulder blade. Shay dropped down to her knees as another popping sound came. This time Dana yelled out and she too felt the pain of something striking her from behind. She also fell to the ground and grabbed her shoulder.

Robert was in the kitchen and happened to look out the window to notice both Shay and Dana on the ground. He called out, "GUYS SOMETHING IS WRONG!" as he headed out the back door.

Robert took three steps out the door when two more pops were barely heard, and Robert grabbed his chest. He looked up and saw a dark hooded figure stepping in from the darkness.

Kevin came running into the kitchen as two more pops sounded. Kevin grabbed his side and looked over at the hooded figure that seemed to have come out of nowhere.

The assassin quickly moved over to the door that led into the kitchen from the hallway. He pressed himself against the wall as Jim came rushing into the kitchen. The hooded assassin stuck his foot out and tripped Jim as he came through the doorway. Jim fell to the kitchen floor and two more rounds found their target in the middle of Jim's back.

Jack entered the kitchen and was met with a gun pointing at the back of his head. "Don't move." The assassin said and Jack froze where he stood. "On the floor." The unknown assassin demanded in a soft but stern voice.

Jack dropped to his knees and looked over at Kevin and Jim. He could feel the end of the gun's suppressor pressed against the back of his head. Then Jack heard Wilson's voice from the doorway.

"Evening Hunter." Wilson said, as he walked into the kitchen.

Hunter removed the hood from over his head and nodded. "How is it going Doctor?"

"What the fuck!" Jack exclaimed as he turned his head and looked up.

Kevin and Jim were leaning against the kitchen counter. They were rubbing the spots where they were shot, as Robert, Dana and Shay walked into the kitchen. They too were rubbing the places where Hunter had shot them.

"Hunter you asshole." Shay said, when she saw Hunter standing there.

"Where are the others?" Hunter asked.

"Sleeping." Jack replied as he stood.

"Well get them up and everyone into the living room." Hunter barked as he walked out of the kitchen and into the living room.

Shay called out, "*Sam Hier!*" (Sam Come!) and in a few seconds Sam came running through the kitchen and into the living room. "Some guard dog you are." Shay said as Sam ran past her.

Nicholas and Red came walking into the living room and saw the others sitting quietly.

"What did we miss?" Nicholas asked, looking around and seeing Hunter standing to one side.

"Take a seat gentleman." Hunter said, as he watched the two walk in.

They all sat there in silence as Hunter slowly looked at each and every one of them.

Dana leaned over to Shay, "He's nodding his head and sucking on his lower lip. Does that mean he's pissed?" Dana asked.

"What happened?" Red asked, as he and Nicholas took a seat on the floor and leaned against the wall.

"We're all dead." Kevin replied.

"You two slept through the entire thing while your teammates were all killed." Hunter replied bluntly.

"Where's your perimeter security?" Hunter asked in a loud voice.

"We have the club members tied up here." Jack said, trying to defend the team.

"Really? Do you have all of them locked up safe? Just how many club members are there?" Hunter shot back.

The group sat there quietly, like a group of school kids, who was just sent to the principal's office.

"What if this Nasir Al-Hadid character had decided to drop in with his army of bodyguards? And you guys are kicked back having a grand old time." Hunter said not mincing words.

Hunter looked at each one as they all looked down at the ground. All but Shay, who was glaring at Hunter.

"You got something to say Shay?" Hunter asked, matching her glare.

"NOPE!" Shay replied, still not looking away.

"Jack what do you have to say?" Hunter asked; looking now at Jack.

"What do you mean? We screwed up." Jack said, not making direct eye contact with Hunter.

"We? What's this we shit? Are you not in charge of this operation?" Hunter asked sharply.

"Yes." Jack replied softly and finally looking up at Hunter.

"Then every one of these team members are your responsibility. Their lives depend on you and your actions. You're lucky I was using an Airsoft gun and not a real one." Hunter said, as he pointed at the others.

"I think they get the point." Came Vicky's voice over the speaker as one of the monitors switched to Omega and Vicky's face displayed.

"You knew about this?" Shay asked; still furious.

"Yes, and we watched the entire thing from here." Vicky replied.

"Who's we?" Jack asked, looking over at the monitor.

"Ray and me. Ray gave Hunter a gun mounted and chest mounted camera, so we could watch from here." Vicky replied.

Jack looked down at the floor and shook his head, "Ray, I know you're there. Thanks Bro, that's twice. I owe you."

Hunter looked at Jack, "I need to see you outside." He said as he turned and walked out of the living room.

Jack looked at the others, then slowly stood and followed Hunter out the back door. Hunter walked up to the firepit and threw a couple of small logs on the fire, causing it to blaze back to life.

Jack walked up and stood beside him. They both stood there for what seemed like forever to Jack.

Hunter never took his eyes off the now blazing fire, "You know kid. You've done a fantastic job leading this operation."

"Didn't sound like it to me just a minute ago." Jack replied, not looking over at Hunter.

Hunter poked at the fire with a stick causing sparks to drift upward and disappeared into the darkness, "I had to do that, you know."

Jack threw a rock into the fire, "What? Embarrassing the hell out of me in front of everyone?" he replied; showing some irritation in his voice.

He turned his head towards Jack, "I bet you will never make that mistake again."

"Nope." He said, still with some irritation in his voice.

"If I had just told you; it would have gone in one ear and out the other." Hunter said and placed his left foot on the edge of the firepit. "My drill instructor did the same thing to me when I was going through basic. I will never forget it."

"Sounds like your drill instructor was a big asshole." Jack replied and tossed another log on the fire.

Hunter nodded, "That he was. That he was."

They both stood there watching the fire burn for several minutes not saying a word.

"I'm starving. Is there anything to eat inside?" Hunter asked, as he turned and started to walk towards the house.

"There should be some left-over pizza and some things to make a sandwich in the refrigerator." Jack replied, "Oh and thanks."

Hunter stopped and turned slightly towards Jack, "For what?"

"Not shooting me." Jack replied, as he walked past Hunter.

Hunter reached into his waistband and pulled out the Airsoft gun; firing two times and hitting Jack in the middle of his back.

"What the fuck man!" Jack shouted, as he grabbed his back.

"You're welcome." Hunter said. He then turned back towards the house and went inside.

Hunter entered the kitchen and walked over to the table where there were two half empty pizza boxes. He checked each box for the contents and selected one piece from each box. He walked over to the microwave and placed the two slices inside.

Hunter retrieved his two slices and went into the living room. The others were sitting, talking, and going about their business. When Hunter walked in; they all stopped talking. Some went back to reading their book or a magazine, while others got up and walked into the kitchen.

Hunter didn't miss a step. He walked over, sat down next to Dana, and proceeded to eat his pizza. He knew they were still upset at the drill he had put them through. But he knew overall it was best.

After about five minutes, Jack walked into the living room. He noticed the cold shoulder that the team was giving Hunter. "Listen up guys, we all know what an asshole Hunter can be sometimes."

"Yep." Shay replied, looking over at him.

Jack smiled a little, "What Hunter did was good. I learned something very valuable tonight. Never let your guard down. We live in a dangerous world and what we do is even more dangerous. We need to be always ready and on guard. It is my responsibility to make sure we remain vigilant. I failed the team, and I'm sorry." Jack smiled and nodded at Hunter.

This seemed to have thawed most of the cold in the room and everyone went back to what they were doing just before Hunter walked in.

"Dana." Wilson said, as he walked into the room.

Dana looked up from her book, "Yes, you need me?"

"I showed Mr. Jamerson the picture of your sister again." Wilson started, but Dana interrupted.

"AND?" Dana replied, somewhat loud.

"He told me that." Wilson paused and took a deep breath. "He told me that the young girl that was sold to Nasir Al-Hadid, is in fact the same girl in your picture."

Dana jumped up and stood there looking at Wilson and then down at Shay. Tears started rolling down her face as she started to cry uncontrollably. Shay immediately stood and gave Dana a big hug and held her tight. The others also came over to Dana and they each gave her a hug.

Jack was the last to approached Dana. When he walked up; Dana looked over at him. He stood there for a second before he said anything. "Now that we know for sure where your sister Katie is; We're going to get her and bring her home."

When Jack told her that, Dana turned and gave Jack a big hug and cried on his shoulder for the next five minutes.

Jack glanced over at Hunter, who was standing about five feet away. Hunter gave Jack a smile and a nod, as a single tear rolled down Hunter's cheek.

Dana took a couple of steps towards Wilson, then stopped and smiled. "Thank you."

Wilson bowed his head slightly, "My pleasure." Wilson turned and started to walk back down the hallway, when Dana asked, "What about the castration band?"

Wilson paused and without turning around said, "I cut off the band after he admitted, knowing about your sister."

"Good." Dana replied.

"However; the band had already remained on too long and irreversible damage has occurred. I'm afraid he'll never be able to use that part of his body, ever again." Wilson then continued to walk down the hallway as the others stood there in silence.

"Would someone like to tell me what's going on?" Hunter asked, looking around at the group.

Kevin started filling Hunter in on the latest information and Wilson's attempts to retrieve the information from Robert and Susan Jamerson.

Jack pulled his cell phone out and called Ray. As soon as Ray answered Jack said, "Ray, we've got a positive ID on Dana's sister. She was sold to Nasir Al-Hadid. Do your thing and have Tony work from his end. We need to get everything we can on him and his entire operation."

"I'm on it." Ray replied and ended the call.

Jack turned towards Dana, "I've got Ray and Tony working on it now. This is going to take time to gather the information and plan the operation."

"I understand. How much time are we talking?" Dana asked.

"It could be weeks or a couple of months before we're able to move." Jack said, trying to reassure Dana that they would do everything possible to get her sister back.

"Why so long?" she asked; looking at Jack and showing disappointment on her face.

Hunter stepped closer to Dana and placed his hands on her shoulders. "This is a big undertaking and extremely dangerous. We are looking at an extremely wealthy sick bastard with his own personal army. Not to mention he's in a country that's not very friendly to Americans. The laws in that country are not the same as they are here. What he does is silently accepted by their government when it comes to people like him."

"I understand." She replied softly.

"We are going to do everything in our power to get your sister back." Jack said.

"At least we now know where she is and who has her." Shay said; taking one of Dana's hands in hers.

Dana nodded her head and broke down in tears again. She pulled herself towards Hunter and gave him a big hug. "Thank you." She said, as Hunter held his arms out to the side slightly, not knowing exactly how to react. But slowly he closed his arms around her and patted her on the back.

"You're family." Hunter said, "We take care of each other."

"Thank you." Dana said softly and squeezed Hunter.

"We still have to wrap things up here and follow the leads we have. Besides, they link back to this Nasir Al-Hadid anyway." Jack said. "What we do here puts us closer to him and Katie."

Hunter looked over at Jack, "What's the status of the questioning?"

"Wilson doesn't think we're going to get anything else out of them." Jack replied.

"Ok, then we need to start wrapping this thing up. I need to make a phone call." Hunter said and walked out the front door. Once he was outside, he reached into his pocket and retrieved his phone.

"Good to hear from you, my friend." Stan said as he answered his phone. "What can I do for you?"

"I need a place to put two people." Hunter replied.

"When you say a place. What are you referring to?" Stan asked, trying to get some clarification.

"Somewhere as close to hell as you can get. Somewhere remote." Hunter replied.

"In country or out?" Stan inquired, with some curiosity in his voice.

"Out." Hunter replied, without hesitation.

"Accommodations for two, correct?" Stan asked as he started writing down some notes.

"One male and one Female." Hunter said.

"Will you need travel arrangements too?" Stan asked.

"That depends on distance."

Stan paused to give it some thought, "Let me make some calls and I'll get back to you. Oh, and cost. Do you have a budget?"

Hunter thought for a second. "For these two, first class all the way."

"Very well, give me a couple of hours and I'll get back to you, with a travel package." Stan said and disconnected the call. Hunter slowly walked back into the house with the others.

Hunter, Kevin, Shay, Sam, and Nicholas were hanging out in the living room reading and watching a movie on Netflix. A few hours had passed since Hunter had contacted Stan when Hunter's phone rang. He looked at the caller ID and saw that it was Stan.

"I've got something for you." Stan said.

"That didn't take long. Where are we talking about?" Hunter asked, with a curious tone.

"My travel advisor has found a place in East Asia. Somewhat tropical and remote." He replied, in a nonchalant voice.

"Sounds interesting." Hunter replied.

"It's an all-inclusive location. Plenty to do; lots of planned activities." He said; in a salesman kind of tone.

"You've piqued my interest. Where exactly is this vacation spot?" Hunter asked, in a joking matter.

"Just outside of Kaechon city." He replied, now switching back to his normal tone.

"Kaechon city?" Hunter replied, "Isn't that somewhere in Korea?"

"North Korea to be more precise. There's a resort there called Kyo-hwa-so, I think your friends will enjoy."

"What kind of arrangements are we talking about? I know we can't fly directly into North Korea." He said, as he looked over at Kevin.

"You'll fly into Incheon International, outside of Seoul. There your friends will meet their travel guide. He'll take them to their final destination."

"Hold on a second." Hunter said as he took the phone from his ear. "Kevin, can the Citation fly us from here to Seoul?"

Kevin looking up from his magazine, "It'll get us as far as Hawaii, but that's about it. It doesn't hold enough fuel to make the final hop from there to Seoul. If you're talking about the one in Korea. Why, are you planning a vacation?"

"Not for me. The Jamerson's are." Hunter replied, raising the phone back up to his ear.

"We're going to need transportation from here to Seoul also." He informed Stan.

"When are you needing this to take place?" Stan asked.

Hunter turned and started to walk into the kitchen, "ASAP."

"The ground transportation won't be a problem. But the air transportation may take several days. I'll get back to you." Stan replied and disconnected the phone.

Hunter looked at Kevin, who was reading a magazine, "What kind of jet will get us to Seoul?"

"I'm assuming you're not talking about commercial." He replied.

"No, something private."

"We're talking about something like the Gulfstream G650 or G650ER. But those things cost a shit load to charter." Kevin replied, putting his magazine down.

"Can you fly one?" Hunter asked, "I'm not worried about the cost. Ray will take care of that for us."

"No, I'm not checked out in that one. We'll need a crew to fly that too."

Hunter stood there for a few seconds, "Guess we can't ship the Jamerson's FedEx."

"How bout the proverbial slow boat to China?" Nicholas said; looking over from the monitor.

Hunter looked over at Nicholas, "Hold that thought. It might come to that. I'm going to give Vicky a call."

"If you're going outside, will you take Sam with you?" Shay asked, without turning her head from the movie.

"Sure thing, come on Sam lets go outside." Hunter turned and walked out through the kitchen and on out the back door, followed by Sam. He placed a call to Vicky and after a few rings she answered.

"What's up Hunter?"

"We have a slight transportation problem."

"What kind?"

"Moving the two Jamerson's."

"Where are you wanting to take them?" She asked.

"A place called Kyo-hwa-so."

"I take it that it's not anywhere local."

"North Korea." Hunter replied.

"What's wrong with someplace here in this country?"

"They wouldn't get the treatment that they deserve here." He replied.

"Why is that?"

"They have too many connections here. And with what they've done; they both need to suffer." Hunter replied in a raised tone.

"What is this place you want to send them; I can't even pronounce it."

"It's a reeducation camp located in the northwestern part of the country." He replied.

"I see. And how are you planning to get them into North Korea?"

"Stan has that covered. He has a connection to get them from Seoul to Kyo-hwa-so. Getting them from here to Seoul is the problem."

"Kevin can't fly them there in our jet?" She asked.

"No. Kevin said it's too far, and that we need a bigger jet. Something like a Gulfstream G650 or something like that."

"And I'm sure you want it by tomorrow." She said sarcastically.

"That would be great if we could do it. The longer we hold these low life's, the greater chance of getting discovered. Someone's going to start missing them."

"I agree, we need to wrap this thing up." Vicky replied with a little concern.

"Another problem is finding a crew to fly this plane that we can trust. We can't just call some charter company and charter a flight."

There was a slight pause before Vicky answered. "I agree."

"Can you call that Sandman character and see if he can help?"

"Hunter, you know I hate doing that."

"I know, but what are our options?" Hunter replied, in a pleading voice.

"Fine! But you owe me Hunter Stockton." Vicky said sarcastically.

"Add it to my tab." He replied and disconnected the call. Hunter sat on one of the chairs near the firepit. He let Sam run and get some of his stored-up energy out before going back inside.

Vicky sat in her chair for several minutes, dreading having to make the call to Sandman. But he told her if she even needed anything to call. He did come through with the account numbers for the Clinton accounts. She reached over and pulled out the cell phone he had given her. She looked at the phone for a second and pressed a preprogrammed number on the phone.

Within a couple of rings, a voice answered, "Vicky; it's been a long time since we've talked. What can I do for you?" the Sandman asked.

"No, no, let me guess. You need a jet, yes?"

"Yes." She replied, somewhat irritated.

"How about tomorrow afternoon; say around 4 p.m. your time?" he replied.

"That should be fine. And the crew, how do we know that we can trust them?"

"They work for me."

"That's not very reassuring." Vicky said in a cautious voice.

"The plane that size will have to land at Easterwood airport. Your Coulter field is far too small."

"Ok, wherever." She replied.

"Tell Mr. Stockton that Kyo-hwa-so is very nice this time of the year."

"I'll pass that along. I'm sure he'll be happy that you're pleased with his selection."

"Also let Mr. Stockton know that next time he's in Frankfurt, we must have dinner together."

"What makes you think he was in Frankfurt?" she started, "Never mind."

"I suggest the next time he's at Zum Gemalten Haus restaurant; that he tries the *Schweinesolber Mit Kohi* (Pork Tenderloin with Cabbage). I think he'll enjoy it much better than the *Rindersolber Mit Kohl* (Beef Tenderloin with Cabbage) that he had last time."

"I'll be sure to do that." She replied, now very irritated that he knows so much about their every move.

She ended the call and tossed the phone down on her desk. She spun around in her chair and faced the window. It was dark outside so all she saw was her refection staring back at her.

After a few minutes she picked up her phone and called Hunter back.

"Vicky, you have something?" he asked.

"Yes, can you have them at Eastwood airport by 4 p.m. tomorrow?"

"That shouldn't be a problem, I'll check with Kevin to make sure. Did he say anything else?"

"Hunter; he knew already that you were taking them to North Korea." Vicky replied, anxiously.

"WHAT! You're shitten me." Hunter exclaimed. "What else?"

"He told me to tell you that next time you're in Frankfurt to try the Rindersolber Mit Kohl instead of the Schweinesolber Mit Kohl."

"That son of a bitch. He knew I was there." Hunter replied with an angry tone.

"He said next time you're in Frankfurt, that you two should have dinner together."

"That would make it easier for me to find him."

"How does he know our every move?" Vicky asked with concern in her voice.

Hunter thought for a second, "He must have our phones or places bugged."

"But how? Kevin sweeps for bugs and devices every couple of weeks."

"I don't know Vicky. The only other way is if there is a mole in our group."

"You mean someone in Omega is working for the Sandman?"

"That or we're missing his bugs somehow. Let's talk about it when I get back. In the meantime, have Ray to start checking everything he can on his end. Use a pen and paper when you tell Ray. Have him start with the main conference room." With that Hunter ended the call.

Hunter walked back into the house followed closely behind by Sam. He asked Jack and Kevin to come with him outside. Once outside, he stopped and turned.

"Two things' guys. First, we are going to move the two Jamerson's tomorrow morning. There'll be a jet at Easterwood airport to take them to Seoul leaving at 4 p.m."

"What kind of jet?" Kevin asked, with a questioning look on his face.

"I don't know. Vicky just told me that transportation has been arranged and it's big enough to make the trip."

"Jack cocked his head slightly to one side, "Seoul? You're talking about Korea?"

"Yes, I'll fill you all in when we go back in. Second, we have a problem." Hunter said, pausing and looking at both Jack and Kevin. "We have a leak."

"What are you talking about, a leak?" Jack said in surprise.

"Somebody outside of our group, already knew about the trip to Seoul and that we needed transportation." Hunter replied, looking over at the house.

"Who knew about it?" Jack asked, showing some anger in his voice.

"Us, Vicky and Stan." Hunter replied.

"Stan... how well do you trust him?" Jack asked, with concern.

"With my life. He and I have been through a lot together, I saved his life once. I know he wouldn't double cross me." Hunter shot back in defense.

The three stood there in silence for a few seconds looking at each other, until Hunter broke the silence.

"When we all get back, we need to find out where the leak is coming from. Until then, let's keep this amongst the three of us for now." Hunter said, looking eye to eye with each one of them.

"Jack, get your plan in action to get this place cleaned and the Jamerson's out of here." Hunter said, letting Jack know that he was still in charge of this operation.

As the three walked back toward the house; Jack asked Kevin, "When can you have the chopper ready?"

"It shouldn't take long at all."

"Good, how about first thing in the morning, taking Nicholas, Robert, Wilson, Hunter and the Jamerson's back, along with their personal equipment."

"That sounds good. After I drop them off and refuel; I'll head back here."

The three walked back into the house and into the living room where the others were waiting.

"Ok guys listen up. Here's what we're going to do." Hunter began, but from behind, he heard someone clearing their throat.

"I've got this." Jack said as he walked past Hunter and gave him a sideways glance.

Hunter threw up both hands slightly and stepped to the side, "By all means kid, this is your show."

Jack looked over at Nicholas, "Nicholas, get Vicky and the others on the line."

After about two minutes, the three, Vicky, Ray and Tony were displayed on the monitor.

"What's up Jack?" Vicky asked, as she took a sip from her coffee.

"Here's what we're going to do. Kevin is going to fly Hunter, Nicholas, Robert, Wilson and the two Jamerson's back first thing in the morning. From there Hunter is going to transport the Jamerson's to their new location. We're sending everything that the rest of us don't need back with them."

"Ok, we'll be ready on this end." Vicky replied.

"Great. Shay, Red, Dana, Jim and I will stay behind and clean the place. Once Kevin returns, he'll pick up the remaining equipment along with Shay, Dana, Jim, and Sam and bring them there."

"Red and I will stay behind and babysit the kids and our remaining guests until law enforcement is on the way." Jack paused; looking around the room to see if anyone had any objections. "How's the planning going on your end?" Jack asked, looking towards the monitor showing Vicky and the others.

Tony opened a folder that was sitting in front of him, "We're going to do the same as we did with the Clinton's. Once we get the go-ahead from you, we'll make the calls. We've got the State police and Marshal service. We're going to contact the state Child Protective Services, since Susan Jamerson works for the local office, and we don't know who's involved out of that office."

"That sounds good. What about the media?" Jack asked.

"We're going with the local media this time. We want to try and keep this off the national networks, so there's less of a chance that this operation might be tied back to the Clinton's." Tony replied; closing the folder.

Jack nodded in agreement, "Good idea. I'm sure something will be leaked out over social media or something. But I agree, it shouldn't be a national story like the other one."

"That's what we're hoping." Vicky replied.

"I'll call once everything is set here and then Red and I will leave with whatever is left."

"Ray, do you have the video's scrubbed and ready?" Jack asked, as he took a seat in front of the monitor.

"I'll send a laptop with the edited video along with one of my instructional videos back with Kevin. Make sure you remove everything else, cameras, monitors, and computers before you leave."

"Jack, did you clean the cabins too?" Vicky asked.

"Yes, we've already taken care of the cabins." Jack replied, leaning back in the chair.

"Good. They are predicting a heavy rainstorm in your area tonight. That should cover any outside tracks that you guys have left." Vicky said, "If there's nothing else; we're going to get some sleep here and I suggest you guys do the same."

"Thanks guys." Jack said.

"I'll see you sometime tomorrow." Hunter said, from the back of the room.

"Ok, you have a safe trip." Vicky replied and the monitor went dark.

Jack turned towards the others as Hunter's cell phone rang. "I need to take this call, go ahead and brief the others." Hunter said, as he stepped out of the room.

"What you got for me Stan?"

"Good news and bad news, which you want first?" Stan replied over the phone.

"Good news."

"The travel guide said he'll do it for hundred thousand U.S. dollars. And the resort wants fifty thousand, for their all-inclusive package."

"Ok, what's the bad news?"

"The earliest I can get you your transportation, is four days because of the cargo and risk that you're asking." Stan said.

"Don't worry about the transportation, I've got that handled. Can you have the travel arrangements from Incheon to Kyo-hwa-so set by day after tomorrow?" Hunter asked.

"That shouldn't be a problem. He needs the money upfront."

Hunter paused for a second before responding, "Tell him he'll get half now and the rest when he delivers our friends to their final destination. The resort will get theirs once they're delivered. Is that going to be a problem?"

"No, I don't believe so. I told him that you are a man of your word."

"Send me the account numbers and I'll have the money wired."

"Sending them now."

"Thanks Stan, I'll call you when I get back." And with that they ended the call.

"Jack, where is Hunter sending the two Jamerson's?" Nicholas asked.

"A resort. He said it's somewhere in North Korea." Jack replied with a smile.

"I didn't know they had resorts in North Korea." Nicholas replied.

"They don't." Shay said and threw an empty drink can at him.

"Nicholas; you and Robert go with Hunter to drop off the Jamerson's. Dr. Wilson, you can fly back to Omega with the first group. Your services are no longer needed at this point, but we may need you again soon, so don't go too far."

Nicholas and Robert both nodded and Wilson just smiled.

"Shay, Jim, Dana and of course Sam will head back on the second trip. When you get back; start working on the next phase of this mission. Red and I will stay here until everything is put in motion, then we'll drive the remaining equipment back in the van." Jack said and looked at each of the team members.

Hunter had come back in just as Jack was finishing.

Robert looked over at Hunter and asked. "We're flying into North Korea?"

"No, we're flying into Incheon International; outside of Seoul. There we're going to turn the Jamerson's over to someone who will take them to their final destination."

Nicholas looked at Hunter, "Where is that, if I may ask?"

"Kyo-hwa-so. It's a reeducation camp located in the northwestern part of North Korea."

"Good, maybe they will get what they deserve." Shay said, smiling.

"Jim, Red, at first light, could you two go and check all the cabins and make sure they are clean?" Jack asked; looking over at the two of them.

"Sure thing." Jim replied. And Red replied with an "Aye."

Jack stood up and said, "Make sure you wipe the place down thoroughly. Every doorknob, and every surface you can find. Clean it twice if you think you may have touched it. That goes for the cabins and this house; inside and outside."

"Don't forget we now have two objectives, one is to break this sex trafficking ring and two, to bring back Dana's little sister." Jack paused and looked at each person. "Hunter, you have anything you'd like to add?"

"No, I think you have everything under control."

Jack gave Hunter a smile and turned back to the others, "Anyone else? Questions? If not let's get some rest; we've got a long couple of days ahead of us."

# Chapter Thirteen

# The Middle East Trip

Ray and Vicky were sitting in the conference room, "I've installed an electronic tracker. It will detect any electronic signal and record its frequency and time of transmission on a dedicated tablet. The tablet is hard wired to the device and has no Wi-Fi or internet connection. That way it can't be hacked from outside. I'll take each person's phone, clean them, and have the unit log their frequency and assign a name to each one. If anything, other than the cleared phones are detected, it will log it. I'll have the tablet beep if it detects any signal that has not been previously cleared."

Vicky nodded as Ray explained the procedure.

"Anything that's planted and transmitted within the room will be detected. And once we have the frequency, we'll be able to jam it or even transmit our own message to whoever is listening." Ray said.

"Can't you just scan the room for transmitters, and it'll be clean?" she asked.

"No, some devices can be turned on and off remotely. If they are off at the time, when we scan the room or item; we wouldn't detect anything. My tracker will be scanning all the time, so at any point someone triggers a transmitter, it will be detected."

"What's the range of the tracker? Can it cover the entire Omega Headquarters or my ranch?"

"It really depends on the structure and the walls. For example; the armory here with the bullet proof walls. The unit wouldn't be able to penetrate those walls. On the plus side, a transmitter inside the armory wouldn't be able to transmit anything out either."

"I want this place covered. The ranch and vehicles, including the jet and chopper." She said.

"I'll put together some smaller mobile units to be used offsite."

"Another issue is the windows." Ray said.

"What about them?"

"Some electronic directional devices can be aimed at a window and pick up the voice vibration off the windowpanes. We don't have that problem here, but at the ranch we'll have to apply another counter measure."

"I can set this room up so that we can activate a unit and it will become a large Faraday cage."

"What in the hell is a Faraday cage?" Vicky asked.

"It's an enclosure, bag or even a room; setup to block electronic and electromagnetic fields. In other words; no signal can get in or out."

"What about us? How will we be able to communicate with the others if we're in this room?"

"I'll setup a relay system that we can turn on and off as needed."

"Can you do the same at the ranch?"

"Sure, no problem."

"Let's do that to the small command center we have there."

"I'll also setup a unit to encrypt anything we transmit in and out of Omega, or the ranch command center." Ray said.

"Then no one can intercept our cell phone or video transmissions?" she asked.

"Yes and no."

"What do you mean?"

"If we send the signal from here or they call into here, yes, we can encrypt the signal. But if they call from their cell phone to another cell phone outside, then no that signal will not be secure. However, if they call here first, I can then redirect their call through the system, encrypt it and send it out to the other cell phone. There are ways to encrypt caller to caller calls, but that's another complete set of equipment. For right now, this will do."

"Sounds complicated."

"Not really, it's like in the old days, when you had to call the operator and then the operator would then connect your call to the other person. It's just slower setting the initial call up. After that it's encrypted."

"Text messages are not a problem, there's tons of applications out there that will encrypt text messages. I'll get all the phones setup with some type of text encryption."

"Ok, whatever you need to do, I don't understand that stuff. Just fix it." She replied.

"That's why you pay me the big bucks." Ray said smiling.

"Vicky, can I ask a question?"

"Sure, what is it?"

"Why suddenly, are we doing all this electronic security stuff. Has something happened?"

She looked at him with a serious expression on her face, "I think we have a spy inside of Omega."

"A what?" Ray replied in shock.

"Someone is letting others on the outside know what we are doing." She said in a concerned voice.

"Who?" he asked.

"We don't know. The only ones that know about the leak are me, Hunter, Jack, Kevin and now you."

"What about Shay?"

"No, she doesn't know yet."

"You don't think she's the one, do you?"

"No, but I've not had time to tell her. It's best we keep everything secret until we get all the new security in place."

"Shit, that sucks. I can't imagine anyone in the group being some kind of a spy. And who are they spying for?"

"We don't know that either. I've received some outside information about things we've done or in the process of doing. Things that only we should have known."

Ray sat there for a few seconds before asking. "Vicky, how do you know it's not me?"

"Ray you're the smartest person I've ever met. I know if you wanted to bug us or whatever, we wouldn't know. Besides, I don't think it's one of the team members. I think it is something else."

"Like what?" Ray asked, in a curious voice.

"I think someone has planted a bug somewhere and that's how they are finding out."

"Ok, that clears things up for me. Now I know what to look for."

"Ray; not a word to anyone else." Vicky said as she heard a noise outside of the room.

"Vicky." Tony said as he entered the room.

She turned and looked at him, "What's up?"

"Hunter and the others will be landing in about five minutes."

"Could you and Ray go out and see if they need any help unloading?" Vicky replied; looking back at Ray.

"Sure thing." Tony replied. Then he and Ray left to head out to the hanger area.

Vicky's phone rang and she looked at the display. It displayed 'Unknown Caller' on the screen. *Wonder who in the heck that is,* she thought to herself.

"Hello." She said accepting the call.

"Vicky, it's Sandman. How are you this morning? Or should I say this afternoon. I forget the time difference."

"What do you want?" she snapped.

"The Jamerson's flight is a little ahead of schedule, it should be landing shortly."

"Thanks for the update."

"My pleasure. Oh, and tell Jack that he's done an excellent job; we're incredibly pleased."

"I'll make sure he gets the message. Anything else?" Vicky replied shaking her head slightly in disgust.

"No. Tell Hunter to have a safe flight and I hope to see him again very soon." With that he ended the call.

Vicky took the phone and placed it in her pocket, took a deep breath and let it out. How she hated that man. But somehow, she was thankful. He has helped them out several times, but how does he know every move they make.

She waited outside as the rotor blades of the chopper were slowly coming to a stop. She watched as Tony pulled one of the black SUVs alongside of the helicopter. Hunter jumped out and slowly walked over towards her. She saw Robert, Nicholas, and Ray, loading the two limp Jamerson's into the back of the SUV.

"Vicky." Hunter said as he walked up and gave her a quick hug.

"How was your flight?" she asked, turning her attention to Hunter.

"Uneventful."

"Your flight to Korea is ahead of schedule and should be landing shortly."

Vicky looked back towards the helicopter as Ray and Wilson climbed into the SUV. Robert and Nicholas were walking back to the hanger as the rotors on the helicopter slowly started turning again.

"Kevin's going to hop over and refuel, so he can head back and pick the others up." Hunter said, as he and Vicky turned and followed the SUV into the hanger.

"How..." The popping sound of the rotors and a sudden rush of air caused Vicky to stop talking and turn as she watch Kevin fly off. "How are the Jamerson's?" she asked after the sound of the departing helicopter dissipated.

"Resting well." Wilsons replied. "I gave Hunter several additional syringes for the trip. If all goes well; they will not wakeup until they've reached their new home."

She turned slightly as Robert and Nicholas walked up. "Welcome back guys. Looks like you'll be heading back out in a few minutes."

"I hope that plane has a bed and shower." Nicholas said; dropping his bags down next to him.

"Tony and I are going to get the truck and pick up the other stuff we dropped off." Ray said as he walked past them.

"There's some food in the refrigerator if you guys are hungry." She said, looking over at Robert and Nicholas. "You know Hunter; we've outgrown that little break area. I think we need a full-size kitchen."

"When I get back, I'll jump on that. I'm thinking we need a bunk area too. We could convert some of the space in the second-floor storage area." Hunter replied, turning slightly as he watched Tony and Ray loading the truck.

"Good idea. We should look at putting in some kind of holding cell too." She said as she looked over at the SUV with the still unconscious Jamerson's.

"That's something we also need." He replied, with a nod. "Have you talked to Ray about that issue we talked about?"

"Yes, he has some ideas on how to fix the problem. He should have some of it addressed before you return. Oh, by the way, your friend said he's looking forward to seeing you again."

Ray and Tony pulled up just outside the hanger door where Vicky and Hunter were standing. As Ray walked past with an arm full of equipment; Hunter asked. "Can you tag those two with some kind of tracking device, so that we can make sure they make it to their final destination?"

"Sure. I don't know how effective they'll be once they reach Korea. It maybe spotty, or we may even lose their signal all together once they enter North Korea."

Robert and Nickolas both walked into the hanger area. Robert was eating a sandwich as he walked.

"You guys ready? We've got a plane to catch." Hunter asked; eyeing the sandwich in Robert's hand.

"Ready." They both replied.

Hunter looked at the sandwiches in both their hands, "Did you bring enough to share? I'm sure all we'll get are some peanuts, pretzels, and some soft drinks."

"I can go back and get you something." Robert replied in an apologetic tone.

"No, no, don't bother, peanuts will be fine. But thanks anyway." Hunter replied and winked at Vicky.

"You guys have a safe trip. Call me when you land with an update." She said as the three got into the SUV.

"You guys ready?" Ray asked as he started the engine.

"Let's go." Hunter replied, as he gave Vicky and Tony a final wave.

It took them a little over twenty minutes to drive from the hanger at Coulter Airfield to Easterwood airport. Vicky had given Hunter the location of where to board the plane that the Sandman had arranged for them.

They pulled up to a beautiful white, blue, and gold Gulfstream G650ER sitting there waiting for them. The jet was sitting off to the far side of the airport, where it would not attract attention to them carrying their unconscious passengers onboard.

As soon as they pulled up, they heard the whine of the jet's engines starting. By the time everyone was aboard and seated; they could feel the jet start moving. In less than five minutes they were airborne and on the long flight to Seoul, South Korea.

After the Jet reached its cruising altitude; Hunter noticed a man exiting the cockpit. As the man made his way back toward him; Hunter assumed he was some sort of flight attendant or something.

"Mr. Stockton, would you care for a drink or anything to eat?" The flight attendant asked.

Hunter looked at the person with a questioning look on his face.

"Charles wanted to let you know that we'll be stopping over at LAX to refuel. From there the flight will take about twelve hours to Incheon International. He wanted to make sure that you, Mr. Bryant, and Mr. Green receive first class treatment."

Hunter looked at the attendant a few seconds before speaking. "Charles? I don't believe I've had the pleasure of meeting him?"

The attendant smiled. "He's our pilot. I'm sure if he gets a chance; he'll introduce himself to you. There is a menu in the compartment next to you with the drinks and meals available; if you would like to take a few minutes to look at it."

After a few seconds of looking over the menu; Hunter said, "I guess I'll have the Smoked Salmon with the roasted Parmesan Asparagus and the cucumber salad."

"Might I suggest a Chablis to go with that?"

"I'll just have a whisky, Kentucky if you have it."

"Yes sir, I do believe we do. And I'm assuming that the Jamerson's will be sleeping during this flight and not be needing anything?"

Hunter glanced back towards the rear of the plane. Robert and Susan Jamerson were out cold on the floor. "No, they'll be fine for the time being."

"Very well. If there's nothing else; I'll check with your friends. If you think of anything else; just press the call button." The attendant took a step and stopped. He turned back towards Hunter, "We have HBO, Showtime, Cinemax and about 10 other movie channels if you like."

Hunter looked up. "Everything but the Playboy channel." And smiled.

"Yes sir, we have that and about fifteen other similar channels, anything that would fit your needs or fetish."

"No that's ok, I'll stick with HBO. I'm sure I can find something on there that will occupy my time." Hunter leaned over close to the attendant and whispered. "My friend Nicholas back there, is into nude midget wrestling." He said without cracking a smile.

"Yes sir, I do believe we have something for him. And I'll recommend a place a couple of miles outside of Seoul, that he might like to visit on your brief layover."

After about ten minutes, the attendant walked past Hunter and gave him a smile on his way towards the cockpit. After he had closed the door behind him, Hunter felt a wadded-up piece of paper hit him on the back of the head.

Hunter turned and saw Nicholas looking at him. "Really Hunter.. . Midgets?" Nicholas said looking at Hunter. Robert was sitting across from Nicholas, trying his best to keep from laughing, as Nicholas gave him a kiss my ass look.

About three hours into the flight the attendant appeared with their food and drinks. He told them that if they needed anything else, to press the call button. Also, that the bar and snacks were available in the galley if they needed anything. He would also be available for a hot lunch or breakfast if they wished.

"Hunter." Robert said.

Hunter turned back and looked at Robert.

"You think Vicky would get us one of these?" Robert said with a half-smile.

"In your dreams." He replied and turned back. He reached up and turned the light out over his head and reclined the seat.

It had been a long day for the three of them and soon after they had eaten; the three were sound asleep.

"Sir, Sir." The attendant repeated.

Hunter slowly opened his eyes and looked up at the person standing over him. It took a couple of seconds for him to become fully aware of what was going on.

"Sir, we will be landing at Incheon International, in about half an hour." The attendant said, once he had realized Hunter was awake and his brain had processed where he was.

"Thank you." Hunter replied as he struggled to raise his seatback up.

After several minutes, the Gulfstream started its approach and soon after that, they landed. As the jet slowed and began to taxi, the attendant approached Hunter.

"Mr. Stockton, we'll be pulling off at the end of runway 33L. You will meet a Mr. Smith there. He'll be waiting to receive your friends."

"Mr. Smith." Hunter replied in a sarcastic tone.

"Can I get you anything?" the attendant asked.

"No, I'm fine. When will we be returning?"

"We should be refueled and ready within an hour. Will that be enough time to say goodbye to your friends?"

"Should be more than enough time."

The attendant turned and as the jet pulled to a stop, he opened the door and lowered the stairs. The jet's two engines immediately started to power down as the fuel truck arrived.

Hunter stood and looked back at Robert and Nicholas. "Nicholas, you stay here and keep an eye on things. Robert you and me will go and meet this Mr. Smith."

As the two exited the jet, they saw a short medium built Asian man approach. He stopped about six feet from them and gave a slight bow. "Mr. Stockton, I presume?" he said in perfect English.

"Yes, and you're Mr. Smith?"

"Yes I am."

The three shook hands and walked over to a military Kia KM450 light military truck. Two other men dressed in military uniforms stood towards the back of the truck. Hunter noticed there was another man in the driver's seat watching.

"I understand you have two friends that would like to vacation in the country north of us."

"Yes, I do." Hunter replied, looking at the truck. "Your English is excellent Mr. Smith."

"I was born here in South Korea. My father was a former Korea ambassador to the United States. He moved our family to the United States when I was three. I attended first through twelfth grade in Washington D.C. From there I spent four years at Georgetown University, studying Journalism. I moved back here with my family, after my father retired."

Hunter smiled and gave him a slight nod. "You're going to drive them into North Korea in this truck with those South Korean markings?"

"No, No. Mr. Stockton. We will remove those and replace them with North Korean markings once we've reached the boarder. I have official documents, that will give us safe passage from there to Kyo-hwa-so."

"Did our friend tell you that you'll receive final payment, once they have reached their final destination and it's been confirmed?" Hunter asked, looking at Mr. Smith and then over at the Jet.

"Yes, that is very acceptable. He told me that I can trust you and that you're a man of your word." Smith replied with a nod.

"And once I've received conformation, I'll also transfer the money to the person at Kyo-hwa-so."

"That too is also acceptable."

"Well let's get this transaction moving." Hunter replied and motioned for Robert to return to the jet and retrieve the Jamerson's.

At the same time, Smith turned towards the two other men and ordered, in Korean, "*Gaseo geuleul dowa.*" (Go help them.) The two rushed over and followed Robert into the jet. He then turned and looked towards the man sitting in the driver's seat. "*Teuleog-eul gakkai gajyeowa mun gakkaie hujinhasibsio.*" (Bring the truck closer and back it up close to the door.) Again, in Korean.

The jet had parked so that the main airport and tower couldn't see what they were doing. Just in case, someone got curious about a jet parked off to the side at the end of one of the runways.

Smith and Hunter watched as the Jamerson's were loaded in back of the KM450. There was a canvas cover, covering the bed of the truck, hiding the Jamerson's and the two guards.

"How long will it take to get them to their destination?" Hunter asked; not bothering to look at Smith. Instead, he watched as Susan Jamerson was lifted into the back of the truck.

"It'll take us about three hours from here to Pyongyang. From there we'll head to Anju and then to Kaechon. The entire trip should take around five hours; providing that we're not stopped." He replied; looking at Hunter and giving him a smile.

A sound from the other side of the plane caught their attention. They both turned as the fuel truck drove away heading towards the main airport area.

"I see that you're all fueled and ready for your trip back home." Smith said as he turned towards Hunter.

"Looks that way."

"Will you be spending some time in Seoul before heading back?"

"No, it's been a long time away from home. I think we'll take a rain check on that."

"Very well. It's been nice doing business with you Mr. Stockton. Please stay in touch and if you ever need my services again; feel free to call."

"I will. Send a text to this number once you've dropped them off. Once I've confirmed, I'll send the rest of the money." Hunter turned towards Smith and they both shook hands.

Robert and Nicholas had finished helping to load the Jamerson's into the truck and were standing next to Hunter.

"You guys ready to head back home?" Hunter asked, as he turned towards them.

"What; no midget wrestling?" Robert replied, glancing to the side at Nicholas.

"Fuck you man, get in the plane."

Robert headed up the stairs into the jet; followed by Nicholas and then Hunter. Once Hunter reached the top of the short flight of stairs; he turned and watched Smith drive away with the Jamerson's.

"Enjoy your stay." He said aloud to nobody in particular.

The attendant closed the door as the jet's engines started powering up. Within twenty minutes they were cleared for takeoff.

About thirty minutes after they left, the attendant exited from the front cabin. "Mr. Stockton, can I get you anything."

"No, I just want to relax and enjoy the flight."

"The captain said that we have a strong tail wind and should be able to bypass LAX and fly directly to Easterwood."

"That will be great. Tell the captain I said thank you."

He leaned back in the seat and picked up the TV remote. He spent several minutes going from one channel to another until he found an old favorite program, Chicago PD. He relaxed and for the next five hours, enjoyed the program.

Hunter's phone sounded, alerting him that he had received a text message. It was a message from Ray, letting him know that the Jamerson's had been delivered. He responded by instructing Ray to go ahead and transfer the money.

Hunter received another text message with a picture of Robert and Susan Jamerson standing in front of a sign that read, Kyo-hwa-so. They were standing, wide eyed and dressed in what looked like oversized dirty pajamas.

Hunter smiled and said to himself, "*It's not easy to outrun your demons.*" and placed his phone back into his pocket. He turned his attention back to watching Chicago PD, for the remainder of the flight.

Ray was waiting at Easterwood airport when they landed. He watched as the jet pulled onto the apron and stopped, and the steps were lowered.

Hunter and the others were gathering their things together, while the pilot stood at the door of the jet waiting as the attendant lowered the steps. He was a distinguished older man, somewhere in his mid-sixties with short grey hair on the sides and bald on the top; which he covered with a pageboy hat. He stood about six foot even with a few wrinkles on his olive color face.

As Hunter and the others approached; the pilot stuck out his hand. "Good evening Mr. Stockton, I hope you enjoyed your flight."

"Yes, it was very nice sir, excellent flight."

"Oh please, call me Charles."

"Very well, Charles." He replied and nodded.

"Thank you for flying Sablehomme Airlines." Charles smiled and nodded back at Hunter. "Perhaps you'll fly with us again in the future."

The three proceeded down the steps where the attendant was standing to the side.

"I hope you gentlemen enjoyed your flight. It was a pleasure serving you."

"Yes, it was great." Hunter replied with a smile and stuck his hand out to shake the attendant's hand. "Oh, by the way, I never got your name."

"Steven Post, sir."

"Mr. Post, we absolutely enjoyed our flight."

"Please sir call me Steven."

"Very well, Steven. You take care and thank you for everything." They both shook hands, then Hunter turned and walked towards the SUV.

As the three approached Ray and the SUV; Nicholas asked, "Were we expected to tip that guy?" as he tossed his bag into the back of the SUV.

Hunter glanced back at the jet as the fuel truck pulled up and the door to the jet was closing. Hunter could see Charles sitting in the pilot's seat looking over at Hunter. Charles gave Hunter a smiled and a wave; before turning back to what he was doing in the cockpit.

After arriving back at Omega; the four walked into the conference room where Vicky, Shay and Dana were working.

"How was the trip?" Vicky asked, as she turned towards the three.

"Very nice. Vicky, you need to get us one of those jets." Nicholas replied, as he put his bag down on the floor.

"Fine, you can pay for it." She replied with a smile.

"How are things moving back at the camp?" Hunter asked as he placed his bag down on the floor next to the conference table.

"Jack and Red left a few minutes ago, Dana just placed a call to the State Police and a call to the local media." Vicky replied, as Hunter walked over to where she was sitting.

"How did they leave things?"

"They pulled all the remaining cameras, but two, and left Mason, Payne and Moon tied up together. Jamerson Jr. was left in a room by himself. The kids were left with plenty of food and drinks. Ray sent back a video with the pre-raid cabin footage and some of the edited interviews."

"Good deal."

"Jack also installed tracking on their cell phones and vehicles."

"Hopefully, they won't need them for many years." He replied as he pulled up a chair at the table.

Vicky looked at him. "If they somehow get away without serving any jail time; we'll revisit them again later."

"We'll see how this thing plays out in the next couple of days." Hunter said as he looked over at Shay; who had not said a word to him yet, "Are you still mad at me?"

Without looking over at him, "Are you still an asshole?" she replied.

Hunter looked at Vicky and laughed, "Guess she still is."

"Give me your old phones." Ray slid a new cell phone over to Hunter, Nicholas, and Robert. "Here are your new phones, they all have been scrubbed and encryption added. If there's anything personal on them, let me know and I'll see about transferring it."

"Ray has turned this room into a fair way room." Vicky said, looking at Hunter and the others.

"Faraday Vicky. Faraday." Ray corrected her.

Robert looked at Vicky then at Ray, and back to Vicky. "What in the hell is a Faraday room or whatever you call it?"

"It's a room, setup to block electronic and electromagnetic fields. No signals can get in or out." Ray said; turning to Robert.

Vicky looked over at Robert. "Ray will go over the details once everyone gets back. He can explain everything at that time."

"Guys, let me and Vicky have the room." Hunter said, looking over at Ray and then at the others.

Hunter turned and watched the three exit the room and close the door behind them. Vicky leaned forward in anticipation to what Hunter wanted to discuss with her in private.

As soon as the room was cleared, Hunter turned back towards Vicky. "Has Ray found any bugs or anything?"

"No not yet, he has just got started. He did sweep this room and setup that Faraday thing in here."

Hunter gave her a slight nod, "Is It safe to talk?"

Vicky leaned back and crossed her arms. "As far as I know it is, but who the hell knows? Ray said it was."

Hunter rubbed his forehead, “Have you given any thought to who our spy is?”

“You think Dana could be our spy?” Vicky asked.

“She joined after you had your first contact with the Sandman, right.” Hunter asked.

“Yes.”

“I don’t think so. He already knew what was going on inside before she joined.” He replied; leaning forward in his chair. “Tell me again what this Sandman looked like.”

“I couldn’t tell, it was dark. The only light on was the one on the desk.”

“So, you didn’t get a good look at him.”

Vicky shook her head. “No.”

“Could you tell how tall he was?”

“When he walked out the door, I could tell he was tall, maybe six feet.”

“Light or Dark?” he asked, leaning over towards her, and placing his right elbow on the arm of the chair.

“Light or dark what?”

“Skin. Hair. Both.”

“He had light colored skin, about your skin tone. His hair was light.” She replied, trying to recall.

“Light colored hair. Blond or grey?”

“All I could really see was the back of his head when he left. He had a hat on, his hair could be grey.”

Hunter looked up towards the ceiling and took a deep breath. “So, we’re looking for a tall old guy, possibly white, with maybe short grey hair wearing a hat.”

She rubbed her temples with her fingers, “I told you it was dark. I know it’s not much to go on.”

“It’s something.” He replied, looking back down at her. He rubbed his forehead with his left hand as if in deep thought.

She frowned, "What is it, Hunter?"

"That description, it almost describes the pilot who flew us to Seoul and back."

"You don't think it was him, do you?" she asked, leaning forward; almost coming out of her chair.

# Chapter Fourteen

# BUGS!

The day after Jack and Red returned; the team met back at Omega. They all gathered around the conference table and prepared for the hotwash of the hunting camp raid.

Jack leaned forward in his chair, "Guys let's get started with this hotwash."

Everyone stopped what they were doing and turned their attention to Jack.

"Before we get started Ray has something to go over with everyone." Jack said, turning towards Ray and giving him a nod.

"Jim, Shay, Red, Kevin, Dana, give me your old phones." Ray slid new cell phones over to them. "Here are your new phones. They all have been scrubbed, and encryption has been added. If there's anything personal on the old phones, let me know and I'll see about transferring it."

Jack picked up his notepad and looked back at Ray. "Is that everyone's phone?"

"Yes, unless Sam has one." When Sam heard his name, he perked up his ears and wagged his tail a couple of times.

"Is there a problem?" Dana asked, looking at Jack and then at Ray.

"It's just a security precaution. We are having Ray update the security of things around here." Jack replied.

Ray spent the next hour going over the new security and calling procedures with the group. They had several questions for Ray and after it was all over; everyone seemed to have accepted the new procedures.

"Did we have a security breach?" Nicholas asked; looking at Ray and then at Jack.

"We just want to secure things. We're getting bigger and expanding our operational area. We just want to take some needed precautions." Vicky replied, while looking at Nicholas and the others.

Shay looked over at Nicholas, "So no more nude midget wrestling on your company phone."

The entire group burst out in laughter, as Nicholas looked at Robert and then at Hunter.

"Man, I didn't say a word." Robert exclaimed, looking at Nicholas across the table.

"OK guys, let's get back to business." Jack said, interrupting the laughter. "Everyone has their kinks. Let's leave Nicholas alone about his."

As the team broke out in laughter again; Ray; never missing an opportunity, displayed two female midget wrestlers on the wall monitors. He had a picture of Nicholas, superimposed in the background, waving money in the air.

When Nicholas saw the picture, he just shook his head and said, "Screw you all." Then he started laughing along with everyone else. "Ok, now that everyone has had a laugh at my expense; can we get back to business?"

Jack began going over the plans about adding some bunk beds and showers to the upstairs storage area. And after that discussion was over, they started recapping the hunting camp mission.

"Well, overall, the mission went very well. No one was shot or hurt this time." He said, looking over at Red and then at Shay. They both nodded their heads in agreement.

"Thank God." Vicky exclaimed; patting Shay on her leg and giving Red a smile and wink.

"I can't say the same for the tangos." He said, looking over at Shay and Red.

"What?" Shay replied with an innocent look on her face.

Red shrugged his shoulders, put his hands behind his head and leaned back in his chair. "Aye, and I do it again."

"What kind of news coverage did it get?" Jim asked; looking at Jack and over at Vicky.

"Very little so far. Only the local stations spent about thirty seconds covering it." She replied, "And that's what we wanted."

"How did the cops respond to the situation?" Nicholas asked.

"They took the video evidence we left them. Moon, Mason, and Payne were taken to a local hospital first and then taken to the county lockup." Jack replied, reading from his notes.

"What about Jamerson Jr.?" Jim asked.

"He assaulted two officers and was taken into custody. That's all we know right now." Vicky added.

"He's going to be a hard case. He's suffering from Stockholm Syndrome. It may take years to save him. If in fact, he can even be saved." Dana replied; looking down and in a somber voice.

Without looking up from his file; Jack said, "Right now, he's in a jail cell waiting on them to sort things out. He and Thomas have been asking where their parents are."

"They are nowhere to be found." Hunter said, with a slight smile and a nod.

"What about the other children?" Shay asked, looking over at Vicky.

"As of our last report; they are with the State Child Protective Services. Ray and Tony are going to keep track with what happens to them." She replied.

"And what if Mason, Moon, and Payne just get a slap on the wrist?" Jim asked, with a concerned look on his face.

"Then we'll address that when and if it happens." Jack replied; finally looking up from his file.

"What about the children?" Shay asked, looking over at Vicky.

Vicky looked at Shay and smiled, "I'm assuming you're talking about financially?"

"Yes." She replied; shifting in her chair.

"They will be taken care of once we find out where they are going. Just like the others."

Kevin looked over at Hunter, "Tell us about this plush resort where the Jamerson's are spending some time at." He asked, with a devilish grin.

"They are relaxing in a place in North Korea called Kaechon Concentration Camp. It's known for its harsh conditions and torture. The guests are used as slave workers at the factories in the camp. They must share their eighteen-by-eighteen-foot room and one bathroom with 80 to 90 other guests. They have to sleep standing up. The only time they can sit is when they are working in the factories."

"Sounds luxurious." Dana replied, in a sarcastic voice.

"I don't think we'll be hearing from those two again." Hunter replied with a smile.

"What about those two jobby heids at that adoption agency?" Red asked, looking around the room.

Jack looked over at Red, "As soon as the story broke, they lawyered up."

"I'm in the process of doing a background check, as well as checking into where they frequent." Ray replied, with a nod at Red.

"When we get enough information; we'll pay them a visit." Jack said, glancing over at Red.

"Aye, and me want to be part of the visiting committee." He replied, with a smirk.

Jack looked back down at his notes, "We'll see what we will do with them, after Ray provides us with all the data on the Kovenski's. Overall, I think it went very well. None of us was hurt and we were able to save five kids." He said; looking up from his notes and around the room.

"Jamerson Jr. is still a question mark." Dana added, with a little concern in her voice.

"That's totally out of our hands right now. We did everything we could." Vicky replied; leaning forward a little in her chair and looking at Dana.

"OK, we'll score it four and a half saves then." Jack replied as he changed the number in his notes.

"Ray, Vicky, and Tony; you guys were great. You kept us informed on what was going on at all times. Ray; would you like to add anything?" Jack asked, looking over at him.

"We did have a few temporary glitches, but for the most part everything went well." Ray replied with a smile.

"Vicky, would you like to add anything else?" Jack asked.

"I thought it went very well. The important thing is that none of us were hurt." She replied; smiling and looking at each person.

Jack looked across at Tony, "Tony, it was nice to hear your voice over the radio. I think it surprised everyone."

"Thank you. I just couldn't stay away. My heart is here with you guys." Tony replied; noticeably choked up a little. "I agree with both Ray and Vicky. I thought everything went well. We still need to fine tune a few things. But I thought it all went well."

"Kevin, my man. Fantastic job getting us in and out without a problem." Jack gave Kevin a thumbs up.

"Aye, but a wee bit sickening. That's gee-in me the boak, almost gonnae whitey. Had to take me a couple of shots of me air sickness medication after we landed." Red replied, with a nod and a smile.

Everyone in the room looked at Red with the same expression of, what did he just say?

"Ok, moving on. Let's review the events as they happened." Jack paused for a second and looked over at Shay. "Someone... decided to jump the gun and run in like a wild crazy idiot and almost got herself shot. If it wasn't for Sam; you'd be dead right now."

"What?" Shay said, looking at Jack and then the others. She motioned with her hands as if she didn't know what he was talking about.

Sam was laying on the floor next to Shay and when he heard his name his ears perked up and he sat up.

"And then you later proceeded to beat the crap out of Mason." Jack added, while looking back down at his notes.

Shay smiled and extended her hand out towards Red, and they gave each other a high-five.

Jack looked over at Red and said, "I'm saving the best for last." Which caused Red to smile and give Shay a wink.

"Jim and Dana; you two didn't have any problems, did you?"

"Everything went well. We had no real resistance." Dana replied with a big smile. She glanced over at Shay and playfully stuck her tongue out at her.

"That's a fantastic job Dana and Kevin. To think that no one was bitten or beaten to a pulp is very impressive." He said; taking a look over at Red and Shay as they both gave him a quick shrug of the shoulder.

While Jack was reviewing the events with Dana and Kevin; a message popped up on Ray's monitor. Ray leaned forward to get a better look at the message and then looked over at the group.

Vicky noticed Rays reaction and was curious as to what caught his attention. Ray's eyes met hers and he gave her a barely noticeably shake of his head. He also had a concerned look on his face. She looked at him, narrowed her eyes and tilted her head slightly to the left; trying to understand what Ray was so concerned about.

Ray leaned back in his chair and placed his right hand in front of his chin. He raised his index finger to cover his lips in a subtle sign for her to keep quiet. Then he turned his attention back to the meeting.

Vicky sat there for a few seconds with a blank expression on her face. Hunter had noticed the concern on her face, and he too was beginning to wonder what was going on. He looked down at the table, then glanced over at Ray, who also had a distant look on his face. He knew that something was up, and it probably had something to do with the spy in the group.

Hunter turned his focus back to the meeting, as Jack was finishing the review of Nicholas and Kevin's dealings with Jamerson Jr. and Bill Mason.

"And this brings us to Red and me and the Jeffery Moon incident." Jack said; looking up at Red who was sitting there like nothing happened.

The room was quiet for a few seconds before Red looked around at everyone staring at him. "What?" he said, with a grin.

"Why did you switch off your equipment?" Vicky asked, with a not so happy look on her face.

"Aye, I must of bumped it or maybe a loose wire or something." Red said, looking at Vicky and over at Jack.

Shay, who was sitting next to Red, covered her mouth with her hand and softly said, "Bullshit." Just loud enough for Red and maybe a couple of others sitting close could hear.

Vicky cut a glance over at Shay, giving her a look to keep her mouth shut. Shay crossed her arms in front of her and looked away.

"And why did you go into the cabin without your backup?" Vicky continued, looking back at Red.

"I thought he was behind me." Red said, looking at Vicky and then at Jack.

Jack gave Red a disbelieving look and shook his head. "And Moon; you said he fell?"

"Aye, that's me story and I'm sticking to it."

"We really don't care what happened to Moon. We're more concerned that you went in alone. Something could have happened to you. That's what concerns me the most." Vicky said, in a motherly tone.

"Sorry Ms. Vicky, it won't happen again."

"See that it doesn't. You're an important member to this family and we don't want anything to happen to you, you've already been shot once... Or to anyone for that matter. We're all a family and we must look after each other."

"It was only a scratch." Red replied; trying to playdown the situation.

Jack leaned forward, "I think the mission went very well. We got in and out without any injuries. Wilson did his thing with some help from Dana. Dana, you did a wonderful job stepping in and assisting Wilson. We could not have done it without you." Jack added with a nod and a smile, and the others all agreed.

"What about her walloping Susan?" Red said, giving Dana a wink.

"I don't know what you're talking about." Jack replied, "I didn't see anything."

Dana turned and smiled at Red and looked back at Jack, "Thank you. I wasn't sure what I was getting myself into, and when Wilson showed up, I really did not know. But after seeing everyone working together and how close you people are to one another; I am sure I made the right choice.

"You are family now." Jack replied with a big smile. "OK, moving on, we were able to get some good intel from this mission. We have Nasir Al-Hadid, Marcus and Alex Kovenski, and we now have a lead on Dana's sister." Jack said while reading from his notes.

"What's the next move?" Jim asked.

"Data collection." Jack replied, looking over at Jim. "We're going to spend the next couple of weeks gathering as much data we can. Then we'll do what we've done in the past; plan and train."

"Does anyone have any comments or suggestions?" Vicky asked; looking around the room. "If not, let's take a break."

Hunter leaned forward and placed his arms on the table, "Someone needs to start working on the new sleeping area and we also need to add a holding cell. So don't wander off too far, we've got work to do."

As everyone stood and started towards the door; Vicky and Ray remained seated. They watched as everyone started filing out of the room, followed by

Hunter. As Hunter approached the door, he stopped and closed the door. He turned and looked at both Vicky and Ray and asked. "Ok, what's going on?"

"Yes Ray, what is the matter? You were acting perplexed during the meeting." She said.

"The computer detected an unknown signal being transmitted from inside of the room." Ray replied, with a concerned look.

"What do you mean, an unknown signal?" Hunter asked.

"I've logged all the frequencies of the new phones and can identify which phone is transmitting. The computer detected an unidentified device trying to transmit a signal." Ray explained.

"You said trying?" Hunter replied, with concern in his voice and on his face.

Ray leaned back in his chair, "Yes, the signal didn't get out. The room is sealed where no signals can exit, except those programed into the relay system."

"And the signal now?" Vicky asked.

"It's gone. As soon as everyone left, the signal stopped." Ray said, as he tapped his fingers on the desk.

"Why don't we bring each person in, one at a time and see if the signal returns." Vicky suggested.

"Good idea." Ray replied.

"Let's have Jack come in first. He is leading this group now. He needs to know what's going on." Vicky said, turning towards Ray.

"I'll send him a message to come back in." Ray said, as he entered the message into the system.

About three minutes later Jack walked into the room. "What's up guys?" he said, closing the door behind him.

Hunter looked at Ray without saying a word and Ray gave Hunter a thumbs-up.

"What's going on?" Jack asked, looking at each one of them with a confused and puzzled look on his face.

"We have a problem." Vicky replied. "Have a seat. We actually have two problems."

"OK, I'm listening." Jack replied as he slowly took a seat.

"Someone had a transmitting device in here during the meeting. Ray detected it and once everyone was gone, the signal stopped." Vicky said.

"So, what are we going to do?" Jack asked, looking at the other three.

"We'll have each person come back one at a time. Ray can go over how the encryption on the phones work with each of them individually." Hunter replied.

"Ok, that sounds good. But you said two problems. What's the other one?"

Vicky looked up at the ceiling and took a deep breath. "Someone has been watching us."

"What!" Jack exclaimed; looking at Vicky and then at Hunter. "What do you mean watching us?" Jack looked over at Ray, who had a puzzled look on his face too.

"Don't look at me. I don't know what she's talking about." Ray said, as he looked from Jack and at Vicky.

"Shortly after we finished the Clinton mission…" Vicky paused a second. "A man visited me at the ranch one night."

"What Man?" Jack asked.

"We don't know who he is. All we know is that he goes by the name Sandman." She replied.

"You said we?" Jack said, looking at Vicky and then at Hunter. "Did you know about this Sandman too?" he asked, looking at Hunter.

"She didn't tell me until after the Jamerson trial was over." Hunter replied as he held his right hand up in an effort to stop Jack.

"He's right. I didn't tell anyone when it happened. I didn't want you to be concerned or possibly lose your focus." She said; showing disappointment in herself for not telling everyone.

"What did this person want?" Jack inquired, still showing a little concern and irritation that Vicky kept this to herself.

"He wanted to help Omega." She replied.

"Help in what way?" Ray asked; leaning forward and placing his elbows on his knees.

"The account codes I gave you to access the Clinton accounts... He gave them to me."

"I knew it! I knew you got them from someone." Ray exclaimed; leaning back in his chair hard and throwing his hands up into the air.

Jack glanced over at Ray, "What else?" he said; looking back over at Vicky.

"The jet to South Korea." Hunter added. "He knew we needed it before I even discussed it with Vicky."

"Who else knew about the Korea trip?" Jack asked, looking directly at Hunter.

"Stan, but before you start accusing Stan, this Sandman knew things before Stan knew anything." Hunter said; before Jack could throw that accusation out.

"You think this Sandman is behind the bugging?" Ray asked, looking back at Vicky.

"I'm sure of it."

"You think that someone on the team is feeding him information?" Ray asked; shaking his head slightly. "That helps me narrow down the problem."

"What do we know about this Sandman dude?" Jack asked.

"Not much at all. That he's an older male, about six feet with short light-colored hair." Hunter replied.

"You said older, like forty?" Jack asked.

"No, older like sixties." Hunter replied, shaking his head slightly.

"When are you planning on telling the others?" Jack asked; addressing the question at Vicky.

"As soon as we find out who is transmitting." She replied.

"Let's get this process underway. Who's going to be first?" Jack asked.

"We'll start with Tony. Jack; why don't you go out and start working on a work detail with the others. We need to get the bunkroom and holding area started." Hunter suggested as he looked over at Jack.

Jack sent each team member in one at a time. After the last one finished; Jack came back into the room. "Well, any luck?" he asked.

"Everyone checked out. We didn't detect the signal again." Ray replied, sounding disappointed.

"Ok, ask Shay to come back in. I'm going to tell her about the Sandman and the leak. She's going to be really pissed off that I didn't tell her before." Vicky said with the sound of regret in her voice.

"Well, I don't want to be in here when you tell her." Jack replied.

"I agree. I think that you need to tell her in private." Hunter added as he and Jack started towards the door. "You coming?" Hunter said; looking back at Ray.

"In just a second, I need to do something first." Ray replied.

A couple of minutes later, Shay and Sam came walking in. "What's up Vicky?" Shay asked; closing the door behind her.

"Excuse me." Ray said as he started to get up. Then something flashed on his monitor that caught his attention. He slowly sat back down and pressed a couple of keys on his keyboard.

"Ray, could we have the room? Please." Vicky said, looking over at Ray, who was glued to his monitor.

Ray held up one finger; asking her to give him one minute. He reached over and opened a desk drawer. He pulled out a handheld electronic device. Ray stood and walked over to where Shay was standing.

"What is it, Ray?" Vicky asked, as she watched Ray slowly walk over towards Shay.

"What are you doing?" Shay asked, as she took a step back as Ray approached.

Sam had been sitting next to Shay after they came in. Once Shay took a step back, Sam sensed that something was wrong. He stood and placed himself between her and Ray. Ray stopped his approach as the hair on back of Sam's neck started to rise.

Ray looked down at Sam standing just a few feet in front of him. "Shay, it's ok. I need to check something on Sam." He said in a nervous voice.

"SAM SITZ!" (SAM SIT!) She said and immediately Sam's demeanor changed. Sam backed up and sat next to her, but still not taking his eyes off Ray.

"May I?" Ray asked, not looking away from Sam and showing Shay the electronic device in his hand. "Just want to check something."

"Sam Platz." (Sam Down.) He laid down and became more relaxed but keeping a watchful eye on Ray.

Ray was slowly running the electronic device along Sam's collar when a green light on the front of the device came on. Ray pulled the device back and the green light went off. Ray again moved the device over Sam's collar and the green light came back on.

"Found it." Ray said softly; while trying to hold in his excitement, so as to not startle Sam.

"Found what?" Shay asked, confused.

"The transmitter." Ray replied; now showing more excitement.

"What transmitter?" She asked.

"Shay, can you remove Sam's collar?" Ray asked.

Shay; now totally confused, looked over at Vicky, "What's going on?" She asked.

Vicky stood and walked over to where Ray was standing. "Just remove his collar."

Shay removed Sam's collar and placed it on the table.

"Let me scan Sam again." Ray said, looking at Shay.

"Sure. Will someone tell me what in the hell is going on." Shay demanded, starting to get irritated.

"He's clean." Ray said, as he ran the device over Sam's neck and body. Ray took the device and scanned the collar that was sitting on the table. As soon as he did the green light came on again. "That's it!"

"Ray, would you give us the room please. Shay, take a seat." Vicky said, and over the next thirty minutes, she proceeded to tell Shay everything that had happened.

They were finishing their conversation when someone knocked on the door. "Come in." Vicky replied.

"Sorry to bother you." Hunter said as he stuck his head in. "If you're finished; can we talk about the transmitter that our four-legged friend smuggled in?"

Shay turned and gave Hunter a look, which most people would have closed the door and left. But Hunter just smiled and walked in. Jack and Ray followed closely behind him. They all took a seat around the table and sat in silence for a few seconds.

"Ray tells us that Sam here is our spy." Hunter said, reaching over and giving him a pat on his head.

"Whatever." Shay replied; folding her arms across in front of her.

"We know that Sam didn't infiltrate us on his own, to gather information about our operation." Jack said, leaning back in his chair.

Shay looked over at him. "Shut up Jack." She said and rolled her eyes.

"Jack you're not helping things." Vicky said shaking her head.

"Tell us were Sam got his collar." Hunter began.

"It's the one that he was wearing when I got him. It has his name and military rank on it. I thought it was nice, so I left it on him."

"Tell us about the person who delivered Sam. What did he look like?" Hunter asked, reaching for a note pad on the table.

"His name was Master Gunnery Sergeant Steven Post." Shay said, after she paused for a second to remember his name.

"Steven Post... Where have I heard that name before." Hunter replied aloud, more to himself than to anyone else.

Hunter looked over at Ray, "Ray can you run a check on a Master Gunnery Sergeant Steven Post? See what you can dig up on this guy."

"Sure thing; give me a couple of minutes."

"What are you thinking?" Jack asked.

"I have a feeling that we've been played." Hunter replied as he sat there looking down at Sam.

"There's no record of a Master Gunnery Sergeant Steven Post currently serving in the United States military." Ray said; turning away from his computer.

Jack looked at Hunter, "Ray, what about a K-9 named Sergeant Sam?" He asked cautiously.

Shay sat there without saying a word. She was obviously mad and confused about the entire situation.

"It says he was KIA along with his handler, a Staff Sergeant Bobby Silvers from an IED."

Shay turned away as tears started rolling down her face. "Now what?" she asked.

Vicky walked over next to Shay and gave her a loving squeeze on her shoulder, "Now we find out who planted the transmitter on Sam."

Ray turned towards the group, "I just did a search on Steven Post and got over nine hundred hits."

"Hold on. Shay what did this Post character look like?" Hunter asked, turning towards Shay.

"He was about six foot tall maybe, light complexion, short blond hair with a narrow face and very strong jaw line. Oh, and blue eyes, I remember the blue eyes. Now that I think of it; his hair was long to be a Master Gunnery." Shay said, turning back towards everyone.

"Damn it! Now I remember, the flight attendant on the flight to Seoul was named Post, Steven Post and he matches your description." Hunter exclaimed, tossing his note pad down on the table.

"Ray, narrow your search to the description that Shay just gave." Vicky said, with a bit of excitement in her voice.

"Thirty hits." Ray said.

"Early to mid-thirties." Hunter added.

"Five hits." Ray replied as he displayed the five pictures on the wall monitor.

Shay stood and walked over closer to the monitor on the wall. "That's him!" She said as she pointed to the second picture from the left.

"That's the flight attendant." Hunter added as he too pointed at the monitor.

Ray selected the picture and the person's bio along with a past military picture, which was displayed on the monitor.

"Can anyone read German?" Jack asked; looking around the room.

"Here I'll have it translated to English." Ray replied and pressed a couple of keys. The words on the monitor changed from German to English.

*Staff Sergeant (*OR-5*) Steven Braun Post, German Special Forces (*KSK*).*

*Awarded:*

*Bundeswehr Cross of Honor for Valor.*

*German Purple Heart.*

*Foreign Duty Medal.*

*The rest of his military history was redacted.*

*Served for 8 years and left due to medical discharge. Wounded on mission, shot in left leg.*

*Father was Richard Post, American and Mother was Sophia Braun, German. Both are*

*deceased.*

*He was born in Frankfurt Germany.*

*Listed as working for Deutschland Marketing as a sales representative.*

Hunter looked over at Jack, "How do you want to handle this kid?"

Jack looked back at him with a bewildered look.

"You're the operational boss. What is our next step?" Hunter added, giving Jack a blank stare.

"I'll have Robert and Jim work with Ray to dig into Post's history." Jack replied; quickly looking at Hunter and then at Vicky.

"And me." Shay said in an almost demanding tone.

"Ok, and you."

"Let's bring the others in and let them know what's going on." Vicky said; walking over and taking a seat. "Let's hold off on the Sandman issue until we find out more about him. We'll keep that to ourselves for right now."

## Chapter Fifteen

# Dungeons and Whips

Jack was about to leave Omega when he noticed a light coming out from under the conference room door. He knocked but there was no answer. He slowly opened the door and over against the wall he saw Ray sitting at the computer.

"Bro, why are you still here? It's past 9 p.m., go home and get some rest." Jack said, as he entered the room.

Ray didn't reply and just kept working on the computer.

"RAY!"

Ray jumped and turned towards Jack, "What?"

"It's past 9. Go home dude."

Ray just turned and went back to work, "I need to finish this. I think I'm on to something."

Jack walked over next to Ray and stopped. "Bro, you stink! When was the last time you took a shower?"

"Wednesday. No Tuesday I think." Ray replied, not taking his eyes off the monitor.

"Ray, it's Saturday night. You've been here since Wednesday?"

"Think so."

"Where are Jim and Robert?"

"They are doing some leg work on the Kovenski's." Ray replied, finally stopping for a second to look at Jack.

"And Shay? Where is she?"

"Don't know. She's not cut out for this research stuff, or for sitting behind a computer. She's more of a taking action and breaking things kind of person."

"Go home and get some rest."

"I've got to finish up on the Kovenski's, Steven Post, Nasir Al-Hadid, Sablehomme Airlines and this Sandman dude." Ray replied, turning back to his computer. "Oh, and I forgot Dana's little sister too."

"Tell me whatcha got on the Kovenski's."

"They are into the bondage stuff, much like the Jamerson's are. Or should I say were."

"Interesting." Jack replied, pulling up a chair next to Ray.

"Jim and Robert are in Atlanta now. They are checking out some of the places the Kovenski's like to visit."

"How often do they visit Atlanta?"

"Tony ran a credit card history on them. He found that they normally take a trip down to Atlanta once a month." Ray replied as he brought up the Kovenski's file on the monitor.

"Any useful pattern?"

"Yes, they stay at the same hotel each time they go. They also frequent the same bar and restaurant too. There's a swinger's club on the west side of Atlanta called Trapeze, that they sometimes go to. And a BDSM club, that seems to be their main attraction, whenever they are in town."

Jack looked at him with a questioning look on his face. "BDSM?"

"Bondage, Dominance, Submission and Masochism are the main ones." Ray replied without missing a beat.

"How do you know this?" Jack asked, leaning back in the chair.

"I've learned and seen some really weird shit since I've worked here."

"When are the Kovenski's due back down in Atlanta?" Jack asked, reaching for a slice of cold pizza.

"If they keep to their schedule, it'll be this weekend."

"Have Jim and Robert keep an eye on them. Have them get as much information as they can on their activities."

Jack leaned over to his right so he could see the monitor better, "Ok, well once Jim and Robert finish up in Atlanta; shoot me the file and I'll start putting a plan together."

"It doesn't look like the legal system is going to be able to do anything to them." Ray replied.

"Nope, that's why we're here. What about the others?"

"I've not gotten much further on them. The company that Steven Post supposedly works for is a shell company. Another shell company also owns Sablehomme Airlines." Ray said in a defeated tone.

"I have faith in you Ray, you'll crack it."

"I don't know. I keep hitting dead ends."

"Why don't you contact some of your Black Hat hacker friends much like you? Maybe working as a team; you can crack it."

Ray turned towards Jack, "Number one; we're not all Black Hats. I'm more of a Red or Grey Hat hacker"

"Black, Red, Grey, blue, purple what's the difference?" Jack asked, seeing that Ray took offence to being called a Black Hat hacker.

"A Black does it for financial gains. Their hacking is normally devastating to a company or person."

Jack squinted his eyes and looked sideways at Ray, "Isn't that what you did to Clinton, Sutton and the others?"

"Yes and No. That was more Red Hat stuff, I wear multiple hats."

"If you say so." Jack replied.

"I have two people in mind that could help. I've used them both in the past. They both are incredibly good. This one dude has a scholarship to MIT for his hacking skills."

"Great, what's his major?" Jack asked.

"His mother won't let him start until he's finished all his high school requirements"

"High school? How old is this kid?"

"He's fifteen, he goes by Starbuck. His mother wants him to get his driver's license before he goes off to college."

"Fifteen?"

"He's off the chain good. He won a contest, put on by some government agency. He hacked the Pentagon's computer in less than 15 minutes. He's been hacking since he was nine."

"Is he one of the Black Hats?"

"No, he's what you would call a Grey Hat. He does it mostly for fun. I've used him to check out the security here at Omega."

"Ok who else?"

"Dark Princess." Ray replied, looking over at Jack with a smile.

"Is she fifteen too?"

"Don't know much at all about her. Met her in a hacker chatroom. She's mostly a Red Hat."

"Annnnnd, are you going to tell me what a Red Hat is?"

"Glad you asked. Red Hats are more into the Vigilante justice. They like breaking into Black Hat systems and turning the tables on them."

"Is she another teenager you've found on the internet? Do we need to start watching you too Ray?" Jack said with a slight laugh.

Ray just ignored the comment and kept working. "I tried to find out more about her. But she sent me a message that popped up on my screen."

"What did the message say?"

"It was a big *STOP* sign and a wagging finger with a devious voice saying, '*No! No! No!*'."

"So, she's better than you. Is what you're saying." Jack replied with a head nod.

"Different!" Ray replied. "We all have our strengths."

"And weakness too, it appears." Jack said; messing with Ray; who wasn't in the mood for joking around.

Ray continued working and ignored Jack's statement.

"Go ahead and contact those two and see if they'll help. Work out some kind of financial compensation with them."

"They don't do it for financial gain." Ray replied.

"Ok, whatever it takes. See if they will help. We're growing and our missions are getting bigger and more complicated. If you trust them, then bring them onboard. But keep what our function is a secret."

Jim and Robert were sitting outside of the Kovenski's hotel when they watched them leave the building and get into their car. They followed them at a distance of about a hundred yards. However, they knew where they were heading. It was their night to go and play at Atlanta's hottest BDSM club, the Forbidden Pleasures.

The couple pulled up to a building that looked like a commercial office building. There were about fifty to seventy-five cars parked around the building.

Jim and Robert watched as the two walked into the entrance and then out of sight. Jim looked over at Robert, "What do we do now?" He asked.

"I guess you go inside and follow them." Robert replied; looking back towards the door of the building.

"Me? Why me?" Jim asked.

"Why not? Someone needs to stay out here in case they leave."

Jim picked up his phone, "I'm calling Jack to see what he wants us to do."

Jack, Vicky, and Shay were all sitting at the ranch watching a movie when Jack's phone rang.

"It's Jim." Jack said as he saw the name on the caller ID. Vicky reached for the TV remote and paused the movie. "What's up? You're on speaker phone. I've got Shay and Vicky here with me."

"Robert and I are sitting in front of this Forbidden Pleasure place. The Kovenski's just went in."

"Is there a question or are you just giving me an update?" Jack asked, looking puzzled.

"What do you want us to do?"

"I'm sorry, what was your assignment again?" Jack asked; knowing where the conversation was leading.

"To follow, observe and document everything the Kovenski's did." Jim reluctantly replied.

Jack looked over at Vicky and at Shay, "And where are the Kovenski's at?" He asked., with a smile on his face.

There were a few seconds of silence, before Jim answered, "Inside the club."

"Are you observing what they are doing?" Shay replied; trying to hold back her laughter.

"Nope!"

"Well then, I guess you BOTH should go in and observe." Jack said, as he too was fighting the need to laugh.

"Vicky, do we have to follow these two into this club?"

"Jack's the boss. If he thinks you both have to go in and observe what they are doing, then I guess you have to go in." Vicky replied. "Oh, and we need a detailed description of what they are doing and as many pictures as you can get."

"I really don't think that they allow pictures inside of this place." Jim replied.

"Didn't you bring your surveillance equipment with you?" Vicky asked.

"Yes."

"Don't you have one of those buttonhole camera things?" she replied.

"Yes."

"Well then, what are you waiting on?" Jack asked; grinning ear to ear.

"Oh, and Jim." Shay said.

"Yes Shay." Jim replied, reluctantly.

"Make sure you get some closeups." She said, placing her hand over her mouth to muffle a laugh. "Did you hear me, Jim?"

"I think he hung up." Jack said, placing his phone back in his pocket.

Jim and Robert grudgingly reached for their electronics bag and placed buttonhole cameras on each of their shirts.

"Hope we're not under or over dressed for this place." Robert said.

"How are you supposed to dress for a place like this?" Jim replied.

Robert looked over at Jim, "Why are you asking me?"

Jim reached for the door and opened it, "Let's just go in and get this over with." He said as he exited the vehicle.

They both approached the door and paused for a second before entering. Neither one knew what to expect. "Here we go." Jim said softly.

As they entered the building, it took a few seconds for their eyes to adjust to the dim lighting of the lobby. A male voice from their left side, caught them by surprise.

"Good evening. Are you two members?"

"Uh no." Robert replied.

"I need to see some IDs please. I also need both of you to complete some paperwork." The man said.

"Sure thing, here's my ID." Jim said, stepping up to the counter.

"Are you two a couple?"

"NO!" they both replied simultaneously.

"Not a problem, we give a discount to couples, just wanted to check." The man replied. "Please read the discloser and the rules and sign at the bottom please."

After the two read and signed the paperwork, Robert turned and asked the man, "How much?"

"Twenty-five dollars each." He replied, "would you like a receipt?"

"Yes." Robert said.

After the man received their money and gave them their receipt, he pointed towards a set of double doors over to the right. "Thank you and enjoy your evening."

"Why did you want a receipt?" Jim asked as they approached the double doors.

"I'm getting reimbursed for every penny for this little adventure." Robert replied as he pushed open one of the doors. They stopped as they entered a large room that looked like a charming hotel lounge. It had chairs and couches scattered all throughout the room. There was a bar located at the far end with about five people sitting there talking with one another.

Robert leaned over close to Jim, "This reminds me of that Star Wars bar scene."

Jim, whispering to Robert, "Yes it does. Is your camera running?"

"Yes." He replied, as a female dressed in all leather approached the two. She was carrying an eighteen-inch Riding Crop, sometimes called a Horse Whip. She stood about four foot three inches tall with long red colored hair.

She stopped about three feet away and looked at both Jim and Robert. "Who is the submissive one?" she asked.

They both looked down and not saying a word; they simultaneously pointed at each other.

She took her riding crop and lightly tapped each one on their chest. "You both are. Excellent! I can use two subs tonight." She turned and motioned with her whip and said, "Follow me to my playroom."

As soon as she turned; both Jim and Robert turned in the opposite direction. They dashed around the corner and into a hallway. "Man, we've got to find the Kovenski's." Jim said as they came face to face with a man dressed in black. He was leading a naked woman by a leash that was connected to a dog-collar around her neck.

They both walked through the club, looking into each room for the couple. Sometimes stopping and watching in disbelief at what they saw. No one was being forced, or seemed to resist, the voluntary abuse they were receiving. It was their thing. A way to escape their everyday dull life, maybe? Ever how bizarre it seemed to Jim and Robert, everyone seemed to be enjoying it. When people weren't doing their "thing," they would be standing around talking and laughing with others in the club.

They finally found their subjects; both were in one of the rooms. Marcus was strapped butt naked with his arms and legs spread apart on what looked like a big X. They saw this woman dressed all in black leather, striking Marcus with some kind of a whip. She wasn't hitting him hard, just enough to leave light reddish marks. It was more of a gentle slap with the whip. He had a gag in his mouth and a blindfold over his eyes.

Alex was a few feet away hanging, also naked, in some kind of cage. It was made of two-inch nylon webbing, interwoven with four-inch by four-inch gaps between. The cage fit tightly around her body; restricting her movement. She too was blindfolded and gagged. She, and the cage were suspended about three feet off the floor. They both watched as the woman took a two-foot rubber paddle from her bag and started spanking her on her butt. The paddle looked as if it was from a cutout piece of a car tire.

Inside the room, and along one of the walls, were five chairs. Two of which were occupied by two gentlemen watching intently. They both watched as the couple took turns being whipped and poked by the masked woman. She would stop every now and then to check on the condition of her submissive subjects. Receiving approval from them; she would continue her work.

Jim and Robert took turns standing and watching as the Kovenski's voluntarily endured over thirty minutes of spanking and whipping. After they were finished, the Kovenski's and their Mistress talked for another ten minutes before they packed up and left.

Jim and Robert stood in the doorway not taking their eyes off the couple. They were astonished and bewildered at how someone could allow themselves to be so humiliated and treated.

Robert poked Jim on his arm, causing him to jump. Robert motioned with his head for them to leave. They didn't say a word to each other as they walked through a large room. There were several people standing around watching, as others were being spanked, or hung from ropes, and various other devices.

They came to a stop as they saw a nude woman on a table lying on her back. She was secured down to the table by her wrist and ankles while her partner was dripping hot wax all over her body. After a few seconds, Jim pushed Robert and they continued out the exit.

"Ok, that was strange." Jim said, as they walked to their car.

"What was?" Robert asked.

"The woman having hot wax dripped on her body."

"And you thought all the other stuff wasn't?" Robert replied as they reached the car.

Jim looked at him before opening the door. "Well, that was more strange."

As they got into the car and closed the doors; Robert asked "More strange? What in the hell is more strange? You mean stranger?".

Jim looked over at him, "You know what I'm talking about. The wax thing was more strange than all the other stuff."

"You mean to tell me that you and your many past girlfriends never got your kink on?" Robert asked, as they watched two women pass their car heading towards the club.

"Well, I've slapped a couple on their butt's a few times and talked dirty. But nothing that comes close to what they were doing." Jim replied. "These people are major league, I'm more like T-ball."

They both laughed and watched as others came and went into the club. "How long you think they are going to be in there?" Robert asked.

Jim looked over at Robert, "Who knows. You think we look strange sitting out here in the car?"

"What do you mean?"

"Two guys sitting alone in a parking lot at night." Jim replied.

"Two guys sitting alone in this parking lot, I'm sure it's fairly common. Just act normal."

Jim chuckled, "After tonight I don't even know what normal is anymore."

"You think any of our people are into this stuff?" Robert asked.

"I don't know. Shay likes to walk around with her riding crop. Maybe she uses it on something other than her horse."

Robert laughed, "Why don't you ask her."

"Hell no! Oh wait, here they come."

They watched as the Kovenski's, and one other lady exited the club. The three stood just outside the club and talked for a few minutes. After they finished, they each hugged and walked towards their vehicles.

"You think that woman was their... whatever they call them?" Jim asked, as he started the car.

"Why, do you want to get her phone number?" Robert replied as he put his seatbelt on.

"Bro." Jim replied, shaking his head.

"Just asking man. I'm sure she can coach you out of the T-ball league. Maybe soft-pitch league or something. Hell, you don't even need a uniform. I'm sure she'll bring all the necessary equipment."

"Just keep an eye on their car." Jim shot back; trying to change the subject.

They didn't say much, as they followed their subjects, making sure they stayed back far enough as to not be noticed.

Before calling it a night, the Kovenski's stopped at a nearby Waffle House. Jim and Robert parked across the street so they could keep an eye on them. They watched as the Kovenski's ordered and ate their meal. After about forty-five minutes, they paid their bill and left. They followed them to their hotel and sat outside until they saw the lights go out in their room.

"Man, I'm starving." Robert said; stretching his arms in the air.

"How does that Waffle House sound to you?" Jim asked as he started the car.

"Sure."

After they finished their late night or early morning meal, they returned to the hotel. They parked where they could keep an eye on the Kovenski's car while they took turns sleeping. The next morning, they followed the couple back to the Waffle House. After they finished their breakfast; they got in their car and hit interstate 85 north. Jim and Robert followed them for about thirty minutes, until they were sure that the couple was heading home.

They took turns driving during the long drive back, to College Station and Omega headquarters. The next morning the team would meet and review the information that they had gathered on the Kovenski's trip.

# Chapter Sixteen

# Rise of the Omega Drakaina

The next morning everyone gathered to review the information that Jim and Robert brought back with them, everyone but Tony. He would be attending the meeting remotely from his office in Houston.

Vicky looked around the room, "I see that everyone is here. Tony, can you hear us?"

"Loud and clear."

"Great, let's get started. Jack it's all yours." She said, looking over at him.

"Ok, as everyone knows, Jim and Robert have been following the Kovenski's, during their monthly trip to Atlanta. They have escaped prosecution for their part in the child trafficking ring. This is due in part, because of hearsay evidence and a sleezy lawyer. It looks like we're going to have to shut them down ourselves." Jack said, looking around the room at each team member.

"What's the status on the others?" Nicholas asked.

Jack looked over at Nicholas, "You referring to, Moon, Payne, and Mason?"

"Yes, and the kids too." Nicholas nodded and leaned forward, resting his elbows on his knees.

"Aye. Especially the wee ones." Red said, looking up at Jack and then over to Vicky.

"The three are sitting in a jail cell awaiting trial. As far as the kids, the state has taken them and have placed them into foster care for now. They are working to find them a permanent home." Ray replied.

"After we finish up with these last two, we're going to focus on Nasir Al-Hadid and getting Dana's sister back." Jack said.

"We need to cut off the head of the snake." Shay said.

"Good analogy Shay." Tony said over the speaker.

"I have my moments." She replied and rocked back and forth in her chair.

Ray picked up his notes, "Tony and I have reviewed the Kovenski's credit card activity. When they go down to Atlanta, they follow the same pattern. Occasionally they pay a visit to the swingers' club Trapeze, on the west side of town. Other than that, they always stay, eat, and visit the same places."

Vicky looked over at Ray, "Any major change in their pattern when they visit that Trapeze club?" Vicky asked; looking at Ray.

"No, whenever they visit that club, they always do it after going to Forbidden Pleasures." Ray replied.

Jack pushed his chair back from the table and looked over at Jim and Robert, "I don't see that as being any issue. Jim, Robert go ahead and fill us in on their activities in Atlanta."

Jim turned towards Jack, "Once they arrived at their hotel and checked in, they went to grab something to eat. They then returned to their room where they stayed for about two hours. At about eight that evening, they both left and headed to the Forbidden Pleasures club. That's were Robert and I observed them entering the club. They stayed inside the club for approximately two hours. We followed them from the club to a Waffle House near their hotel. After leaving the Waffle House, they returned to their room for the night. The next morning, they checked out of their hotel at nine forty-five that morning. They then proceeded to the same Waffle House for breakfast. After eating, they left and headed north on interstate 85. Robert and I followed them for about thirty minutes to make sure they were heading home. We then turned and made our way back to Omega." After reading their report, Jim looked up at Jack.

"You have anything to add Robert?" Jack asked, turning towards him.

Robert gave Ray a nod, to signal him to bring up the pictures on the monitor. "Here are some pictures of their vehicle, hotel and them arriving at Forbidden Pleasures." Several pictures flashed up on the monitor as twenty to twenty-five pictures of the Kovenski's displayed one by one on the monitor.

"Anything else?" Jack asked.

"Nothing other than, I saw some stuff that will keep me up at night." Robert replied shaking his head.

"Aye, what kind of stuff did ye see?" Red asked.

"Yes, tell us." Nicholas urged.

Hunter had been sitting quietly over in the corner watching. "I hear you have a video for us to watch."

"Ray let's see what they brought us." Vicky said; looking over at Ray.

"I've not had time to edit the video, so this is the entire video from start to end." Ray replied as he moved the mouse on the computer and brought up the video.

"Wait, wait. Don't start the video yet." Shay said as she stood and rushed out of the room.

"Where are you going?" Vicky asked.

"We've got to have some popcorn for this. Give me a couple of minutes." She replied.

Kevin stood and followed, "I'll help. Wait on me Shay."

Dana looked around the room, "Does anyone want anything to drink?" she asked as she too stood and started walking towards the door.

"I'll take a double shot of bourbon please." Robert said. "I think I'm going to need it."

"Aye, bring me a whisky." Red piped in, never missing a chance to have a drink.

A few minutes later Shay and Kevin returned with several bowls of popcorn. Dana followed with an arm full of drinks and sat them on the table next to the popcorn.

"Sorry Robert and Red, couldn't find what you wanted." Dana said, looking up at Robert.

"Never ye mind, I've got me own." With that being said, Red reached into his back pocket and pulled out a flask. He raised the flask into the air in a toast and took a swig.

After everyone settled into their seats, Ray looked around the room, "Is everyone ready?"

"No." Jim replied. As Ray pressed the play button on the screen.

The video started playing as Jim and Robert exited their car and walked towards the club. Everyone laughed as they discussed if they were properly dressed.

The cameras that they were wearing, switched to low light mode as they entered the club.

"Oh, he's cute." Dana said, as the man sitting inside the door came into view.

"Robert, you know you get reimbursed for all your expenses." Vicky said as she watched the two awkwardly enter the lounge area.

"Yes ma'am." Robert replied, softly.

"You could have said that you were a couple to save the company some money." Nicholas replied, tossing a wadded-up piece of paper at Robert.

As they entered, the group watched as a noticeably short lady approached the two.

"Oh look, Nicholas's girlfriend." Hunter said aloud, which caused the entire room to erupt in laughter. The comment was in reference to the joke Hunter played on Nicholas during their recent Korea trip.

Nicholas was sitting across the table from Hunter. His right elbow was resting on the arm of his chair with his chin resting in the palm of his right hand. When Hunter made the comment; Nicholas cut his eyes over towards Hunter and slowly slid his middle finger up; flipping Hunter the bird.

The group sat and watched the video, with very few of them saying a word. Occasionally, they would look at each other, as they watched people whipping, being whipped, and what appeared to be torturing each other.

The video then showed Jim and Robert exiting the club and walking to their car, "Ok, that was very interesting." Jack said, as he turned towards the group.

The video continued to play in the background as the team watched. They heard the conversation between Jim and Robert as they sat in the car waiting for their subjects to leave. Some of the team members started talking amongst themselves about what they had seen on the video.

"Excuse me.... Did I just hear my name mentioned?" Shay said aloud. The room got quiet as everyone turned their attention to Shay.

"Ray, will you rewind that for me?" Shay said; pointing up at the monitor and motioning with her hand.

"Sure thing." Ray replied.

Robert looked over at Jim, "You didn't turn your camera off asshole." Robert said as the room got quiet, and they all turned their attention back to the monitor as it started to play.

They could hear Jim laugh in the background, "After tonight I don't even know what normal is anymore."

"You think any of our people are into this stuff?" Robert was heard asking.

"I don't know. Shay likes to walk around with her riding crop. Maybe she uses it on something other than her horse." They all heard the comment that Jim made.

Robert was heard laughing in the background and saying, "Why don't you ask her."

"Hell no! Oh wait, here they come."

Everyone turned towards Shay, who was still looking at the monitor.

"Was that far enough?" Ray asked.

"Yes, I think it was just far enough." Shay replied slowly.

"This is going to be good." Jack said; leaning back in his chair, smiling ear to ear.

Shay turned her attention to Jim and Robert, her jaw jutting out slightly. Jack, who was sitting next to Jim, leaned over, and whispered. "Bro, I would quietly slip out the back door if I were you. Also, make sure you lock your doors before you go to sleep tonight."

As Jim stood, Vicky asked, "Going somewhere?" she said with a smile.

Jim looked back at her, "Yes, sorry, I remembered that I have something to do."

"I know where you live and work." Shay said, sitting there with her arms crossed, eyes narrowed and not taking her eyes off him.

Robert stood and followed Jim out the door. As the door closed behind them, they could hear Robert, "I can't believe you forgot to turn the camera off!"

Jack threw-up his arms, "Well... I guess the meeting is over." He said, as he watched the door close behind the two.

"Before everyone else leaves, Hunter will be heading back tomorrow on his other assignment." Vicky added.

"How about taking Jim and Robert with you." Shay said; looking over at Hunter.

Jack had been working for over a week on a plan to take out the Kovenski's. He thought about hitting them at their hotel room, but there were too many cameras in the hotel. Maybe a shooting or robbery while walking to or from the restaurant or club. After all, Atlanta is a very violent city, and it would be written off as just another robbery gone wrong. Stuff like that happens daily in large cities like Atlanta. Inside the club, he thought to himself. It's semi dark, no cameras but a lot of people. How would they escape unnoticed?

He determined that the Forbidden Pleasures was the best place to do it. But how? Who?

"Hey Jack, what are you working on?" She asked as she walked in.

Jack looked up, "Oh hey, come on in. I was just working out a rough idea on what to do with the Kovenski's."

"What have you come up with so far?"

"I think doing it at the Forbidden Pleasures club is the safest way, but I'm not sure how yet."

"How about have someone stab them?" she suggested.

Jack shook his head, "No, too much blood and someone might see it."

"I hear some like to be choked. Maybe that's a possibility."

"That's a possibility." Jack replied, "But we need to make it look like an accident. We'll need to get out before someone discovers the bodies."

"I know what you should do." She said, leaning forward.

"What?"

"Call Wilson. I'm sure he has some ideas."

Jack thought for a second and nodded, "That's a good idea. Hold on a few seconds while I call him."

Within a couple of rings, Wilson answered. Jack went over the idea that he had about taking the Kovenski's out at Forbidden Pleasures. The conversation lasted for a few minutes and when Jack ended the call, he looked over at her.

"Wilson has a couple of ideas. He wants me and whoever is going to assist, to come to his place." Jack said, looking at her. "Are you up for it?"

"Not sure what he has in mind, but I'm in." She replied.

"Good, we'll drive up tomorrow morning." He replied with a devilish smile.

Jack sent a text to Ray, "Hey man, how about sending Wilson a copy of the video from Forbidden Pleasure. Edit out everything outside of the club. Also send him the notes we have on the K's too."

A few minutes later, Jack received a text from Ray. "Done."

The next morning, they followed the directions given to them by Wilson. They were both excited and curious. No one from Omega had ever visited Wilson's place. They drove for a couple of hours until they turned into what looked like an industrial office park. They stopped in front of a two-story building that was surrounded by a ten-foot security fence. They were not sure if they were at the right address, but it was the address that Wilson had given them.

The sign on the front of the building read, S & W Pottery and Ceramics. Jack pulled up to the security gate and pressed the intercom button. The gate started opening, she looked at Jack, "I guess we're at the right place." A voice over the intercom instructed them to enter and drive through the larger open door on the side of the building.

He looked back at her, "I guess so." They proceeded through the gate and around the side of the building. They drove into the large open door leading into the building. As soon as they entered, the door started to close behind them.

"Well, I think we're in the right place, I see Wilson's motorhome." Jack said, looking over to his left.

As soon as the door closed, the lights came on inside the building. They could see, parked next to Wilson's motorhome, several vintage cars.

"Welcome my friends." Came the voice of Wilson. "Please get out."

They exited the car and met Wilson, who was standing in the doorway leading into the rest of the building.

"Is this where you live?" She asked, looking around.

"Why no. This is my workshop my dear. Although I have spent many of nights working here."

"What's with the name, S & W Pottery and Ceramics?" Jack asked.

"Who would break into a pottery and ceramics warehouse?" Wilson replied, as he led them into a kitchen area.

"And the fence?" she asked.

"Keeps the vagrants, salespeople and shoppers out." He replied, "Please have a seat. Can I get you anything to drink or eat?"

The three sat and talked as Jack brought Wilson up to speed on the status of the people at the camping retreat. He filled him in about the thoughts he had concerning the take down of the Kovenski's at the club.

"You want to eliminate them at the club?" Wilson asked.

"I think that's the best option."

"And how are you going to get away?" Wilson asked; as he started cleaning off the table.

"That's where it gets tricky. Getting in and out without anyone knowing." Jack replied. "That's where we need your advice."

"You have three targets to eliminate not two." Wilson said, as he placed some things in the refrigerator.

She looked at Jack and then at Wilson. "Three? Who's the third?"

"The dominatrix."

"Why her?" Jack asked with a curious look on his face.

"It's obvious from the video that she has worked with the Kovenski's many times before. She knows what they like, and they know and trust her. The BDSM community is built on trust." Wilson explained.

"I don't understand. I thought it was about getting whipped and whipping someone." She said; looking as confused as Jack.

"Follow me to my research area." Wilson said, as he led the two up some steps and into a large room. He turned on the lights exposing its contents.

"You have your own dungeon." She exclaimed.

"I prefer to call it my research area."

"Looks like a dungeon to me." Jack said; looking around at all the torture devices.

"Most of the BDSM tools; shall we say, are based off medieval torture devices. I too, use many of these devices to do my work. Tools of the trade; I guess you'd say."

Looking at Wilson, "Well tell us what your thoughts are." She said.

"I noticed in the video that they liked The Saint Andrews Cross. They used it, as you saw, to flog people and perform other more torturous things. If you would like; I will demonstrate how it was used. If you would step up and allow me to tie your arms and legs to the cross bars." He said looking at her.

"You talking to me?" she asked; stepping back and putting up her hands.

"See trust plays a very important part of the dominatrix and Submissive role. That is a hurdle you must bridge if you're going to pull this off."

"We'll come back to that later. Let's... see... the other stuff." Jack said; taking a closer look at the cross.

"I'm assuming my dear, that you'll be the one going in?" Wilson asked, glancing back at her as they walked to the next device.

"Me! Why me?"

"I assumed that's why you came with Jack. The Kovenski's seem to prefer a female dominatrix. To introduce a male at the last minute might spook them, and then your plan won't work."

Looking at Wilson; she said, "I don't know a thing about this stuff."

"I will teach you everything you need to know. Jack will assist by being your submissive."

"I WILL!"

Wilson smiled and looked at Jack, "Yes, how else is she going to learn where the proper threshold of pain is?"

"What's wrong Jack... you don't trust me?" she asked with a smile.

"Don't worry Jack, I'll make sure she doesn't hurt you, too bad. You'll have a safe word, and when things get too bad; you'll use your safe word, and everything stops."

"My safe word will be. Ouch that hurts."

"Come on Jack. It'll be fun." She said.

He looked at her, "For you maybe."

They spent the next several hours going over the various devices that she would be using. They strapped a dummy onto the cross, while Wilson gave her the proper techniques in using the tools.

"I think that will be enough for today." Wilson said.

"Thank you very much for the instructions." She replied, as she handed him the horse whip that she had been using.

"Oh, my dear, this is just day one of your training. You're going to need much more training if you're going to pass as an experienced dominatrix. Tomorrow; Jack will be your subject and you'll learn the commands and manners that you must have.

The next morning; they arrived back at Wilson's 'Play Palace', as they had dubbed it the evening before. "You ready to get spanked?" she asked Jack.

"You're looking forward to this aren't you?" he replied without looking over at her.

"Every bit of it." She said as she gave him an evil laugh.

They noticed a silver Ford SUV parked next to Wilson's motorhome, as they pulled into the lot.

"Wonder who this is?" she asked.

"Looks like some soccer mom's SUV." Jack replied. There was a family of stick figures on the back window. Father, Mother, three children, dog, and a cat. Also, a sticker that read, 'Proud Parent of an Honor Student at Riverside Middle School.'

"Maybe it's Wilson's girlfriend here to watch." She replied.

They walked into the building and up the stairs into Wilson's 'research area' as he called it. As soon as they entered, they saw a tall dark-haired woman standing next to Wilson. She was dressed in knee high-black leather boots and fishnet stockings from her knees up to her crotch. She had on a G-string that barely covered anything. Above that she wore a black leather long sleeved top that was cutoff just below her nipples. She wore a black police patrol hat, and she held a riding crop in her right hand.

Behind the woman was a man wearing only underwear and sporting a dog collar and leash, which the woman held in her other hand.

"Please come in. Allow me to introduce you to Mistress Phoenix, she'll be your dominatrix trainer for today."

Jack stood there with his mouth wide open; mesmerized by this tall beautiful mysterious woman.

"Come in you two." Wilson said.

"Jack... Jack... are you coming?" she said as she nudged him on his side.

"Oh, yes sorry." Jack replied; snapping out of his trance to follow her.

They walked over to them, and Jack extended his hand to shake the Mistress's hand. "Hi, I'm Jack."

The Mistress looked Jack up and down and gave him a slight nod.

Jack dropped his hand and said, "Allow me to introduce you to my colleague..."

"QUIET! No one gave you permission to talk." The Mistress replied in a firm but soft voice. "You will speak only when spoken to."

"OoooooKaaaay" Jack replied, eyes wide open as he took a step back.

"From this point on; your name will be Mistress Drakaina. I will teach you how to discipline your pet whenever he misbehaves." Phoenix said; smiling at her new apprentice Drakaina. "You may refer to me as Lady Phoenix."

"What does Drakaina mean?" she asked.

"Female dragon." Lady Phoenix replied.

"Ok. I can live with that."

"I'll let you four proceed. I'll be downstairs if you need me." Wilson said, as he turned and walked out of the room.

"What's next?" Jack asked, as he looked at the leather clad woman.

"Did your Mistress say you could speak?" Phoenix snapped. "Lady Drakaina, you must control your pet."

"Did I give you permission to speak?" Lady Drakaina replied, looking at Jack who was giving her the stink-eye look.

"Come Lady Drakaina, we will find something more appropriate to wear." Phoenix said as she turned and walked towards the back room. "Tell your slave to strip down to his panties and to be ready to be disciplined when you get back for being a very naughty boy."

She stopped, turned, and looked back at Jack. "Strip down to your panties like a good little slave. You will be ready for your punishment when I return." Lady Drakaina commanded; getting into her new role.

Jack stood there looking back at her and mouthed the words, "Hell No. Go to Hell!"

They were gone for almost forty-five minutes, when they both appeared. "Introducing your Master and Mistress, Lady Drakaina." Lady Phoenix announced as she stepped aside.

She appeared from behind the door and stood next to her teacher. She was dressed in a black leather corset with garters holding up thigh high stockings. Black leather boots, with four-inch heels and a black mask covering the top of her head, with two openings so she could see. She held a twenty-four-inch-long whip in her right hand and was slapping the side of her right boot with it.

She walked over to where Jack was standing, took her whip and lightly tapped him on his chest. "Why are you not undressed like I commanded?" she asked.

Jack looked at her and smiled, "I think there must have been some sort of a communications problem."

She took the end of her whip and placed it under his chin and lifted it up a couple of inches. "And what, slave is that?"

He looked at her, "I said, No. Would you like for me to spell it for you? N... O..." He pronounced each letter slowly.

"How dare you disobey your master." She said as she drew back her whip and started to strike him with it.

"STOP!" Lady Phoenix yelled.

Just before Jack was to receive his lashing; she stopped and turned towards Phoenix. "What is the problem?" she asked, with some puzzlement.

"Lessen number one, and the most important one. We do not force our submissive to do anything. This is a 100% rule to follow, with no exceptions." Phoenix said, as she slowly walked over to her. "What's very, very important for this to work, is to realize that the submissive isn't forced to do anything they don't want to do."

"But?" she asked, before being cut off by Phoenix.

"No buts. It's not like you see in the movies. This is a mutual agreement and either one can stop at any time. Now if Jack doesn't want to be your submissive; we will use mine. Is that ok with you. Pet?"

"Yes, Mistress Phoenix." Phoenix's submissive replied.

Jack watched as the two Mistresses took turns, "disciplining" the person strapped to the St. Andrews Cross.

Jack stepped out of the room and walked downstairs to talk to Wilson while the other three were doing their thing.

"Hey." Wilson said, as Jack walked in. "You're not up there participating?" he added as he went about his business.

"Nope, not my thing." Jack replied.

"You should try it, it's not as bad as it looks."

Jack shook his head, "No thank you."

Wilson had been waxing one of his cars that was in his collection when Jack came in. "Jack; you'll also have to go in with her at the club. You'll need to act as a blocker in case she must leave in a hurry, or she needs help. All you'll have to do is just watch and be one of the spectators or voyeurs as they are called."

Jack placed a call to Ray. He asked him to review the video and see if he could pull the license plate from the mistress' car who worked on the Kovenski's. He wanted to see if they could track her down and get her name, address, and phone number.

Ray did his best but because of the angle, he couldn't get a clear picture of the license plate.

"Ray can't get the tag, all we have is a picture of the Kovenski's Master, Mistress or whatever you call her." Jack said; looking over at Wilson.

Jack heard a noise behind him and turned. The three from upstairs were approaching. However, now they were wearing their regular clothes.

"Sorry I didn't recognize you." Jack said looking at the three.

"Hi, I'm Peter and this is my darling wife, Janet." The man said as he approached and stuck out his hand.

"Did I hear you say you're trying to identify someone's Mistress?" Janet said as she walked up to Jack.

"Well yes. All we have is this picture." Jack said as he held his phone up.

"What club and where?" Janet asked.

"Forbidden Pleasures in Atlanta."

"Let me see... Isn't that Linda?" Janet said; looking over at Peter and showing him the picture.

"Yes, that's Linda." Peter replied, nodding his head.

"She goes by Mistress Victoria. Here; I'll show you. Here's her webpage. May I?" Janet asked as she started to reach for Jack's cellphone.

"You're asking?" Jack said with a surprised look. "I thought you would have demanded it."

"Jack, Jack... That's only when we are playing." Janet smiled and gave him a wink.

"Only when we are getting our kink on; as we like to say." Peter replied.

"Well, I'm not into that dominant and submissive stuff." Jack said, shaking his head.

"Did you have parents growing up?" Peter asked.

Jack looked at him, "Yes, why?"

"Did they discipline you?" He asked.

"Yes of course."

"Teacher... Boss?" Janet added.

"Yes, again why?" Jack asked; looking at the two of them.

"Did you submit to their rules, even if you didn't agree with them?"

"Yes, I had no choice."

"Then you're submissive." Wilson replied, answering for them.

Janet and Peter nodded their heads in agreement, "The difference with us and others like us, is we agree beforehand on the rules and when and where it happens. It's also about trust."

"What about these guys that beat their wives." Jack replied.

"That's totally wrong. That's called abuse and that's nothing about what our relationship is about. Or others like us."

"Still not my thing." Jack replied, shaking his head a little.

"Tell me Jack, have you and your girlfriend or significant other ever gotten a little physical in the bedroom? Ever slapped them on the butt a few times?" Peter asked.

"Girlfriend, and maybe a few times. But nothing hard."

"Then you were the dominant one. Really no different as to what we do." Janet said. "I sorry we've got to go. I've got to pick the kids up at practice and Peter needs to run by the church. Same time tomorrow, Mistress Drakaina."

"Sure, looking forward to it."

"Are you going to be here too Jack?" Janet asked as she grabbed her bag and walked towards their SUV.

"I guess."

Janet opened the front passenger door and started to get in. "I'd love for you to watch tomorrow." She said and closed the door of the SUV.

# Chapter Seventeen

# FORBIDDEN PLEASURES

The next day the four met for their final session. This time Peter was the dominate one and Janet was his submissive. Jack still didn't participate in the fun. He just sat over in the corner and watched. They ended their training session shortly after lunch. Before Janet and Peter left; they answered some last-minute questions from her and Jack.

"Well, it's been a very interesting last couple of days." Jack said.

"Yes, it has been. What's the plan now?" she asked.

"Ray hacked into Mistress Victoria's website. He's set up a trap on her website. Whenever the Kovenski's register for their next appointment at Forbidden Pleasures, it will redirect the appointment to a mirrored site he's set up." Jack replied as they walked into Wilson's kitchen.

She was leaning against the counter when Wilson walked in, "Are you one of Lady Phoenix's pets?" she asked, as Wilson took a seat at the table.

"Pet? No, but I have been on the receiving end of her whip." Wilson replied as he scooted his chair up to the table.

"Wilson, you're submissive? I would never have imagined." Jack said, as he looked over at him.

"On the contrary, my dear boy. I am a master of my trade; an artist so to speak. A true artist must know his canvas and his brushes."

Jack looked intently at him, "What do you mean?"

"In order to know and perfect my trade; I must know what my tools can do and to what extent they can be used to achieve my end goal. In other words, the canvas is my subjects, and my brushes are the tools I use to extract the information I'm after."

"Gotcha."

"What are your feelings on this Dom/Sub stuff?" she asked Wilson.

"It has been prominent throughout history in every country and culture. Many countries and religions still today, use some level of Dom and Sub relationship. The Western culture has either slowly moved away from, or have looked down on, that form of relationship."

She nodded her head slightly, "I guess so."

"Omega has taken up the fight against the dominate child predator, so the submissive sex slave can be freed." Wilson said. "In that instance; you have forced submission. Whereas with Janet and Peter, that's a totally voluntary form of submission."

"We need to still come up with a plan to eliminate the Kovenski's somehow." She replied; taking a seat at the table.

"Isn't there something we would be able to give them so that they will have a heart attack?" Jack asked, looking at Wilson.

"Heart attack would only eliminate one. The chances of both having one at the same time is very remote." Wilson replied. "Besides, you don't want to be around when they die."

"Well, what then?" she asked.

"You're going to need something that you can give them during their session. Something that will take effect hours or even days later." Wilson paused in thought. "Something that will allow any contact at Forbidden Pleasures to be out of the picture, as far as being connected to the cause of death."

Jack leaned forward and said, “That’s in your ballpark.”.

“Ricin.” Wilson said softly; thinking aloud to himself.

She looked at him with a questioning look. “Ricin?”

“That’s something we don’t know anything about.” Jack replied.

Wilson smiled, “Here’s the short version. No antidote exists for ricin, and the amount of ricin that would fit on the head of a pin could be enough to kill an adult. Within a day or so, vomiting and diarrhea will start. Next come the hallucinations, and seizures. The person's liver, spleen, and kidneys would stop working, and the person would die.”

“I don’t want them to infect anyone else or infect me either.” She replied with concern.

“They can’t transmit this to others, and unless you ingest the ricin; you’re not going to be at risk either.”

“How do you expect me to get this ricin into them?” she asked with concern evident in her voice.

“Water bottle.” Wilson replied, lifting his water bottle off the table. “You’ll give each of them water bottles tainted with ricin. Before you start and when you finish your session; you’ll give both of them the bottles of water to drink.”

“Sounds simple enough.” Jack replied.

Wilson smiled, “By the next day, they should be starting to feel the first symptoms. By then it’ll be too late for them to do anything. It’ll be a slow and painful death for them.”

“Where do we get our hands on this ricin stuff? I’m sure the local Walmart or CVS doesn’t carry it.” She asked, beginning to feel a little better about things.

Wilson smiled and stood, “I’ll be back in a couple of minutes.” He left the table and walked out of the kitchen. About fifteen minutes later he returned with four DASANI water bottles.

“Here you go.” Wilson said, as he placed the four water bottles on the table.

“Those have ricin in them?” Jack asked, studying the four bottles.

“Yes”

"How do you know they will drink them?" she asked.

"My dear, if you'd studied the video your colleagues took; you would have noticed at the beginning and the end of the session Lady Victoria gives them both a bottle of water to refresh themselves."

"Wait a second." Jack said, "You have water bottles back there with ricin already in them?"

"No, no. I had some water bottles back there. I've got a large supply of.... shall we say additives on hand. Just in case I need them."

"Additives?" she asked.

"Ricin, VX the nerve agent, used to kill Kim Jong Un's brother, Botox, Hemlock, Aconite from the plant monkshood, Tetrodotoxin from the blue-ringed octopus, Cyanide, Botulinum, Fentanyl and Arsenic." Wilson said proudly. "Each has its advantages and uses."

"I just give them the water to drink before and after the session and that's it?" she asked.

"That's it. You chat a little, walk with them outside and get in your car and leave." Wilson replied, calmly and with a devilish smile.

"That simple?" She said.

He looked at her, "The hard part is convincing them that you are a true dominatrix. Giving them the poison will be the easy part."

"Ray's going to trap any phone calls from the Kovenski's to this Victoria and any calls from her to them just in case they try and contact each other. He has it going to a voice mail he's created." Jack said, looking at both of them. "He's going to send them a last-minute message, informing them of the change and giving them a big discount. She'll let them know that Lady Drakaina will be replacing her and that she has full confidence that they will be pleased."

"Well Mistress Drakaina, I think you have everything you need. Any more questions?" Wilson asked.

"No, I don't think so."

She looked over at Jack, "How about you?"

"Nope, I'll be along for the ride. You'll be doing all the work."

"Speaking of which... I don't want any of the others to know anything about this. If you tell anyone, you'll regret it. Do I make myself clear?"

"Not a word Mistress Drakaina." Jack replied with a laugh.

"I'm serious Jack Davidson!"

Wilson looked over at her and then at Jack, "I'd do what she says."

"I think this is a two-person mission. So, we don't need to involve any of the others." Jack replied with a nod of his head.

She smiled at Jack and said, "Good let's keep it that way."

"Yes, Mistress Drakaina." Jack said, as he drew back in anticipation of being hit.

"Keep it up Jack. It's going to be a long drive back home."

They sat around for another hour, making sure they had everything they needed before heading back. The drive back was uneventful because Jack kept his mouth shut about the Mistress Drakaina thing. They did discuss their roles in the mission and a backup plan just in case.

The next morning Jack walked into Ray's work area, "What's up man?" Jack asked.

"Same old thing, trying to find out what I can dig up on this Sandman dude."

"Any luck?"

Ray turned to face Jack, "Not really. The guy's good at covering his tracks."

"Where is everyone?" Jack asked.

"I've only seen Red and Nicholas the last several days. They're finishing up the bunk room and shower area."

"Anything on the Kovenski's?"

Ray turned back towards his monitor, "Nothing useful yet. Do you have a plan on how to deal with them?"

”I’ve got a couple of ideas. I think it’s going to be a two-person operation.”

“Hunter’s back in Frankfurt, trying to follow-up on some leads on the Sandman.” Ray said.

Jack turned and walked towards the door, “I’m going to have Robert and Jim to help you out. They can dig through the data you find so you can concentrate.”

“That will help, the others are not cutout to do that kind of work. They only slow things down.”

She and Jack had paid a visit to the Forbidden Pleasures Club two weekends before the scheduled meeting with the Kovenski’s. They wanted to learn the layout and get use to what was going on inside. They reserved the room for the scheduled weekend and time when they would meet.

Now it was time to wait for that weekend to arrive. They have now put the plan in motion to eliminate Marcus and Alex Kovenski for their part in the child sex trafficking trade.

The fateful day arrived, and they parked near the far end of the parking lot of Forbidden Pleasures. The lot was already over half full with about thirty cars. They sat there for a few minutes not saying a word.

Jack looked over at her, “Well, are you ready to go in?”

“As ready as I’ll ever be.” She replied.

“The Kovenski’s will be here in about thirty minutes. Why don’t you go in and get acclimated to the place? You still need to get your outfit on.”

“I guess I should.” She replied with some hesitance in her voice.

“You’ll be fine. Just remember what Lady Phoenix taught you.”

“I’m just ready to get this over with.” She said as she opened the car door.

“I’ll contact you when they arrive. Do you have your earpiece in?” he asked, leaning over in his seat.

"Yes, and my button camera is on too. Check the reception, test, test, 1, 2, 3, 4." She said as she slid out the door.

"I copy and video is coming in clear, have fun." Jack said as she closed the door and started walking towards the building.

"I can hear you too." She replied. "OK... here we go." She approached the door and paused for a second before opening it.

She remembered most of the layout of the building and where everything was, from their previous recon visit two weeks prior. She just wanted to make sure that everything was still as it was before. She found the changing room and entered. She had all the equipment that she needed stuffed into a medium size rolling suitcase, along with a backpack that held her Mistress Drakaina outfit.

She started to leave the changing room when a terrible thought went through her mind. "*Shit, did I forget the water bottles*?" her heart started racing as she opened the backpack and looked inside. To her relief she saw the water bottles; four with blue caps and two with green. The blue ones contained the ricin, and the green ones were clean for her to drink. "Thank God." She said quietly.

"Did you say something?" came Jack's voice over her earpiece.

"No, I thought I had forgotten the water bottles, but I've got them." She closed her eyes and took a deep breath. She pushed open the door and walked from the changing room into the lounge. She felt like everyone was watching her as she slowly walked through the lounge area.

"*Stay calm*." She told herself, "*You've got this. Just make it to the room, close the door and wait for the Kovenski's.*"

"Excuse me." Came a voice from behind.

She froze in her tracks and slowly turned. She saw a middle-aged man about six foot tall, standing there dressed in regular street clothes. Her mind went blank for a second and then she spoke.

"Are you talking to me?" she asked, looking the man up and down.

"Yes." He replied, with an excited look on his face.

They stood there looking at each other; neither one knowing what to say next.

Jack had been in the car watching and listing to what was going on. "Remember who you are, you're Lady Drakaina. Get into the role." He whispered over the earpiece.

She looked at the man and said in a polite but stern voice, "Who gave you permission to speak to me?"

He looked down and said, "I'm sorry my lady... But I was wanting to know if you were available?"

"Available for what?" she asked.

"What else, you dummy." Jack said, in her ear.

"I've been very bad and need some discipline. I was hoping that you would discipline me." The man replied, without looking up.

She released her suitcase and raised the riding crop that she had in her right hand. She took the crop, remembering what she saw the short lady do when she approached Robert and Jim. She placed the crop on the man's chest and raised it up to his chin. "I am already booked for today. You're going to have to find someone else."

"Thank you, my lady. Would you happen to have a card?" He asked, without looking up.

"A card?" she replied.

"Yes, a business card. I would like to schedule a session with you."

"No sorry, I'm all out."

"Business cards." Jack said, we didn't think about that.

"Look, I've got to go and get setup for my appointment, maybe next time." She replied and turned around and started walking towards the room, but this time in a more determined pace.

"We're going to have to get you some business cards for next time." Jack replied.

"There's not going to be a next time." She said in a whisper.

"Sure thing. You'll be back here next week, trolling for someone to spank." He said, playfully over her earpiece.

"I'm going to shove this riding crop up your ass, if you don't shut the hell up."

"Oh, come on, you're getting off on this and you know it." He replied, as he laughed.

"Jack!" she said in a serious but playful muffled voice.

"The Kovenski's are here. Are you ready?" he said in a hushed voice.

"I'm getting setup now." She replied, sounding somewhat nervous.

"As soon as they get inside, I'm coming in too. I'll be hanging right outside the room."

She paused what she was doing and asked with a concerned tone in her voice, "What if they change their mind at the last second and leave?"

"Then I'll follow them and see where they go."

"What about me?" she asked.

"I'll come back and get you."

"And what in the hell am I supposed to do in the meantime?" she said in a raised tone.

"I don't know. You can find that guy that wanted to hire you a few minutes ago. After all, you have the room already reserved, it would be a shame to waist it."

"JACK! If you leave me here, I will hunt you down and"

Jack cut her off, "Ok they are in, and I'm about to walk in the door now."

In a couple of minutes there was a knock on the door. She took a deep breath and slowly let it out. "Enter." She said as she turned toward the door.

Marcus and Alex walked in and left the door open. "Hi, I'm Marcus and this is my wife, Alex. Lady Victoria said that you will be our Mistress today.

"I am Mistress Drakaina, and you will be my obedient submissive today. She told me everything that you like, and I will do my best to make sure you are taken care of in the same fashion that Lady Victoria would have. And your safe word is what?"

"Red velvet." Alex replied.

"We have this private room for one hour, same as usual." Marcus asked.

"Yes, we do. Do you not know how to properly address your master?"

Marcus lowered his head, "Sorry Mistress Drakaina."

"You will drop down before me and lick the top of my boot."

Marcus at once dropped to his hands and knees. He licked the top of his Mistresses right boot three times, before stopping. He remained on all fours at her feet, awaiting further instructions.

She reached down and grabbed the hair on the back of his head and pulled his head up. "You remain there until I get back. I will deal with your disobedience later."

"I have water bottles here. You will hydrate before we start."

Alex looked down at the ground, "Yes, Mistress Drakaina."

She grabbed one of the tainted water bottles and handed it to Alex. "Drink."

"Yes, Mistress Drakaina." Alex replied as she reached for the water bottle.

"Damn girl." Jack said, over the earpiece.

"You miserable excuse for a man, you drink this water and then take your position on the cross." Mistress Drakaina commanded.

Marcus jumped to his feet and grabbed one of the tainted water bottles without making eye contact with his mistress, opened it and downed half of the bottle.

"Both of you strip down. I don't want to see anything but skin." She demanded.

She turned her attention back to Alex. "Now it's your turn." She reached down and opened her suitcase and pulled a small carrying case. Inside the case was a hanging nylon cage. She removed the cage and placed it on the ground underneath a cable, that was attached to a pulley on the ceiling. The bottom of the nylon cage had a twelve-inch diameter wooden support, so that the person inside could stand.

Alex stepped onto the wooden support and gave Mistress Drakaina a big smile. She reached down and pulled the nylon cage up to shoulder height. Mistress Drakaina took the cable hanging down from the ceiling and attached it to a large metal ring on the top of the cage. Once attached, she walked over to the wall where a control box was located. She pressed the up button and the cable that was attached to a winch started to tighten. Alex dropped her arms to her side as the nylon cage started to close in around her.

Slowly the cage tightened around Alex, and she couldn't move her arms and legs. She was now suspended two feet above the ground in what looked like a cocoon. Small parts of her body protruded out between the four by four-inch openings. She was totally immobilized, and at the mercy of Mistress Drakaina.

She walked over to where Marcus was standing and stopped next to him. She leaned over to within inches of him. "You call yourself a man?" she asked, mockingly.

He looked over at her and said, "No Mistress."

"You dare to look at me!"

"Sorry Mistress." He replied now looking down.

"That will be an additional thirty lashes."

"Thank you, Mistress Drakaina." Marcus replied. "I deserve it, Mistress."

"Yes, you do. You both deserve everything you'll get tonight." She replied.

She took the rope bindings, attached to the top of each cross post, and tied each one of his arms, high over his head. His back fully exposed to the wrath of Mistress Drakaina's whips.

She walked over to her suitcase and pulled out a three-foot long braided leather flogger and positioned herself directly behind Marcus. She hesitated for a few seconds; looking at the naked body of the sexual pervert tied in front of her.

By this time Jack had entered and had made his way to the doorway of the room they were in. "Think of all the children they have sold off into sexual bondage through their adoption agency." Jack said into her ear; low enough that others standing close by could not hear.

She looked back at the door and saw Jack standing there. As soon as they made eye contact, Jack gave her a slight nod. She turned back, and with the leather flogger in her right hand, struck Marcus across the back. This left faint pink marks across the upper part of his back, where each one of the narrow leather straps struck.

Jack stood just a few feet away as he watched, "Think about Jackson, Thomas and Robert Junior." He said softly, but with a hint of hate, into her earpiece.

She turned her head towards Jack, this time with fire in her eyes. She swung her arm back and then with force struck Marcus across his back; this time leaving dark red marks across the previous marks.

Marcus screamed out in pain, "THANK YOU MISTRESS DRAKAINA! THANK YOU!"

She repeated the strikes fifteen more times and with each strike, Marcus replied the same, thanking her. Dark red marks covered most of Marcus's back as he softly cried. She looked back at Jack, who was bewildered, and motioned over towards where Alex was hanging. She dropped the flogger on top of the other items in her suitcase and picked up a two-foot-long paddle made from rubber. She approached the back side of Alex and took a hard swing. Connecting to the flesh of her butt where it poked out between the nylon webbing of the cage.

After she gave Alex twenty-five strikes with the rubber paddle; she returned over to where Marcus was. She looked over at Jack, still standing in the doorway. She noticed someone walking up and stopped next to Jack in the Doorway. She could hear the conversation between the two of them over her earpiece.

"Hello handsome." Jack heard someone say over his right shoulder. He turned his head to the right, to see who was talking to him. Standing about a foot away was this tall incredibly attractive blond with hair down below the shoulders. Jack immediately turned his attention to the blond on his right and noticed the nice firm bare breasts.

"Are you a dom or a sub?" the person asked.

"Uh, uh why you ask?" Jack stuttered.

"I just wanted to know if I can spank you or better yet, can you spank me?"

Jack just stood there not knowing how to answer. Then a voice came over his earpiece. "Jack, you know that's a guy you're talking to."

Jack turned his head quickly and saw his cohort laughing as she stood next to Marcus.

"Jack, looked down." She said trying to regain her composure. "He, or she has junk between their legs." She said, smiling as she looked at Jacks reaction.

"No! No!" Jack said as he took a step back. "I'm here just to watch."

"Oh, you're a voyeur then. Feel free to come and watch me get spanked. Maybe you might decide to take a lick yourself... If you know what I mean." With that the person turned and walked away into the darkness of the club.

Jack just stood there not moving and after a few seconds, he looked back into the room where the Kovenski's were. She was finishing using the rubber paddle on Marcus when Jack looked back in.

"Our time is up." Mistress Drakaina said, as she stopped and tossed the rubber paddle into her suitcase. She released the bindings around Marcus's wrists. She then walked over and lowered Alex and the cage down to the floor.

Once freed, Marcus and Alex retrieved their clothes and started to dress.

She handed both Alex and Marcus another tainted water bottle. "You've received what you disrespectful and poor excuses for human beings deserved. Here, drink this bottle of water." Mistress Drakaina commanded.

"And we both so deserved it, Mistress Drakaina." Alex said. She then took a big swig of her water.

"Giving people what they so deserve gets my heartrate and breathing up." She replied. "I will join you in a drink." She reached into her bag and pulled out a clean and uncontaminated bottle of water and downed almost half the bottle.

"Mistress Drakaina, we are heading home now. May we call you again?" Alex asked, mustering up a smile through the pain.

"Sure, you may. I have your contact information. I will send you a link to my website so that you can schedule another session." She replied with a smile.

As soon as Jack saw them packing things up; he turned and slowly made his way to the exit and then into their car. He watched as the Kovenski's exited the building and slowly walked over to their car.

"Jack." She said, over her microphone. "I'm going to shower and change. Give me about ten minutes."

"Ten-four Mistress Drakaina. Your driver awaits."

"You can cut the crap now Jack. Mistress Drakaina is officially retired." She replied in a matter-of-fact tone. "Oh, and if you ever tell anyone about this, I'll tell them about your blond boyfriend."

The next morning Marcus Kovenski called his office, at Loving Arms adoption agency. He told his secretary that he and Alex weren't coming in for a few days, and for her to reschedule all their appointments for the rest of the week.

Those were the last words that were ever heard from them again. When they didn't show up for work or return any calls from their office; their office secretary called the local authorities and asked if someone would go and check on them. The police discovered their lifeless bodies when they went to check on them.

# EPILOGUE

It was a very cold and windy evening in Frankfurt as Hunter made his way from his hotel. He was staying at the Maingau Hotel, about a ten-minute walk from Zum Gemalten Haus, a restaurant he frequented whenever he was in Frankfurt. He turned and headed down Schifferstraße towards Brückenstraße. He stopped in front of a store, so that he could check around to see if anyone was following him, without making it look too obvious. Satisfied that he wasn't being followed, he turned to his left and continued to Schwanthalerstraße.

Hunter continued walking down the sidewalk for several more minutes, stopping a couple of times to check for a tail. Once in front of the restaurant, he stopped again and took a quick glance. Still satisfied, he opened the door and entered the restaurant.

"Willkommen Herr zu Zum Gemalten Haus. Wie viele sind in deiner Gruppe?" the maite'd said.

Hunter looked at the man for a second. "I'm Sorry, I don't speak German, I'm American."

The maite'd smiled, "Yes sir, I too speak English. I said, Welcome sir to Zum Gemalten Haus. How many are in your group?"

"It's just me."

"Very good sir." The maite'd replied and motioned for a close-by waiter to escort Hunter to a table.

Hunter smiled and gave the man a nod as he followed the waiter.

"How is this sir?" the waiter said, in English but with a strong German accent.

"Do you have a table facing the entrance?" Hunter asked, looking around at the other patrons eating.

"How about this one sir? Are you expecting someone to join you?"

He looked over at the waiter, "Oh, no I just like to see who is coming and going."

"Very good sir. May I ask what you are having to drink today?"

"Tea please, with lemon." Hunter replied as he took his seat.

"And here is your menu sir. I will be right back to take your order."

A few minutes later the waiter returned with his tea. "Sir, are you ready to order?"

"Yes, I'll have the Beef Tenderloin with Cabbage please."

"The Rindersolber Mit Kohl, a very good choice sir." The waiter smiled, turned, and walked towards the kitchen.

Hunter checked his phone and looked around at the other patrons enjoying their meals. There was a family sitting a couple of tables away. The son, who looked to be about ten years old, was telling his parents about the video game he wanted. To the side of Hunter there was a young man and woman sitting very close together, as they talked and slowly picked at their food.

You could hear the hustle and bustle in the kitchen and occasionally you herd the chef barking out orders to the cooks.

A few minutes later the waiter returned with Hunter's meal, "I'm sorry sir, I was told that you might like the Schweinesolber Mit Kohi... Sorry, my apologies, the Pork Tenderloin with Cabbage better." He said as he placed the plate in front of Hunter.

Hunter looked up at the waiter, "And who was that?"

"Good evening Mr. Stockton." Came a voice from behind Hunter.

Hunter turned slightly in his chair in the direction of the voice.

"Let me guess, you're the Sandman?" Hunter asked, as the man walked around and took a seat across from him.

"Yes, I believe so. Charles Sablehomme Pascal, you may call me Charles."

"Sablehomme Airlines. Go figure. Do you always pilot your own jet?"

"I like to stay current." Charles replied with a smile.

"And I'm sure you remember my colleague Mr. Post." Charles said as Steven Post walked up behind Hunter and placed a hand on his right shoulder.

"Yes, the steward on the plane." Hunter said, turning his head slightly towards the man behind him.

"Among other things... He's also my bodyguard." Charles said.

"Also, Master Gunnery Sergeant Steven Post." Hunter replied.

"Not one of my favorite rolls." Post replied.

"Mr. Stockton, may I call you Hunter?"

"Sure, why not. I feel like we're old friends." Hunter replied; looking back at Charles. "Oh, why do they call you Sandman?" Hunter leaned back in his chair and crossed his arms.

Charles smiled, "Sablehomme in English translates to Sandman."

"So, your name is, Charles Sandman Pascal?"

"Yes, you can say that."

"What is it you want?" Hunter asked.

"In time." Charles replied. "But for now. Eat! Enjoy your Schweinesolber Mit Kohi."

"Aren't you going to eat?" Hunter asked, looking up from his meal.

"No, I ate before you came."

The two sat without saying a word until Hunter finished his meal. Steven stood directly behind Hunter the entire time. Once Hunter finished his meal, he slowly wiped his mouth off with a napkin and finished off his tea. He placed his empty tea glass on the table and looked at Charles.

"Now what?" Hunter asked.

"Please Hunter." Charles paused and smiled. "Lift your arms so that Steven can relieve you of your weapon. You know Hunter, carrying a weapon here in Frankfurt can put you in a lot of trouble. Trouble that your friends back at Omega can't get you out of; not even Ray or your FBI team member Tony."

Hunter lifted his right arm and Steven reached inside of his jacket and pulled Hunter's 9mm Sig P365xl Spectre Comp pistol.

"Very nice." Charles said.

"Well, it's a dangerous world out there; what can I say. You never know what kind of scumbags you'll run into nowadays." Hunter leaned back in his chair and crossed his legs at the ankles.

Charles looked over towards the waiter. "*Dürfen wir bitte den Scheck haben, Sir*?" (May we have the check please sir?) The waiter immediately walked over to the table and placed the check on the table in front of Charles. "*Danke*." (Thank you.)

"Thank you, Charles, you didn't have to pay for my dinner." Hunter said sarcastically.

"My pleasure. Also, your backup weapon, please Hunter. The one on your left ankle." Charles said, without looking up from signing the check.

"Don't know what you're talking about."

"The 380 Sig P238 in your ankle holster. Two fingers please and slowly. While you're at it, give Steven the dagger in your left pants pocket too." Charles placed the pen down on top of the check and slid it over towards the waiter.

The waiter smiled and nodded his head and removed the check, "*Danke*."

Charles looked up at the waiter, "*Danke, Hans, gib Anne und dem kleinen Gunther bitte eine Umarmung für mich*." (Thank you, Hans, give Anne and little Gunther a hug for me please.)

"*Ich werde Sir, gibt es sonst noch etwas?*" (I will sir, is there anything else?) the waiter replied.

"*Nein danke, mein Freund und ich gehen gleich.*" (No thank you, my friend and I are about to leave.)

Hunter sat up in his chair and placed both hands on the edge of the table to push himself back. "I hate to break this happy reunion up, but I've got to leave." As he pushed back, the chair stopped as it bumped into Steven, who was standing behind him. Steven placed his hands on Hunter's shoulders.

Charles smiled, "Hunter, if you will, come with us."

Hunter looked at him and up at Steven, "Do I have a choice?"

"You always have a choice. If you make the right or wrong choice, it's totally up to you." Charles laughed.

The team was eating at a local restaurant, in College Station. It had been over a month since the hunting camp and the Forbidden Pleasures mission had successfully come to a conclusion. Jack was in another world as the events of the past few weeks ran through his mind. Suddenly he was startled by the waitress putting her hand on his shoulder and giving it a slight squeeze.

"Sweetie what would you like to order?" she asked, as everyone at the table started laughing.

Jack was having a flashback about the time he and his stepfather were eating dinner at a restaurant with his stepfathers' hunting buddies. His stepfather asked the waitress to take Jack and pop his cherry. The waitress replied "sure" and grabbed Jacks arm, trying to pull him up from the table. Jack resisted and the waitress ended up just giving Jack a big kiss. His stepfather and his friends laughed at him. Jack was only thirteen at the time.

After they finished their dinner and were about to order dessert; Jim asked "Jack, whatever happened to the Kovenski's?" Before Jack could answer, his phone rang: It was Vicky.

"What's up Vicky?" Jack asked, still thinking back to the dinner with his stepfather.

"Jack we've got a problem." Vicky said, noticeably upset.

"Vicky, what's wrong?" Jack replied, with concern.

Everyone at the table stopped talking and turned their attention towards Jack.

"Slow down Vicky. Now tell me what's wrong?" there was a slight pause, as Jack waited for her to calm down. "Say again." Everyone could see the concern on Jack's face, as he repeated what Vicky said.

"HUNTERS BEEN KIDNAPPED!" Jack yelled out, as he looked at the others.

# ABOUT AUTHOR

*David J. Story, author of The Omega book series, A Jack Davidson and Shay Lynn Adventure. "The Creation" was the first book in the series. As I mentioned in the first book, I began writing soon after Sharon, my dear wife, Soulmate, and partner, was struck down in the crosswalk in a Walmart parking lot, while leaving the store on March 23rd, 2020. She remained in a coma until she succumbed to her injuries on July 17th, 2022. This was also during the outbreak of Covid 19. I started writing to occupy my mind and time while trying to cope and deal with Sharon's injuries and later passing.*

*I've continued the series because I feel this is an important topic. There's not enough written or talked about this major worldwide epidemic of Human Trafficking. There are three major classifications of human trafficking: Sex trafficking, Labor trafficking and Domestic servitude.*

*This is happening all over the world. Here in the United States, both U.S. residents and foreign nationals are being bought and sold like modern-day slaves. Traffickers use violence, manipulation, or false promises of well-paying jobs and other ways to exploit victims. Victims are forced to work as prostitutes or to take jobs as migrant, domestic, restaurant, or factory workers with little or no pay. Human trafficking is a heinous crime that exploits the most vulnerable in society.*

*Thank you for taking the time to read my book and hopefully my other books in the series. Omega II – A Cry for Help.*

*Omega I – The Creation,* ***Omega II – A Cry for Help,*** *Omega III – The Head of the Snake (2023), Omega IV – Inside the Belly of the Snake (2024), Omega V - Border Crisis (2024)*

# ACKNOWLEDGMENTS

I want to thank, Eric Bruce for his assistance in helping me with story ideas. I want to also mention Kellie Keefe, Sharon's best friend, and who helped me through Sharon's tragic injury and passing. I also want to thank Gregg Stephenson for his input and editing.

I also want to thank the men and women of the many worldwide agencies that are fighting the daily battle against human trafficking.

Made in the USA
Columbia, SC
19 January 2025

51071167R00161